Country Inn, Dead and Breakfast

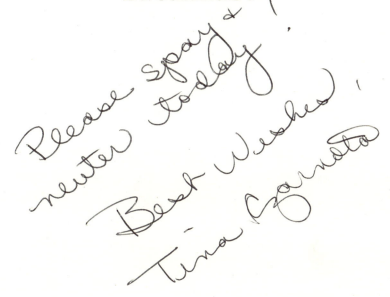

Please spray & neuter today!

Best Wishes

Tina Gonnata

Country Inn, Dead and Breakfast

by

Tina Czarnota

1stBooks - rev. 01/25/01

DISCLAIMER:

Because the author has no formal medical training, all health and diet related information in this book is used strictly for creative purposes. You are advised to consult with a health professional before starting on any vitamin or preventative medicine program.

The author and publisher are not responsible for any adverse reactions caused by following Katrina's regimen of natural supplements, vitamins, regular indulgences of chocolate, coffee and flavored brandy. Enjoy at your own risk.

The author

Dedication

For Dad and Mom. Family past and present. For Bruce. Diane and Tony. Lou and Dee. For "The Adventurers" — especially Bud "Bibs" and "O'Sauch". For Kim.

Acknowledgements

My special thanks to the people who allowed me to use bits of their likeness' in the creation of some of my characters. They are: James and Vaughn — without you there wouldn't be a Tim and Song Versay. Kim, who is the inspiration for Katrina's partner-in-crime. Paul Kloc of Kloc Blossom Chapels, W. Seneca, NY — who doubles as Lieutenant Joseph Klonski.

To: Norman, my Florida panther, and B & W Kat — thanks for the company all those nights. But, I could've done without the three a.m. catfights outside my window.

To: Author Monk Rose — so glad I took your class first. One of the many gifts I got there is my good pal, author Laura Arbeit.

To: All you fine hosts who keep the country inns and bed and breakfasts of the world percolating. Thanks for providing us "big kids" a refuge. Especially, the Bishops, innkeepers of the beautifully restored Bailey House in Amelia Island, Florida. Your support means so much to me. Bob and Lois Davenport, Cindy and the staff at Cedar Key Bed & Breakfast, Cedar Key, Florida. "The call" was a turning point. Love your coffee and waffles. Dwyer O'Grady who gave of his time and for "turning me on to" P.O.D. Sonny Howard, former innkeeper of the Herlong Mansion, Micanopy, Florida. You deserve a fun retirement. However, the ghost must miss you as we humans do. Christine and company, you did a great job.

To: Ruth C., Larry F., Daniel P., you are all fine friends. My neighbors who are there for each other. Thank you.

To: Our local law enforcement agents who answered several of my queries, even if only to say, "I haven't seen it done that way before." Some procedure carried out by my fictional police force is just that. The folks at our local public library who are so helpful. The staff at my favorite coffee haunts — thanks for letting me "hang". My clients who overlook my sleeplessness due to late-night writing. Sara M. and all teachers past and present. The staff at 1st books.com — you've made it so easy.

About the Book

Excitement and the fragrance of orange groves permeate the air at the grand opening of the Tudor Grove Inn. Katrina, an attractive health buff, is a novice innkeeper who sets out to entertain the guests of her newly acquired B & B establishment. Helping her is her fiancé, Bruce, and his parents, Song and the ornery Tim Versay. Katrina's niece, Kim and Kim's boyfriend are among their first guests.

Merely hours into the first day of operation, Mindy, a guest is murdered. Katrina realizes that she has welcomed a killer to her supposedly idyllic country inn... or did she? Perhaps the murderer is one of her own, residing under the same roof, or worse, sharing the same bed.

Leery of everyone, Katrina begins searching for clues. She eventually dismisses the idea that Bruce would be capable of murder, but considers everyone else. She soon entertains the idea that Mindy wasn't the intended victim—it was her future father-in-law, Tim. While realizing Tim can irritate people with his orneriness, she wonders who would want to kill him. Between dodging Tim's barbs, chasing ghouls, matching wits with a relentless, sexy reporter who wishes to destroy the inn, and playing hostess, Katrina guards her independence—all this on top of trying to find the killer and also liberate Song, Tim's hopelessly dominated wife.

With the inn's future at stake, Katrina tries to assist the police unaware that she is one of their prime suspects.

Tudor Grove Floor Plan

First Floor

BACK YARD

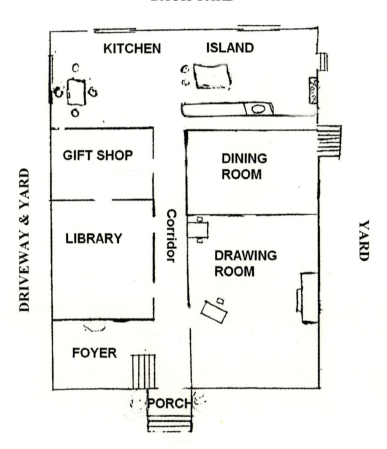

KITCHEN

ISLAND

DRIVEWAY & YARD

GIFT SHOP

DINING ROOM

LIBRARY

Corridor

DRAWING ROOM

YARD

FOYER

PORCH

Second Floor

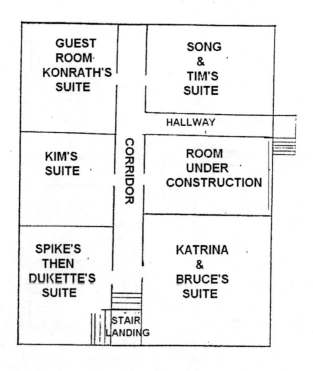

PROLOGUE

Summer 200-

It was a perfect night for a rain dance. An otherwise black, velvet sky illuminated by a near full moon transformed the heavens to a sapphire blue. A soft, summer drizzle kissed the earth, creating a misty stage only nature could fashion.

Draped in a silken sash, she pranced about the glistening, grass, felt the moist earth beneath her feet. Her shiny hair bounced around her shoulders.

"Adonis," she called his favorite namesake, "have you ever danced naked in a moonlight mist? You really should, you know."

"Aphrodite," he answered. He admired how the soft fabric clung to her near perfect figure. His fantasy maiden ceased cavorting and whirled around to face her god.

"I hate that name," she pouted, while stomping over to him. "I told you not to call me that. I am the Love Goddess"

"Sshhh... You're messing it up, you're spoiling the whole thing," he said. "Okay then, Love Goddess it is."

Gazing into his eyes, she kissed the tip of her finger and pressed it to his lips. "That's better," she murmured, flashing him a bewitching smile and dashing away before his mesmerizing gaze could render her powerless.

Bitch, he thought as he watched her sway from side to side, this time holding the silken sash above her head. If I wasn't in so deep I'd...it's too late now. He despised the power she wielded over him, yet that was the very thing that captivated him. He, after all, resented women who were better than he was at his own game.

"Adonis, my love, come join me," she beckoned.

Unwilling to ruin the night, he allowed his mind to fill with amorous intent. Earlier, he remembered, he had hidden a white box behind a convenient shrub, waiting for the right moment. "Aphr–Love Goddess," he called out to her, "I've something to show you, but first I want you to do something for me." He picked up the iridescent heap. Grabbing it from him, she covered herself with the cloth. "I want to wrap you in this," he said of the silken sash she held close to herself.

"I can do it myself," she said with a confident air.

"Go now, my love." She proceeded to twirl the long sash around her ankles. As she maneuvered the cloth upward around her body, he walked toward the shrub and glanced over his shoulder. His love goddess tucked away the loose end into her bosom and he wondered how many times she had done this before.

Retrieving the flat, white box, he adjusted the gold ribbon and attempted to revive its wilting bow. Returning to his mummy-fashioned paramour, he saw her adjusting her damp hair, anxiously awaiting him and the gold-ribboned parcel.

"It is the season, it is right for you to know now," he said in his own archaic manner as he presented her with his offering. With both hands free, she tugged at the ribbon, all the while envisioning gifts of cashmere, expensive lingerie or tickets to an exotic island getaway. Dropping the white cardboard cover, she eagerly began lifting the edge of white tissue paper. The bottom of the box fell away and she held up the contents. "Oh–how nice," she said in forced enthusiasm, "a floral wreath. Whatever for, my love?" She was unable to hide her disappointment.

With one arm outstretched to the heavens, he thundered, "What do you mean?" His eyes now widened as he roared in near rage. "This is to be the eve of your coronation." He faced her now, holding the garland clutched in both hands up to her face. "That is if you still want to be my Love Goddess?"

"You're really workin' it this time, aren't you?" she said meekly. "I've never seen you like this before."

He hadn't heard her at all. "That is if I still find you worthy." He held the floral wreath above her and gently placed it on her head. Lifting her chin slightly, he kissed her lips and looked deeply into her eyes. "It is done."

"Whew," she breathed while her lover caressed her face and continued to hold her gaze. Hearing her breath and sensing her anxiety, he couldn't control himself and began to shake with laughter.

"You and your sick fantasies," she blurted while fumbling for the end of the sash and the beginning of her freedom. "I'm getting out of this stupid thing."

Not wanting her to, he moved close to her and grabbed the cloth out of her hand. "The gods will be angry if we don't complete the act," he whispered softly, holding her firmly in his right arm.

"Tough."

Finally convincing her to stay, as he knew he would, he let go of her with his free hand, continuing to hold the sash in his left hand. Reaching deep into the pocket of his fitted jeans, he withdrew an airline ticket envelope and waved it in front of her face. "This is bestowed only to Aphr–my Love Goddess."

Snatching the envelope out of his hand, she attempted to scamper away, all the while ripping at the sealed flap. Still holding the silken cloth in her hand, he yanked at his fleeing goddess. Running away from him, she whirled around and around. Once free she broke into a playful prance. Again his goddess would dance for him.

This time is different, he mused, for you have willingly accepted the crown and title of slave goddess. "Let's go now."

"I don't want to."

"I said let's go. Someone may see us. With your giggling, you're bound to be heard."

"Oh, like you were so quiet," she countered. "My mirth was unlike your roar, Adonis."

"What was that?" He turned his head quickly, scanning the night. The moon still shone brightly, but the rain had stopped. "I heard a noise–something in the bushes."

"Oh, probably a cat or something."

"I guess, let's just get inside."

A door clicked shut behind the couple, then bush branches cracked and rustled. Allowing his breathing to become deep and heavy, a lone figure whispered malignantly, "She never did that with me." Straightening up from a crouched position, his knees creaked this time.

An arm rose slowly behind him. "And she never will."

A dull thud and a low moan escaped from the body now lying face down in the bushes.

CHAPTER 1

"We did it, we did it," shouted the two women as they whirled each other around, barely missing the stove. This was no time for decorum, for at last their dream was realized; their country inn was ready to move into.

Procurement of their vision, like most, was not without sacrifice. The deaths of immediate family members, and the estates that were left to the two, were the bitter-sweet vehicles with which they could afford their dream.

Katrina, the youngest child of a strict European upbringing, prided herself on being very "American." At thirty-six years, she still "dug" the Rolling Stones and still loved to wear form-fitting dresses and high heels. Managing to keep the weight low on her nearly six-foot frame, she sometimes passed for a fashion model, something she always dreamt of becoming.

Song, too, was pretty, appearing younger than her sixty years. Cotton was the staple of her wardrobe. No frills for this blonde, she dressed for comfort.

"Let's go around one more time," gushed Katrina.

"Well, just once more and..." Song barely uttered her last word when she felt herself being scurried off outdoors through the side kitchen door.

Rounding the front of the two-story building, they stood back once more to get the full view of their Tudor treasure. The place was a strong, well-built mistress. With steeply pitched roofs, stucco wall cladding and brown half-timbering, this inn was sure to be a welcomed sight for many a modern traveler.

"Isn't she beautiful?" Katrina said, marveling at the gracious structure. The warm, clear autumn day, with a profusion of white, billowy clouds added to the stateliness of the magnificent structure. The grass-covered acreage on which the house was situated, with a cluster of trees strategically planted around all four sides of the building, was completed by a huge bottlebrush tree gently caressing the front of the shingled roof.

"My heart skips a beat every time I realize this place is ours," said Song.

"Your heart is gonna do more than that if you don't get started on lunch soon," teased a masculine voice from behind them.

"Oh-h... just ignore him," Katrina said lightly.

"It's after one o'clock, I should get something cookin'."

"He's not helpless," Katrina groaned. "Can't he make a sandwich? Or let him open the icebox door and inhale the contents."

"I heard that," laughed the man. Joining the two women, Tim Versay, Song's husband, put his arm around his wife's tiny shoulder and gently directed her up the path to the house. "How many times are you going to stare at the place?" he asked.

"Oh, let us have our moment in the sun," Katrina said. The light breeze lifted her brown hair off her shoulders. "Haven't you ever been excited about anything in life?" She looked at the man who might be her father-in-law some day. She tried to like him, but often didn't understand him. He was unlike her own father and she wasn't used to his way of thinking.

In his prime, Tim had been a good-looking man, tall and slender with sandy blonde hair and blue-grey eyes that twinkled when he smiled. Having seen pictures in the family album, Katrina knew why Song was attracted to him.

Unlike his wife, Tim lost his trim physique to a pot belly, a flabby backside and at least thirty unwanted pounds. Just as long as Bruce doesn't become his father, Katrina thought, I may still keep him. She smiled to herself while she lingered behind. Looking up at the sky, she closed her eyes and inhaled deeply of the fresh air. This was a moment to savor.

Smell the roses, she mused. Impulsively, Katrina broke into dance, amused by her thoughts.

Twirling around like a clumsy ballerina, Katrina glided across the front lawn of the inn. Eyeing the front door, she saw she had attracted the attention she hoped to.

"Look at her," declared Tim. "What the hell's she doin' now?" He laughed out loud.

Finishing his sentence at the doorway, Katrina heard what she had wanted.

"I'm being what you wish you were...a free spirit," she said.

"A crazy broad! I'll pass." Tim shook his head and laughed, especially when he noticed a silver sports car drive slowly past the inn. Turning, he went to see how his meal was progressing.

Inside Tim was joined by his son, Bruce.

"Where's Trina?" he asked. Looking out past Tim at the spectacle in the front yard, the tall, younger man smiled and continued to watch the entertainment.

"Your girlfriend's havin' a fit," Tim said. "Better bring her in before she hurts someone."

"Dad, she likes to mess with you; just play back," his son replied.

"Well, I don't have to live with her, Bruce..."

"She says the same about you."

Tim squinted as he glanced from Katrina, out at the road. "Well, if it's attention she wanted," he said, "she got it."

Bruce nodded as he watched a silver coupe proceed slowly past the estate.

"They must've come back for another look," Tim chuckled, inching away from the door. "It's the second time that car's gone by the inn." Tim shook his head and walked off for the kitchen.

Bruce went outside. "You should help her," he said, approaching Katrina.

Katrina stopped prancing. "If you feel so strongly about it...you help," said Katrina, running her hand through her lengthy brown hair. She was out of breath. "Oh hell, why doesn't your dad pitch in some? With all that lub he has around his belly, he could use the exercise." Katrina resented the amount of work

Tim put on Song, as if she was a servant. "I swear, if you ever get like him..."

"Yeah, yeah," Bruce said. He was well aware of Katrina's feelings and equally aware of his father's habits.

"Besides," Katrina said, folding her arms across her chest, "the plan was, she cooked, I cleaned, you did repairs. I did the bookings, and we all supervised the finances. But guess what? The only one not carrying his weight is Mr. Primadonna."

"Katrina, we agreed they'd only kick a few bucks into this place. As far as he's concerned, he did it for my mom."

"Big sacrifice," she pouted, "we do all the work and in a few years he retires and gets waited on. Talk about investments paying off."

Bruce stretched his tanned arms skyward, then folded them across his chest. "Look, I've talked to him...he won't be here full-time; he'll stay in Tampa and drive out on weekends."

"When's he leaving?" Katrina asked. Her gaze sought his brown eyes. "He is staying for the opening, isn't he? Your mom will be hurt if he doesn't, at least till we get the place going. I...I'm sure he could help out somehow."

"I don't believe it; you actually sound disappointed."

"You know how I feel about your dad," Katrina said more gently as she and Bruce shuffled across the lawn toward the house. "One minute I'd like to hug him, the next minute I'd like to choke him. I can't say I'm not happy with these arrangements. Besides, he'll kill us with his smoking." She struggled with her feelings. "Actually, it'll be good for your mom. She won't have to wait on him constantly and she can enjoy the inn more. When's he leaving?"

"At the end of his vacation," Bruce said. "In two weeks."

"I feel bad now," Katrina said. "I don't want him to think he's being run off. He is welcome…"

"Don't worry," said Bruce, "he never does anything he doesn't want to."

"True," Katrina said. "Well, let's go in. They're probably wondering what happened to us."

Katrina climbed the three steps to the small wooden porch, stepped across it and lingered at the heavy front door.

"Think we should put a screen door here?" she asked Bruce.

He didn't reply, for while he lingered behind surveying the face of the old house, he noticed the curtain moving in the right-hand window on the second floor. He tried shielding his eyes with his hand, hoping to get a better look, but the movement stopped.

"What's up?" Katrina asked, noticing him eyeing the second floor.

"Nothing. I just think I have another job to add to my list. Seems there's a draft up at our bedroom window," he motioned. Bruce stared at the window a moment then went indoors.

CHAPTER 2

Song stood alone in the English country kitchen and marveled at the new white appliances set against freshly painted butter yellow walls. She ran her hand across the smooth, white counter tops and stooped to compare the texture of the white tile kitchen floor. Steadying herself upon rising, Song went to the back wall and opened the double-hung windows, letting a warm Florida breeze enter and add to her delight. The white cotton Priscilla curtains swirled and danced, and the woman smiled. At the end of her own private tour, Song admired the collection of cream-colored bowls, kettles and pitchers that sat atop the matching yellow shelving that Bruce made for her. She sighed. It was time to make lunch.

Song was assembling the makings for sandwiches when she heard her husband shuffle toward the kitchen. He was laughing deeply, then started to cough.

"Damn cigarettes," he mumbled, while popping a throat lozenge into his mouth. But Tim liked to smoke, and didn't plan on giving it up. "What's for lunch?" He was standing in the kitchen doorway.

Just then the phone rang. Song wiped her hands and hurried past Tim to answer it. "Uh, Tudor Grove, may I..." Song returned the phone to its wall base. "No one's there," she said. "So what are the kids up to?" she asked, heading back to the counter and her sandwich making.

"The usual," he grunted. "Katrina's in her age regression mode, Bruce is explaining it away, and…"

"Sometimes I think she's good for him and others…well I just don't know," Song said, shrugging. She was proud of Bruce. Tall and nearly handsome, he could build wonderful things out of a few pieces of wood and a couple of nails. She was glad his

7

expertise lay in the construction field, which she considered a very macho field indeed.

Bruce's happiness was important to her and, though she went along with his choice of Katrina, she secretly wished he'd find a real woman, one that could make a good home for him and who liked to cook and do needlepoint. A woman much like herself.

"How can I help?" asked Katrina, now joining the two in the kitchen.

Tim had already sat at the kitchen table and waited for service. Bruce soon joined him.

"You know," said Katrina, while producing paper plates and plastic forks from a grocery bag, "if everyone does his share, we can really get this place going."

"I gotta wash my hands," Bruce said. He got up and went to the sink. Katrina shook her head.

Tim's wheezing chuckle was the predicted response. Bruce was a chauvinistic father's dream come true and Tim was enjoying the fruits of his parenting... or lack thereof.

Sensing an impending family altercation, Song intervened with a tray of sandwiches, potato chips and pickles.

"This is it?" said Tim, trying to revive the mood that had been interrupted.

"What a mule." Katrina dug in the pocket of her faded jeans. She took out two vitamins and handed one to Bruce. "Flu season's almost here. We should be taking extra Cs."

"You believe that crap?" Tim was back in the game, between mouthfuls of sandwich. "She takes all those vitamins and then eats cake and junk. Just look in that grocery bag–"

Katrina lifted a cake box from the bag. "It's okay to have an occasional dessert," she said. "But, I guess I should abuse my body all of the time, instead of occasionally, huh Mr. Fizz Fitness?"

"Occasional?" chortled Tim.

Katrina waved the cake box under Tim's nose. "And, if it bothers you so, you don't have to eat any." Katrina laughed as Tim waved her away.

Song grabbed the cake from Katrina and began to slice it and dish out servings.

"When's your niece comin' in, Trina?" she asked, trying to steer the conversation on to more pleasant issues.

"Tomorrow. I can't wait to see her. I miss that kid."

"She anything like you?" Tim asked.

"Yeah, so watch it, Versay. You're gonna have me in stereo."

"Now I do need a cigarette."

"On your way outside, at least walk your dirty plate to the recycling bin."

"Katrina, I'll get it," Song said.

Tim looked back at the younger woman with satisfaction, opened the side kitchen door, and let himself out.

Katrina turned toward Bruce and stared him down.

"Okay, okay," he said as he grudgingly collected the soiled paper plates and threw them in the recycling bin.

"What were we... oh yeah," said Katrina, "my niece. She's coming in tomorrow night about eight. Last I heard, she was bringing this guy she's been dating on and off for about a year. He's a cop. She's got this thing for cops."

"She's an airhead," said Bruce. "Remember the time she sucked wet cat food into your new vacuum? It stunk for days and we couldn't figure out where the hell the smell was coming from."

"She's a good kid though," said Katrina. "She's just a bit...carefree, that's all."

Song was intrigued. She'd never met any of Katrina's family and this was a chance for her to see what type of background Katrina had come from.

"I think you'll like her," said Katrina. "She's sweet. Besides, what could be better than having a cop and a hair technician on the premises?" She wiped the table clean with a damp cloth.

9

"Personally, I think she's wasting her time... it's not that hairdressing isn't worthwhile, it's just that I'm sure she could make it in modeling. She's so photogenic. But, maybe that's not what she wants in life."

"Yes, you'll have to let her make her own choices," said Song.

"Or," Katrina went on, "I'd love her to open a shop right here at the inn. We could convert some of the downstairs space into a styling room... say, next to the gift shop. That would be a good draw for us." She rubbed a spot on the table.

"You have big ideas, Katrina," said Bruce. "Kim's only coming for a week or so, and you got her moving in already. She's lived at home for twenty-some years. She won't leave it to come live here."

"It doesn't hurt to dream," Katrina said.

"So, is she flying in? Do they need a ride from the airport?" Bruce asked, edging toward the same escape route his father had used.

"I'm not sure," Katrina said. "I'll call her tonight and find out if they need a ride or if they're renting a car and what time their flight's due in. You don't mind if we have to get them do you, Bruce?" Her answer came in the form of a gentle click of the screen door closing, heralding the successful escape of yet another male prisoner held in domestic captivity.

Katrina tossed the last few crumbs into the trash can and shook her head. She glanced at Song.

"He's amazing," Katrina said, folding her arms across her chest, "he can tear down walls, put new ones up, construct buildings... now if I could only get him to put his dirty socks in the hamper."

Just as Katrina figured, Song didn't reply. The older woman remained busy at the sink rinsing some dishes. Katrina sighed. "You know what I do when Bruce doesn't pick up his dirty clothes?" she asked Song directly.

"What?"

"A wise woman taught me this one. I ask him twice, and if they're still laying on the floor, I pick them up and throw them in the garbage."

"Garsch," exclaimed Song. That word came from her Ohio roots. "Who was the woman?"

"You don't know her... so don't get upset if you see me throwing his clothes out in the trash."

"Does it work?"

"No, but it's better than resorting to drastic measures!" Smiling, Katrina left the kitchen. Halfway down the corridor, Katrina heard the phone ring. When it stopped, she figured Song had answered it. Katrina hurried off to the drawing room.

Tina Czarnota

CHAPTER 3

"Yes-s," Katrina sighed as she kicked off her sneakers and sank back into the cushiony couch. Propping her legs up and folding her hands behind her head, she closed her eyes and felt the strains of the day melt away into the sofa. Doubts and fears tried to invade her serenity, but she flushed them out with daydreams of her successfully managed bed and breakfast inn. Opening her eyes, she stared at the brick fireplace before her and fantasized about the time when the old hearth would once again, on a snappy winter's night, be ablaze with a warm, crackling fire. Guests would linger over light conversation, cocoa and hot toddies. Strains of soothing classical favorites would softly weave their way throughout the air, never being so bold as to interrupt mellow chit-chat.

Katrina glanced about the spacious drawing room and proudly concluded that they all did a good job of decorating, in spite of the budget they had to work with.

Song's love of antiques and shrewd bargaining netted the deeply stained mahogany table, the ornate front desk with chairs and the downbridge lamp. Never straying far from contemporary preferences, Katrina's love of rich colors and new fabrics were evident in the deep green, floral printed couches that were set against patterned carpeting of a moss hue. Tim had insisted on the high-backed winged chair, footstool and cut glass chandelier. Warnings were issued upon purchase, that aside from the guests, Tim got first dibs on the high-backed chair. Bruce, not caring much about interior design, contributed by handling repairs and making renovations.

Katrina heard footsteps coming toward the drawing room. She hopped off the sofa, ran to the door, and turned the key in the old-fashioned lock. Hurrying to the back door, she repeated the process and sealed off the entries to all possible forms of intrusion.

That should do it, she smiled and reclaimed her spoils... the vacant beckoning couches. This time, she pounced on the right sofa, settled in and checked the vantage point from this angle.

Three raps on the door were followed by Song asking, "Katrina, ya in there?"

"Damn, just as I was..."

"What's wrong?" asked Tim from down the hall.

"I think the door's locked."

But before Tim got to the entrance, Katrina hurried to the door, unlocked it, and scurried back to the couch.

"Let me try," he said.

With the turn of the knob, the door opened and in came the intruders, Tim and Song.

"The door wasn't locked," he chided Song.

"Oh... sometimes it sticks," Katrina said, unwilling to admit what she had done. Katrina asked Song about the phone call.

"Bruce can fix the door," Tim interrupted. "I have enough with the gardening," he grumbled, gesturing toward the kitchen. " Possums must've come out of the woods and got the dead fish. My impatiens under the kitchen windows got trampled."

"Dead fish?" Katrina sat up straight and eyed Tim. He was busy jiggling the doorknob.

Song moved away from the doorway. "It's that fish Tim bought the other night. He heard the scraps could be used as fertilizer. Tim guesses," she said, approaching Katrina, "that possums dug 'em up and ate 'em. He must've not buried the scraps deep enough."

Katrina grimaced and sank back into the couch. "So, who was the phone call from?" Katrina sat back up.

"No one," said Song. "That's happened twice today."

"What's up?" It was Bruce.

Song told Bruce about the phone calls. Tim told Bruce about the door. As the two men checked the door, the phone rang.

"What the... ?" muttered Bruce.

"Hopefully, the reception phone works," said Katrina.

"Hopefully, it's our first guest," said Song.

Katrina knew this was her job and hurried to the front desk.

"Good afternoon, Tudor Grove Inn. May I help you?"

In response to the caller's answer, Katrina waved her hand in excitement.

"Someone must be calling about lodging," whispered Bruce.

Katrina picked up the reservation log and flipped to the current date. As she continued listening to the caller, her determined expression gave way to a quizzical smirk. Was someone messing with her?

"Hello… hello, are you there?" the caller asked. The woman, introducing herself as Mindy Konrath, had a high-pitched and nasally voice.

"Oh… yes, I have an available king-size suite for this weekend."

"What amenities do you offer? Is this a smoke-free establishment? Are there animals on the premises?" The caller went on and on.

Katrina winced and held the phone away from her ear. The others could hear the high voice babble on and began to chuckle among themselves.

"Are you there?" the anxious woman appealed. "Why aren't you answering me?"

Katrina smiled, inhaled deeply, and with composed charm began to answer every one of the caller's queries right down to the fact that each suite came with its own ionizer.

"Perfect," the woman said. "Are you health buffs too? My husband and I are into health food. Do you serve organic grown produce by any chance? We eat pesticide free foods whenever possible."

Katrina answered that arrangements could be made for a special diet. "I have you down for Saturday late morning or early afternoon arrival. That's for two adults. Will you need our van to pick you up at the airport?" The woman wasn't sure. "Just let us know when you decide. If there's nothing else, we look forward to your arrival."

The hand piece hardly connected with the phone's cradle when the questions flew at her in rapid succession. Katrina sat back in the reception chair and tossed aside the pencil she had been using. "Just let me clear my head," she said. Again doubt was vying for equal time with fear. Aware that most new ventures came with an element of uncertainty, she decided to embrace the joy of her dream come true. Katrina drew on motivational tapes, and self-help books she had learned from, and in the echoes of her mind she recalled snippets of advice from speakers past. She sent a thought up to Heaven.

"Well?" asked Song, drawing her back to the present. By now, Bruce, Song and Tim had assembled around the desk.

"Sorry. Just rebounding from my initiation."

Katrina relayed the details of their first prospective guests to the others. Enthusiasm started to return to Katrina as the sting of their new undertaking began to wear off.

It was reminiscent of the time when her mom passed away, almost two years ago. She felt strong until the reality of her mother's death met her head on, in the form of the woman's lifeless body lying there at the wake. Although running an inn was a happy adjustment to make, it was a big undertaking, filled with responsibilities and obligations.

The group chattered a while, then began to disperse. Tim made for the door the moment Song said she would go upstairs and do more unpacking.

"Well, I guess I'll take a quick run to the hardware store before it closes," said Bruce. "What time we going to dinner?"

"You'll make it," said Song. "We won't leave for another hour or so. You gonna ask your dad along for the ride?"

"Naw," Bruce said. "He'll just hang out the window so I'll let him smoke on the way to the store."

Katrina chuckled. "Good, then you can take a corner on two wheels and dump him in an orange grove somewhere."

Bruce frowned, but she could tell by his eyes that he approved of her humor.

Finally alone, Katrina picked up the phone and called her niece. She needed to talk to someone back home.

"Hello?" a sweet voice answered.

"Kim?"

"Aunty Trina? I was just thinking about you."

"You're still coming down, aren't you?"

"Yeah, I'm almost all packed. Our plane will arrive at your airport at 7:59 p.m."

"You need us to pick you up? I mean Spike is still coming, right? You guys didn't quarrel or anything did you?"

Kim giggled. "Not yet. And no, you don't need to pick us up, we're renting a car."

"You did buy me sponge candy and Charlie Chaplin, right?" Katrina asked, referring to her favorite chocolates found in upstate New York. "Don't board that plane without my chocolate," she teased.

"You kidding? So how's the new inn? You sound a li'l freaked."

Katrina told Kim about the phone situation. "The last call was from a woman asking about a room. At first I thought someone was messing with me 'cause she asked all kinds of questions and stuff. Turns out, she and her husband will be our first official guests... paying guests that is."

"Spike and me don't count?"

"We're not charging you. Everyone agreed on that. Anyway, I can't wait to see you, you brat."

"Me or your sponge candy?"

"Um-m?" Katrina chuckled.

"So things are okay?"

Katrina became serious. "Kim, the initial shock of running an inn has me nuts. I just might bolt and keep running. You better show up; I need you for my emotional rescue."

Kim laughed, knowing how unwound her aunt could get while striving to uphold a cool exterior. "If we see you on the road, we'll pick you up," teased Kim. "What about Bruce's family?"

"His mom's okay, but Bruce is numb and his father needs his own personal valet."

"Cool," laughed Kim.

"Yeah. Well, I should go. Gotta get ready for dinner. We're going to some li'l steak joint in town. Let me tell you this place is not Boca Raton."

"No hot dress shops?"

"No, the chickens don't dress around here. I'm teasing, you can go into town for that stuff. Bring lotsa mousse and mascara though, it's a long walk to the mall if you run out."

"You mean you intentionally left Boca for that place?"

"I'm messin' with you. It's nice, you'll see."

"Gotta rock, Aunty Trina."

"Have a safe trip. Call for directions from the airport. Bruce is gone and you'll land up in Georgia if I guide you. Bye."

Katrina hung up the phone, stretched, and passed through the foyer to join Tim out in the front yard.

"Gorgeous out here isn't it?" she murmured, walking down the front steps. Tim was gazing at the yard, smoking.

"Yeah, it is."

"I was thinking, shouldn't we be putting our shingle up? I know we have other things to do, but a shingle will announce our inn… a vacant inn desperately seeking business."

"I s'pose," Tim said. "We also need more flowers or shrubs around the front of the inn. It lacks color." He turned to face the building.

Just as Tim ended his sentence, the two heard a scrapping noise. It grew louder.

"What's that?" Katrina asked with a start.

The pair looked up at the roof in time to see a stack of renegade bricks come hurtling down toward them.

"Look out!" Tim yelled, grabbing her arm.

CHAPTER 4

Silence crushed around them as dust rose from the rubble.

"You all right?" Tim asked.

They were lying on the ground, a pile of bricks not three feet away.

With a dull moan, Katrina winced and carefully raised her right hand over her shoulder. "I think I wrenched my back. What about you? Are you okay?"

Tim rose slowly and surveyed the heap of debris. "Yeah. I'm just stunned." He started to laugh and cough at the same time. "Those sons-of-bitches coulda killed us."

Katrina stood up and began to brush the soot off her jeans. She wanted to cry but listening to Bruce's father, she shook her head. She couldn't believe this guy. They narrowly escaped getting pulverized, and he was laughing.

"Quit laughing and move yourself around... see if you're hurt." Katrina couldn't help feel concern for Tim. After all, he was Bruce's father.

"I'm okay," he said.

"What happened anyway? Did you see them fall?" Katrina was starting to thaw, and realized how close they were to being killed. "Who was so stupid to leave bricks on the roof like that?" she demanded.

"Bruce," Tim said. "Katrina, when a bricklayer works on on a wall or chimney, he generally leaves a pile of bricks right at the site so when he comes back to finish, he has 'em right there to start on."

"Well that's stupid." She slapped her jeans to get the remaining dust off. "Someone could get killed that way. What if this fell on a guest? The only grand opening would be on the visitor's head."

19

Tim shrugged.

"Shouldn't we move these?" Katrina said, and she stooped to begin picking up the bricks. A pain shot through her shoulder and she dropped the few pieces she held. "The hell with it. Bruce will just have to get them later."

"Good idea," Tim said, lighting up a new cigarette. A few moments later they heard a vehicle driving up the road toward the inn.

"Oh good, it's Bruce," Katrina said.

As the van wound its way up the drive, Song appeared at the front door all set to go to dinner.

"You aren't ready yet," she said. Seeing the bricks, astonishment came to her face. "What happened?"

Katrina waited until Bruce arrived, then told Song and him about the bricks.

"I'm just glad you two weren't hurt," Song said.

"Sure you're okay?" Bruce asked Tim. He hugged Katrina.

"Bruce, you're not gonna leave those bricks up there any more, are you?" Song said. "With guests walkin' around the grounds... well, we don't want to lose the place the first week of operation."

"Yeah, I just wonder how they got loose," he said. "They were secured. I made sure of that."

"Not secured enough," Katrina said.

"I guess."

"What did you buy?" Katrina noticed he wasn't carrying any supplies or packages.

"Nothing... I just priced building material for the first floor bathroom and got ideas for the cottage we talked about." Bruce looked at his watch. "I better get ready for dinner. I'm starving." He started across the lawn toward the front porch.

"I should do the same." Katrina took the route Bruce had, all the while looking up at the chimney. As she neared the porch, she decided on a detour, and went around to the back of the inn.

Everything looked in place. Katrina glanced at the makeshift ladder at the back of the house and moved in closer. This is nuts,

20

she thought, running her hand over a rung on the ladder. I've been reading too many headlines. Besides, what do I hope to find… a clue? To what?

The only thing her inspection produced was a clump of mud clinging to the bottom rung. Rolling it around her fingers she couldn't decide whether it was fresh or old, damp or dry.

Katrina eyed the ground beneath the ladder. She noted at least a dozen footprints, but none were discernable. In the movies, her favorite female sleuth, with the same meager evidence, would've by now deduced the identity of the "perp," or perpetrator.

Katrina exhaled deeply. There was no perp and those bricks just fell off the roof, she concluded. As for the phone calls, that was just another bug to work out.

Katrina's stomach growled, reminding her that it was time to get moving. As she stepped back, her gaze swept across the mound beneath the rear kitchen windows. Most of the bright pink and orange impatiens that had been planted there were now reduced to squished stems. Frustrated, she went indoors.

Up in their suite, Katrina found Bruce pacing while buttoning up his shirt.

"Are you okay?"

"Yeah. I'm just a little sore," said Katrina.

"How long till you're ready?"

"Not long."

"You know my father gets nuts when he doesn't eat on time."

Katrina shook her head. "The restaurant's casual, right?"

"Yeah, my dad heard their steak is great."

Katrina sat on the edge of their king-size bed and toed at her shoes, trying to put them on, while running a brush through her hair.

"I hope our phones aren't messed up," mused Katrina.

"Somebody probably just dialed wrong."

"What do you make of those bricks?"

"What do you mean?" asked Bruce.

"Well, isn't it weird those bricks just falling down on us?"

He shrugged. "Not really. I just messed up. Hey," he said, looking away from his key ring, "you're not thinking the place is–"

"Bruce, I saw it this afternoon– "

"The driver was probably lost or something."

"Wha… ? I was talking about the curtain. I saw it move, I just didn't say anything. You know there's no draft there." She looked toward the windows. "And no one could've moved the curtain. Our room was locked. Then the brick thing… " she added. "Now what's this about a car?"

Bruce laughed. He explained, how earlier, a car drove by the inn, probably entertained by her dancing out on the front lawn. "I know," he said, "a ghost moved the curtain and the driver willed the bricks to fall... from behind tinted windows."

"Things are a little weird, and he jokes."

"It's... sometimes your imagination kicks into overdrive."

"Yeah, right. Let's go," she said, figuring it was futile for her to assert the value of one heeding one's intuition, especially when it was female based.

"It's getting dark out already," Bruce said, locking the door to their suite.

"It is autumn. Thanksgiving's just around the corner."

As they descended the carpeted, wood staircase, they saw Tim and Song sitting in the drawing room, waiting for them.

"We're ready," said Bruce.

"About time," mumbled Tim.

The quartet filed out the front door. Song, Bruce and Katrina began to discuss inn repairs, thus drowning out Tim's grumbling about how hungry he was and how late it had gotten to be.

As Tim navigated the car past serene farmland and down winding country roads, the group steered their conversation on to the official opening of the inn.

"I hope we did enough advertising," Katrina said. "I didn't want to overdo it, but yet I wanted adequate coverage."

"It'll be enough... we don't want to bite off more then we can chew," said Song.

"It's cool that the paper's sending someone down to do an interview," said Bruce.

"Yeah, but don't count on a huge article. You may see a paragraph and that's it," said Tim. "The inn ain't big news."

Everyone agreed that Tim was probably right, but just the same they were elated at the chance of being photographed and interviewed by the local newspaper.

"Well, here we are. I can hear that steak sizzling now." He turned the ignition off. In a heartbeat, he was out of the car heading for the restaurant, rubbing his hands together.

"Dad can really move out," laughed Bruce.

"Does he get that excited over sex?" Katrina asked, climbing out of the back seat. The trio laughed at Tim as he rushed through the front door.

"Phil A. Minion's Steak House," Bruce smirked while reading the sign on the door.

"Leave Tim alone for a while," said Song. "If he gets a bug up that butt of his, we're all gonna suffer."

Bruce and Katrina looked at each other and laughed as they followed Song into the steak house.

The trio found Tim settled in at a window table, anxiously summoning a waitress.

"Dad, what's the hurry?" Bruce asked.

"I'm hungry."

"Let's relax and enjoy this meal," said Song, "'cause once the inn gets goin', I'll not get out much for dinner."

With their dinner orders taken, the conversation returned to the inn.

"I gotta get used to the idea of going to bed early," Katrina said, toying with the straw in her root beer. "I'll miss staying up late... even if it's only to read a book or take a bubble bath."

"You're not sorry now, are ya?" said Song.

"No-o." Katrina fingered the hem of the red and white checked tablecloth. "Am I the only one who's unglued about this venture?" Katrina omitted what really was on her mind.

"I'm a little jittery but I'm also excited," said Song. "This was always a dream of mine and it's finally come true."

Tim was more interested in the salad placed before him and waived his right to respond.

"About the seating on Sunday morning," Katrina said, "our main table will handle six. But if my niece and her friend sit there, the guest couple may feel left out, being at a table off by themselves."

"Maybe they'll want it that way," Bruce said between bites of lettuce.

"It might be rude," Song said. "Tim, what do you think?"

"Should you be eating with the guests?" Having finished his salad, Tim lit a cigarette.

"It's our grand opening," said Song. "We're making an exception."

"I'll ask my niece and her friend to sit at their own table," said Katrina. "I'll explain why. She'll understand. That way the other couple won't feel neglected. There'll be time when she can move to our table later and sit. What do you think?"

"Sounds okay," said Song.

When their waitress arrived with a large tray carrying four thick, sizzling steaks, Tim grunted.

Katrina laughed. "The beast... they should've just flung it at him and let him catch it with his teeth."

Tim ignored Katrina's remark as he methodically covered his steak with a layer of butter and followed up with a generous sprinkling of salt.

"Yuck," Katrina muttered.

Bruce caught her eye with a look of disbelief.

Katrina felt guilty enough about occasionally indulging in a queen-sized cut of meat, let alone burying it in butter and salt.

Key lime pie with coffee rounded off the meal, and it wasn't long before the group was on their way back to their new home.

The return trip to the inn was pleasant. The country night air was fresh and the dark sky was replete with twinkling stars.

Katrina pulled her head inside the window after taking a deep "hit" of fresh air. They were all feeling the effects of a long day and she urged them to do the same.

"It'll revive you, you'll feel better," she said. "Bruce," she whispered, "make conversation with your dad to keep him alert. He's yawning his brains out and I don't want to land up in a ditch or something."

Engaging in small talk, Bruce managed to get a discussion going, and steered it towards Tim.

"Dad, did you tell the guys at the office about our inn?"

"No," he said. "I just stuck a brochure up on the board in our break room."

"Your dad's afraid the guys at work are gonna razz him," Song said sleepily.

"It would blow Tim's image," teased Katrina. "Now, if he were a drug czar that would command respect."

Tim snickered. "Did the guest who reserved say how they heard about us?" he asked Song who's head began to nod.

"Yeah, how did they hear about us?" asked Bruce.

"I forgot to ask," said Katrina. "I'd like to know if it was the magazine ad that did it or just local talk. Anyway, it's great that we got a booking already."

Tina Czarnota

CHAPTER 5

"Wake up Song, we're here." Tim had a hard time referring to the inn as home.

Everyone stretched and yawned as they got out of the car.

"I hope when I hit the pillow, I feel as tired as I do now," Bruce said.

"Sure you will," said Song.

Katrina noticed Song seemed more awake now. "Are you going to bed?"

"I've some things to unpack yet," said Song.

Inwardly Katrina frowned, but she said, "I'll be right down to help." Katrina followed Bruce upstairs to their suite. "I need to splash water on my face to wake up," she told Bruce.

Tim was gone, but with his door open, his gargling echoed down the hall, telling everyone where he was.

"Imagine guests booked next door to him hearing that at night?" Bruce laughed. "Well, if there's early checkout, we'll know why."

"Your dad's so suave. I'll get washed and go down to help her."

Katrina tied the belt on her white terry robe and descended the dimly lit stairs. Shadows danced about the staircase walls, slowing only when she reached the landing. Katrina stopped. She looked up at the second floor and around the stairwell. They were definitely going to need more nightlights. Katrina hurried down the rest of the way.

God, this place can be creepy, thought Katrina. She felt spooked by her dim surroundings, and recalling earlier events didn't help any. Katrina moved down the carpeted corridor. A ticking wall clock and some creaky floorboards broke the obscure stillness. Quickly, she followed a soft light coming from the kitchen. ,

Katrina swung open the door. Song's back was to her.

"How can you see in so little light?" she asked Song.

The woman faced Katrina, her eyes moist with tears. She turned and wiped them.

"What's up?" asked Katrina.

"Honestly? I guess I just miss the old place in Tampa," Song said. "I felt I was adjustin' and all of a sudden, I got the blues."

"I was beginning to think I was the only one with these feelings," said Katrina. "Anyway, why don't I make us some cocoa? We can talk a bit and we'll both feel better."

Soon, the teakettle whistled. Hot water sputtered as Katrina added it to the brown, instant mix.

"This is topped, of course, by lots of whipped cream," Katrina said, shaking a chilled can of topping. "Want some?"

Song shook her head and the two women huddled over their cups of the steaming chocolate.

"You know," Katrina started, "we've handled other changes in our lives. All we have to do is draw on those experiences and get involved in living life. Before long the inn will feel like home to us."

"We've adjusted before, we can do it again."

Conversation soon turned to the following day's itinerary.

"Are the bikes ready for the guests' use?" Katrina said. "I don't want to promise things in our ads and then not deliver. Remember that inn we visited? Their brochure boasted a breakfast that was only served when media people came to visit."

"Yes," Song agreed, "every guest should get V.I.P. treatment." She smiled. "Well, Katrina, I think your cocoa did the trick. I've just a few more things to put away before I turn in."

"I'll help."

"No, it's okay. In fact, I'd rather do it myself. I'm trying to get familiar with this kitchen and this is the best way do it."

Katrina wasn't going to protest. She rose from the table, took her empty mug to the sink and bid the woman goodnight.

Katrina felt better. Even the creaking corridor floor didn't sound as threatening as it did earlier.

It's all how we view a situation, Katrina thought while climbing the staircase.

Once in their room, Katrina closed the door behind her and groped around in the darkness, finally tripping over shoes and a pile of clothing.

"Dammit!" she muttered, but Bruce didn't hear her.

She settled into bed and got comfortable. Reaching for her cassette player lying on the nightstand, she donned the headphones, adjusted the volume and closed her eyes. Who needs sleeping pills when you have these? mused Katrina listening to the soothing voice of the motivational speaker coming across with his tips on succeeding in life.

Katrina fell into a light sleep and was awakened by a shrilling sound coming through her earphones. In her grogginess she reached up to remove the headpiece and found she had removed it before falling asleep. Bolting up in bed her eyes flew open as a second shrill pierced the night, this time louder.

Katrina turned on a lamp and caught Bruce hopping out of bed, hurrying to the door.

"Something's happened!" he said.

Katrina threw on her robe and ran after Bruce. Stepping out in the hall, they almost collided with Tim.

"What's goin' on?" he demanded.

"We heard a scream," said Bruce.

The three rushed down the staircase. Song was running toward the steps in their direction. Seeing them, she waited till they reached the bottom then ran to Tim trembling and mumbling.

"What's wrong?" he asked. "Calm yourself, and tell me what's wrong."

Song covered her mouth with her hand and pointed down the hall toward the kitchen.

With that, Tim left in effort to find out what happened. The younger couple tried to calm Song and get information from her.

Katrina left Bruce with his mother and went about turning on lights in effort to rid the downstairs of its eerie darkness. On her way to the kitchen, Katrina heard Song mumbling something about "a face." When Katrina reached the back kitchen door, she saw Tim walking around outside, flashlight in hand, inspecting the yard.

"...Then you three came down," Song was telling Bruce as the pair entered the room. Song inched behind him as they passed the island range and approached the site of her horror.

Meanwhile, Katrina caught up with Tim and relayed what she'd heard from Song. "She said something about a face," Katrina told him. Seeing Bruce coming down the back steps, Katrina asked, "What's this about a face?"

Bruce walked up to the rear kitchen windows and studied them, then the ground. Katrina and Tim joined him.

"She said after she'd put some things away, she shut off the kitchen lights, turned toward the windows and saw what looked like a man's face. When he saw she'd spotted him, he ran off to the left—our right." Bruce eyed the thicket that separated their drive and yard from the next-door property. "She said she screamed, ran down the hall and screamed again. That's when we came running down."

The trio looked up at the kitchen windows. Song was pacing the floor and wringing her hands.

"Those curtains don't close all the way," Katrina said. "We need to draw the shades at night. Anyone can look right in."

"Let's find out what happened first. You can decorate later," Tim said, aiming his flashlight at the mound beneath the windows. "Bruce, look at all the footprints down here." Tim cursed when the light rested on his ruined impatiens.

"There's been a bunch of traffic here lately," said Bruce. "It's hard to make out anything."

The men headed around the back of the house and up the side. Katrina hurried after them, knowing that if they found

30

anything, they'd probably keep it from her and Song, fearing they'd frighten the women.

Walking right up alongside the men, she asked flatly, "Did you find anything?"

Forgetting that Katrina had invaded male territory, Tim answered no, and they continued their inspection of the grounds surrounding the house.

The trio circled the inn and ended their search in the backyard. Except for Katrina. She left the two men discussing the situation. In minutes, she returned and grabbed the flashlight Tim had left on the ground. Katrina moved past them and edged up to the kitchen windows. She dropped to her knees, her robe brushing the ground.

Tim and Bruce closed in, and stepped into a stream of light that filtered out the back windows. Tim chortled as Katrina dug up the dead plants with her right hand, while training the flashlight with her left. When her hunt produced no more than disturbed soil, father and son went back to the house chuckling about Katrina's stalled career in crime detection.

Katrina threw her garden spade down and brushed at her knees. It was just a hunch, she mused, and she wondered if beasts ruined the impatiens, or did the peeper–if there really was one. If it was the latter, how long had their privacy been violated? She shook off a shudder and made for the back stairs.

Katrina paused at the top step and scanned the night. Oddly enough, the estate appeared tranquil in its cloak of midnight blue. Katrina breathed a clipped sigh. Or was it hushed by a shroud of Gothic black? Katrina opened the back door and went in.

Inside, Song was sitting at the table, looking calmer but still anxious. Tim and Bruce were telling her of their findings. Katrina went about the kitchen and pulled the shades down on the windows.

" ...those footprints could belong to anyone," Tim was saying. "Song, you sure you saw something?" You could... thought you saw a face? Tim stopped. "Was it a fish face by any

31

chance? It seems Katrina's lost one…" Bruce chuckled along with his father.

."No," Song said hotly. "I'm sure as I'm sittin' here. I saw a man's face lookin' in that window. When he saw me he ran off toward the left. That's when I ran out the kitchen… you know the rest."

Katrina glowered at the men as she sidled up to the kitchen sink. "We need to report this to the police," she said, turning on the faucet.

"No," Tim said. "The cops won't do anything except look around and make a report. They can't tell us anything more than we already know."

"She's right, Tim," said Song. "At least they'll have it on file."

"Yeah, and your inn's off to a great start with bad publicity," Tim said. Pulling the pack of his cigarettes from his shirt pocket, he took one out and lit it.

"It may serve as a positive thing… like a draw for excitement seekers," said Bruce.

"I don't think it's a good idea," Tim said, shaking his head. He drew heavily on the cigarette, the smoke swirling up from the lit end. "The locals may not appreciate us coming in here and stirring things up."

Katrina dried her hands in a towel and turned to them, "This is one time I'm gonna agree with you, Tim," Katrina said. "Maybe we shouldn't report it. But any more weird stuff and I'll be the first one on that phone."

"This feels like one of the longest day's of my life," said Bruce. "Let's go to bed."

"Help me lock up and turn off the lights so we can all go up together," said Song.

As lights were turned off and doors got locked, Song reached inside a cabinet and shook out one of her sleeping pills. "I really need one of these tonight I'll tell ya."

"Well," said Katrina, "see you in the morning–I hope."

Song wasn't sure whether it was the sound of her husband's morning cough, or the sun that sneaked through the slit between the shades that woke her from her sleep. She blinked and looked at the clock. It was nine o'clock. She hadn't slept that late in years. Throwing the covers off, she got out of bed, mentally reviewing a list of things she had to do before the guests arrived.

Make breakfast, clean up after, and put out fresh flowers, thought Song. The plush, thick rug felt cushiony against her toes as she stood and stretched.

But there was no time for such pleasure, though she longed to do so as she glanced about the bedroom and admired the peach painted walls. Stalling, but still being productive, she reached behind the floral lace curtains and drew up the shades, blinding herself with the strong sunlight.

"At least we've nice weather for the opening," Song mused as she went to make the bed. Song pulled back the cream-colored eyelet comforter and the blankets. Fluffing the matching pillows and adjusting the off-white draping on the mahogany canopied bed frame, Song backed up and admired the completed look of the room.

"Song," followed by a ripple of coughing, interrupted her thoughts as she made for the bathroom. "Song, you up?" boomed Tim, opening the door and entering the bedroom.

"Yes dear, I'm getting washed."

"Good. I've been up over an hour. I'm hungry."

"What time were you up, Tim?" she asked through the bathroom door.

"About eight."

"Why didn't you wake me earlier? I've much to do."

"We were up so late I thought I'd let you sleep."

"What about the kids. They awake?"

"Yeah. Bruce and Katrina are getting washed. He'll make the coffee. She takes too damn long to get ready. Besides..."

Song opened the door. "I didn't hear all ya said."

"I started to say that Bruce makes better coffee than Katrina does. Her scrambled eggs are good though."

Song scurried past her spouse, opened the bedroom door, and headed down the hall past the guest and Bruce's rooms.

"Mm-m, coffee's on," she declared, savoring the aroma as she reached the staircase.

"Yes-s-s. Coffee," Katrina said. She was stepping out of her room.

"Good mornin', Katrina. Well, today's the big day."

"Good morning, sunshine," Katrina said to Tim as he hurried past her to catch up with his wife.

"Yeah," came the mumbled response.

Katrina closed the door behind her and joined in the procession heading downstairs.

Once in the kitchen, Tim sat down at the table and waited for service.

"Let's grab a small breakfast, guys," Katrina said. "We have lots to do before the guests and the newspaper people arrive; we don't have time to play around."

"I want sausage and eggs," said Tim.

"Sausage and eggs. Sausage and eggs," chanted Katrina. "No cigarette? Don't you need a cigarette to go with that?"

She started to feel testy, still unsettled from last night.

"I'll have one after my sausage and eggs."

"Sheesh," said Katrina. "Can you grab these mugs from me and set them on the table?"

"Yes, Katrina," sang Tim.

Katrina watched him get up and do as she'd asked. "There is a God."

The sound and the aroma of links sputtering in the frying pan were enticing to Katrina, but her appetite was diminished.

"They smell good… but no, I'm not having any," Katrina said, more to herself than the others.

"Should I make more?" Song asked, cheerfully.

"No thanks, I'm cutting back," lied Katrina. "My jeans are getting tight." That one was not a fib.

While Song cooked breakfast, Bruce and Tim enjoyed coffee and a discussion of gardening and repairs.

Katrina stole glances at each. It's odd, she thought, everyone's acting as though nothing happened last night. Is this a case of don't talk and don't feel? Or are they keeping quiet as not to upset Song any more? Hell, what about me? Some guy's face in the window didn't exactly make my night. And what about those bricks, weird phone calls and cars slowly driving by. Prudence wasn't always Katrina's strongest virtue and she fought the urge to bring up last night's incident.

Katrina would let someone else do it, and she sipped coffee while reviewing her to-do list for the day.

"Whatcha got there?" Song asked, setting filled plates before Tim and Bruce.

"My to-do list for the day," replied Katrina.

"Yeah, shave her tongue and brush her legs," chuckled Tim.

"You're sick."

"You two stop it," said Song. "Eat and be quiet."

No one had to tell Bruce, for he was content just to wolf down his breakfast all the while hiding behind the morning's paper. Besides, he'd made his contribution to breakfast chit-chat earlier and was now ready for some serious comic strip enlightenment.

"Bruce," said Katrina, "you left a pile of clothes on the floor. Can you get them before the newspeople get here? We don't need some photographer coming along and capturing them on film." Katrina exhaled. "Did you bring down our vitamins?"

"Yeah." Reluctantly Bruce put down his paper, dug in his pocket, and produced a small plastic bag with several capsules.

"So, what do you want me to do?" Bruce asked.

Katrina knew Bruce didn't offer twice. "Let's get together on this one. Who wants to do what?"

"I guess I'll put up the banners out front," Bruce said.

"I'll get the kitchen," said Song.

"Tim, what about you?" said Katrina. "Can you check the exterior and see that everything looks good?"

"Yeah," he sighed. "What about you?"

35

Tina Czarnota

"I'll go through the inn and finish cleaning and vacuuming."
Katrina smiled. "How 'bout us? How do we look?" Katrina
ignored Tim's expression. "Should the newspeople or guests
arrive, we can't look rough around the edges."

"Yes, Katrina," sang Tim.

"Wise guy. Don't you want us to make a good impression?
This is it, Bubba."

"Katrina, this is your dream, not mine. I'm not," he twirled
his finger in the air, "gung-ho about this as you are."

"Then do it for your wife. And if you can't, at least don't let
the guests see your puss."

"Tim, just do the best you can," said Song.

"Yeah, yeah."

"Well," said Katrina, "I'll start upstairs." She picked up her
plates, set them in the sink, passed the others at the table, and
gave them each a mini-hug. When Tim grimaced, she playfully
pinched him and left the kitchen.

"I should start on the banners," said Bruce. "You coming,
Dad?

"Yeah." Tim was already fishing in his shirt pocket for a
cigarette as he got up from the table. Pushing his chair back, he
made for the rear kitchen door.

Song was left alone and surveyed the dirty kitchen. Once
again the mess was left to her, except for the dishes that Katrina
picked up. She shook her head. There was much to do.

In a short time the inn was bustling with the activity of busy
workers. Song cleaned the kitchen, accepted fresh-cut flowers
from the delivery service and set about arranging floral
centerpieces. Bruce, with Tim's help, erected two deep teal and
emerald green banners announcing the grand opening of the
newly remodeled Tudor Grove Inn. Katrina freshened the suites
and put out fresh guest soaps and chocolates. The inn was about
ready for their first official business.

"Katrina, Katrina," Song called up the stairs. "They're here.
The folks from the newspaper are here."

"I'll be right down. Can you greet them at the door?"

Katrina's heart beat faster as she took a final look at herself in the long mirror. Smiling at her image, she reeled around to head for the bedroom door. Then, her gaze caught the pile of soiled clothes that hadn't been picked up.

"Dammit." Katrina heard Song's and two unfamiliar voices, followed by footsteps, heading up the carpeted stairs in the direction of the guest suites.

Katrina kicked the offending pile under the bed just as the door swung open to reveal Song and her two new arrivals.

"Hi... welcome to Tudor Grove," Katrina trilled and smiled. She pulled her leg back and walked over to the trio.

After exchanging pleasantries, Song introduced the couple as Jessie Hodgkins, the staff writer, and Lou Smagatino, the photographer, both from the local newspaper. While the photog was about thirty and great looking, the writer was young, blonde, and pretty–so pretty that Katrina wondered why she wasn't in modeling.

"Well, I'd like to see the rest of the inn and proceed with a few snaps of the rooms," Smagatino said. "The exterior and then maybe a group picture and some individual shots, if that's okay?"

Song and Katrina agreed, and ushered the two out of the room and down the hall toward the remaining guest suites.

While Song toured the upstairs with the newspeople, Katrina saw the opportunity to rush downstairs and make sure the rest of the inn looked perfect. Figuring she had just a few minutes, she quickly plumped up pillows, adjusted draperies and straightened anything that was just a centimeter off.

Seeing a photograph of Tim and Bruce, Katrina stopped and grimaced.

"Oh boy. I wonder what those two look like? The bargain basement boys in a photo shoot... they're probably ripe after working out in the sun."

Hurrying outside and across the front lawn she sighed at the sight of the father-son team out on the lawn, sitting and talking. "And I was worried they'd be dirty from all that yard work. Hey, you guys... " Katrina called as she approached them. She was slightly out of breath. "The people from the paper are here. Are you dressed okay? They're gonna take our pictures. Sitting out there on the grass can take a toll on a guy's wardrobe."

The men laughed. Tim especially seemed amused by Katrina's worry.

"Come on, you guys, let's see what you look like."

"I don't want my picture taken," Tim said, dismissing her with a wave of his hand.

"Tim, please. Cooperate."

"So what do you think?" Bruce looked in the direction of the road. Katrina followed his gaze.

"They're beautiful."

For the moment Katrina forgot about the duo and ran down the remainder of the lawn out to the road. There she looked upon the two brightly colored flags that heralded the opening of the inn and a large teal wooden sign with the words, "Tudor Grove Inn, Bed and Breakfast," pitched in the ground for all the world to see.

Katrina was admiring them from all angles when she remembered she had left Song alone with the visitors. With a glance at the empty road, she turned and hastened toward the inn.

"Guys, they look great but we do have guests," she said, hurrying past the duo that still lolled on the grass.

Watching Katrina running up to the front of the house, Tim laughed and thanked Bruce for the diversion.

"They're making a big deal of this whole thing," Tim said.

"Yeah," sighed Bruce as he rose to his feet, "and I got some pictures to pose for or I'll never hear the end of it."

"You know, if women didn't bitch so much, maybe we'd do more."

"Yeah, Dad," Bruce laughed, deciding his father's excuse was better than none.

"Go have your picture taken. I'll be right in." Tim lit up another cigarette.

CHAPTER 6

"Katrina, there you are," Song said. "I wondered where you'd gotten to. They're ready to take the photos and we're deciding the best places to do that in."

"I was rounding up Bruce and Tim," Katrina said. "They'll be along in a few minutes."

As the photographer adjusted the lighting in the drawing room and Song freshened her make-up for her "shoot," Bruce entered and picked up the jangling phone at the reception desk. Covering the mouthpiece he asked, "Should I answer it? Or do you want to?"

"You're holding it," said Katrina.

Smagatino smirked and proceeded to tilt Song's head gently to expose her more photogenic side.

"Uh-h, Tudor Grove," Bruce said. "Okay, uh huh… That's good. Bye."

"Who was that?" asked Song.

"The guests due in… Konrath somebody or other. Anyway, they'll be late he said. He wants us to hold their room for them."

"Mrs. Versay, just relax and smile," said the photographer. "That's good."

Tim finally joined the group in the drawing room and watched the whole scene, hardly ever taking his eyes off Jessie, who was inspecting the chess table across the room.

Katrina saw Tim's hungry stare and eased over to him. "Sheesh, you're gonna bore a hole through her," Katrina hissed in a loud whisper.

"Don't worry what I might do," said Tim.

"If you were my husband I'd have dumped your ass a long time ago."

39

"You'd never have a chance to be my wife." He said it loud enough for the others to hear. They turned toward the two.

"Sorry," Katrina said, her face reddening.

"You're pretty frisky," Smagatino said. "How about you going next? What room have you chosen to use? Remember, select the room that most reflects your personality."

"The bathroom," Tim said and laughed.

Katrina ignored him and approached the photographer.

"Well, I love the fireplace, but Song already used the drawing room. Besides it lacks something without a fire blazing in it. My next choice is the gift shop or library." Katrina started to babble as she typically did when she was nervous. "Um... I really don't know, let him go next." She pointed at Tim.

"I don't want my picture taken."

"Dad, just have the thing taken already," said Bruce.

As the family bickered, Jessie took out a pocket recorder and started to talk into it.

Noticing this, Katrina became silent and motioned to Bruce.

"I'll go next," Katrina said. "How about in the library? Yes, the library will do just fine."

Everyone followed Katrina out of the drawing room except Jessie.

"Bruce," Katrina whispered as they entered the library, "did you see her talking into that recorder? She's probably making notes on the most dysfunctional family-owned-and-operated bed and breakfast in North America. Can you see what she's up to? And keep an eye on your dad. The way he stares at women makes him look like he hasn't seen one in years. I'll bet he tries to sneak back with her."

"You worry too much, but I'll go," he whispered back.

"Make sure he doesn't try to hit on her... or something. All we need is to have some smut printed about this place."

She was right. Tim, trying to appear nonchalant, was quietly backing out of the library.

Bruce nodded at Katrina and followed a few steps behind his father.

"You're next, Miss," said Smagatino to Katrina.

When the photo shoot was completed, Katrina realized that neither Jessie Hodgkins nor the men had returned to the library.

"Excuse me," she said.

Katrina's imagination was running wild. She envisioned both Tim and her boyfriend acting like fools and hanging on the blonde babe in the other room. Stopping at the doorway, Katrina stood there and watched Bruce and Tim sitting on the sofa with the reporter between them, engaged in light, happy conversation. It was several moments before Bruce noticed his girlfriend glaring at him.

"You're next," Katrina said.

"Oh Katrina," Bruce said quickly. "Ms. Hodgkins was just telling us about her position with the paper."

"I'll bet."

Bruce rose from the couch and followed Katrina out.

"Great," she said. "I ask you to keep an eye on your dad and you land up acting worst than him... if that's possible."

"Katrina, she's engaged... or something."

"Good, don't forget it. The photographer's waiting for you. Where are you having your picture taken?"

"I don't know. My workbench in the pantry isn't much of a backdrop."

The couple entered the library when Song announced that Lou had another appointment and needed to get on with the booking. After discussing settings, Bruce agreed to use a makeshift backdrop to give the illusion of a work area.

"Do you have a shop to do your construction work?" Smagatino asked.

"Not yet," Bruce said. "But I plan to build a free standing workshop soon as my blueprints are approved and we get this place going."

"Bet you're anxious about that one." Smagatino was setting up his equipment.

"Where's Tim?" asked Song, becoming aware of her husband's absence.

41

Excusing herself, Song went to fetch her husband.

Katrina smiled at Bruce who now posed for the camera, then left to catch any possible action.

"Honey, you're next," Song called to Tim. "Honey" never heard her, for he was laughing and talking with his new friend.

It was Jessie Hodgkins who ended the conversation. "I'd better start my interview." She began scooping up her belongings while rising from the couch she shared with Tim.

"When Lou is through with the photos, we'll proceed with the interview. In the meantime I'll set up in the library." The writer smoothed her tight red skirt and walked past Song, never glancing her way.

"I'm not getting my picture taken," Tim said, hoping to dodge any conversation regarding the pretty blonde.

"What were you doing in here so long?" Song asked.

"Yeah, Honey, what were you doing in here so long?" Katrina joined in Song's defense.

"Jessie... er... Ms. Hodgkins and I were talking about things... pertaining to her job," Tim said.

Katrina exaggerated a cough.

Tim avoided looking at Katrina and continued his protest about having his picture taken.

"Well, I can't force ya into it," Song said. "Come on then, let's do the interview instead."

While the group assembled in the library, Smagatino was busy taking various pictures of the exterior of the inn.

"Now then," said Jessie, "will one of you be spokesperson for the group?"

"How about if we all share in the input?" said Katrina.

"Yes, I'd like that," said Song. "Tim, what about you?"

Tim stood in the doorway glancing in Jessie's direction. "You go ahead, I'll be fine right here."

After asking the novice innkeepers the obligatory questions regarding their likes, dislikes, hobbies and vital stats, during which Katrina quickly pointed out that Tim was married and

Bruce was engaged, the reporter asked Song how the group decided to go into innkeeping with so little experience.

"Well, I always had a desire to operate a B and B, especially after it became a popular thing to do. I mentioned it to Katrina one day while she and Bruce were visiting us and we looked at a house that I had an eye on. Katrina had a similar interest, but wasn't impressed with the place. Since we didn't have enough money anyway, we brushed off the idea as a dream. A few years went by and my dad passed away, and Katrina's mom did also. Anyway, after settling our parents' estates, we came into a little money and well here we are."

"So, Katrina," Jessie said, "how did you folks happen to settle on this particular site?"

"We never could get away from our jobs for a stretch of time, so the Versays and Bruce and I would meet at a halfway point between Tampa and Boca, which happens to be somewhere around Lake Wales and these parts. I don't know if it was sentimental reasons, the fragrance of the orange blossoms, the area itself–I suspect it was a bit of all–but we started looking at real estate and as Song pointed out, here we are."

After asking Bruce a few questions on his experience in construction and his new career at the inn, Jessie glanced in Tim's direction, and noticed he was gone. A barrage of coughs echoing from outside the library door revealed that Tim was experiencing one of his coughing spells and was heading outdoors all the while trying to stifle the hacking noises.

The pretty blonde grimaced and continued with her questions.

"So tell me, how will you be distinguished from other bed and breakfasts?"

"Well," Katrina answered, "I will introduce into our breakfast menu some dishes that have been favorites of our family for generations. On special occasions we'll serve candlelight dinners, again including some favorites that my grandmother handed down to my mom and down to me. Some of our ingredients will be organically grown and pesticide free."

Song would not be outdone. "I'll be doing most of the cookin', for I've over five years of cafeteria experience and I'm able to turn out large volumes of food. My German chocolate pie is to die for. Also, my menu will boast special items quite often. And my dear, I just may invite you to one of our special breakfasts."

"That would be nice," said Jessie, though it was clear she was unimpressed. "So, let's say it's a year later and I am interviewing you. What do you hope to report to me about this venture? This inn?"

"That it isn't haunted," mumbled Katrina, as a curtain fluttered in her mind.

"Why would you worry about such a thing?" Jessie said, her interest sharpened. "Come on. I'm a good listener."

The curtain flapped wildly then stopped. "Why do you ask?"

"You mentioned it. Look, it's my job, that's all."

Bruce bit back a smile, and watched the two sparring females.

"Are you sure that's all?" Katrina said, her green-grey eyes narrowing.

"Look, I don't know what you're implying but this house does... well it has sort of a history."

"What sort of a history?" Now Song's curiosity was piqued.

Bruce got up and headed for the kitchen. He always enjoyed a snack with his entertainment.

"Well, let me ask you this. What do you know about this house, or inn, rather?" Jessie asked. She turned off her recorder and put it into her leather bag. "Off the record. All right?"

"We were told that in the early 1900s a young doctor built this place for his new bride," said Katrina. "Actually quite a nice story. Why?"

"And that's all you were told?"

"Yes. Why?" Katrina said.

"You're correct so far but there's a part that's left out. The story goes on that this same young doctor came home early one evening to surprise his new wife. It seems that he was the one that got the surprise. When he entered the dim house no one was there. Calling out to his spouse, he received no answer. As he entered the kitchen, from the window, he noticed a light coming from the barn. Going across the backyard, not knowing what to expect, he heard noises. Peering through a knot in the wooden door, he could make out a man embracing his wife. According to the story, he went into a rage, scared the wife's lover off, and killed her."

By garsch," said Song.

Katrina remained silent.

Jessie glanced at her watch. "Just look at the time," she said. "Has anyone seen Lou? We'll be late for our next booking." She rose from her chair and extended her limp hand to both Song and Katrina. "Well, it's been a pleasure. Good luck and have a nice day."

Tina Czarnota

CHAPTER 7

The hot red convertible, with its radio cranking out rock tunes, sped up the driveway, hesitated, then pulled up farther. The male driver turned down the music.

"This is it," the attractive young woman in the passenger seat announced.

The young man turned off the ignition.

"Is that a pile of clothes on the front lawn?" he asked.

"Yeah. It's my aunt's doing. When Bruce leaves his dirty clothes laying around, she picks them up and throws them out the window... or sometimes in the garbage can."

"I'm staying at a hotel," her companion said.

Sitting in the car giggling between themselves, the perky woman glanced over at the inn and tapped her beau's arm. "Look."

Following her pointing finger, he looked up in time to see a beat up, old sneaker come flying out of an upstairs window, bounce off a lower roof and land squarely in the middle of the already formed pile.

The young couple laughed uproariously.

"Okay, Song, it's your turn," said Katrina.

"Oh Katrina, I can't do that." Song was quite upset at this.

"Sure you can. Just think of all the times you had to pick up their dirty clothes. All those meals you cooked and never got a thank you for..."

Song trembled while holding on to the big, dingy, tennis shoe, reflecting gravely on Katrina's comments.

"That blonde from the newspaper..."

The sneaker went sailing through the air and plopped on the ground just short of the heap of clothes.

Screaming and laughing ensued as more clothes were tossed out, followed by the two women jumping around. A high-five sealed their emotional triumph.

"That was fun," said Song, smiling broadly.

"Doesn't it feel good? It's a great way to vent your frustrations."

"Katrina, did you hear a horn beep?"

Sticking her head out the open window, Katrina saw a red convertible parked in the driveway.

"Oh no." She pulled herself back inside. "Someone's parked in the drive. God, I hope it's not our guests."

The horn sounded again.

Katrina poked her head out the window once more, and watched the occupants get out.

"It's Kim... it's my niece. Song, come on, she's here."

Grabbing Song's arm once again, Katrina headed for the bedroom door and half dragged the woman down the stairs.

"Katrina, careful."

Letting go of Song, she jumped the stairs two at a time, ran out the front door, across the porch and down the steps in the direction of the driveway.

"I didn't think it was you. I thought you were coming later," Katrina squealed, hugging her. "Did you have a hard time finding the place?"

"A little. Your sign is gorgeous, Aunty Trina, but we could barely read the lettering in the sun. Those flags helped though."

"So this must be Spike." Katrina hoped she got the name right; keeping up with her niece's boyfriends was a tough job. "I recognized you from a picture Kim sent me, the one with you at the beach."

Katrina extended her hand with a welcoming smile. She'd heard her niece gush openly about this man several times. And for good reason. He was a tall, strapping "dude" with a good build. His training with the police force back home insured this. Being a jock, he was tough, but his blue eyes could melt the iciest of hearts. Spike was a few years younger than her niece, but his buzz-cut gave him the appearance of a more mature man.

After exchanging greetings with Song and helping with the luggage, Kim produced the much-anticipated chocolates–sponge candy and Charlie Chaplin.

"Song, you've got to try this stuff," said Katrina. "But I need to get these inside out of the heat."

"Where's Uncle Bruce?" asked Kim. Even though Katrina and Bruce weren't married yet, Kim considered him to be an uncle.

"Where else? At the hardware store," said Katrina.

"I see you haven't changed your cleaning methods," Kim said with a nod at the pile on the front lawn.

They all laughed and walked on the crooked path toward the inn.

"So, what do you think of the place?" Song asked as they reached the front of the house.

"It's "jammin'," said Spike.

"He said he likes it," said Kim.

Spike stopped. "Is there wildlife living back in those trees?" he asked, straining a trained ear. He listened intently.

"Why, do you hunt?" asked Katrina.

"Not really, I just thought I heard a wounded animal or something."

Just then a horn-like noise sounded, followed by the appearance of Song's husband stuffing a railroad hanky into his pocket.

"There's your animal," Katrina whispered to Kim as they began to giggle like schoolgirls.

"Oh, there's Tim," said Song. "I'd like you to meet my husband. Tim, come here and meet Katrina's niece."

"This I gotta see," said Tim, further wiping his muddy hands on his pants.

Introductions were made and Tim stared at the young woman, not only taken with her beauty but with the striking resemblance to her aunt. Looking straight into Kim's green-grey eyes while shaking her hand, he felt as though he was greeting a more petite, prettier, version of Katrina. He smiled as she brushed a long wisp of medium brown hair from her face. Her full red lips parted as she smiled back at him.

"So your a cop?" Tim said, turning to Spike, conscious he might be getting into more trouble. "I used to be a state trooper myself."

Spike grinned. He felt he had met someone on common ground.

The group went inside, the two men walking behind and comparing law enforcement of years past to present times. Once inside Song offered to make some snacks and headed down the hall.

"Let me show you your room," Katrina said, then added quickly in a low tone, "Okay, she's gone." Katrina looked to make sure Song had actually gone into the kitchen. "Let's go upstairs. I'm so glad you're here. I need someone to talk to."

"What's up?" Kim asked curiously.

"Maybe it's nothing, but there's been some craziness going on around here. I should put this candy down. It's gonna melt in my hands. Want a piece?"

"No thanks. So go on."

After quickly recounting the events of yesterday, Katrina realized they were still standing in the hallway, holding onto several small packages.

"I'm sorry, I never even let you see your room. Some hostess I'm turning out to be. I'm sure it's nothing, Kim, and I'm probably a little more sensitive than usual, but just keep your eyes open. Now, here's your room."

Radiating pride but trying to appear cool, Katrina opened a door to reveal a beautifully decorated room.

"Aunty Trina, how elite and it's done in my favorite color."

"You like it?"

"Are you kidding?" Kim entered the room. She put down her small suitcase and immediately began exploring her surroundings.

"The closets are over there and the bathroom is to the left," said Katrina. "I'll let you settle in. When you're ready, come downstairs and get something to eat. We'll talk later and I'll show you the rest of the inn."

"If you see Spike send him up here."

"Okay."

"I could get used to this," Kim said as Katrina left. She basked in the essence of the English country-styled room. She approved of the white, lavender and pink repeat floral patterned walls that were mirrored in the ballooned valance curtains and plushy comforter. The light pickled, sturdy pine bedroom set rested on thick, lavender carpeting, and at once Kim claimed the satiny white chaise for her own. Stretching her legs out and laying her head back against her folded arms she sighed deeply and visually retraced the room once more. She realized that her aunt spared few expenses as she looked at a vase full of white and pink roses. Sitting on top of the bed pillows were two foil-wrapped chocolates and next to the nightstand stood a tall ice bucket with a bottle of champagne.

Kim adored Katrina, who had always lavished her with gifts and love. Only when she became a woman did Kim realize this was because Katrina never had children of her own.

Kim got up from the chaise and decided to check out the bathroom. Clicking on the light switch, she was greeted by the sight of an old-fashioned slipper tub with a gooseneck faucet and matching brass claw feet. A white pedestal sink and toilet completed the line of necessary fixtures. Little baskets containing toiletries were located conveniently near the tub and sink. Thick peach colored terry towels added just enough color to the almost all-white room, and a basket of peaches and cream potpourri emitted its unmistakable fragrance.

Peeking at herself in the mirror and liking what she saw, Kim decided that the rest of the inn must be as elite as her rooms were. She clicked off the light and went downstairs. She found Tim and Spike in the kitchen, eating sandwiches and enjoying cop talk.

"Where's my aunt?" Kim asked.

"Catching a nap," said Song, who was busy at the sink.

"Uncle Bruce come back yet?"

"Yes," said Song.

Stealing a pickle from her boyfriend's plate, Kim tried to get his attention but failed. Bored, Kim decided to help Song and got a quick tour of the kitchen. She wasn't surprised to see that it matched her suite with similar stunning charm.

Kim turned. "Aunty Trina, you're up. Did you rest?"

Katrina stood in the doorway, and stretched. "A little," she said, stifling a yawn. She noticed that Tim still had Spike engrossed in cop talk. "You like your suite?" Katrina asked Kim.

"It's gorgeous, I want to see the rest of the place."

"Let's go," said Katrina, beating a hasty retreat, for Tim was starting on his routine of worn-out, trooper jokes.

"Song, join us if you want," Katrina said, standing in the hallway. "We'll be goin' through the inn."

Song had just sat down with a cup of coffee. "I'll catch up with you later."

"This place is so elite," Kim said, admiring the hand-hooked runner that they walked on. "I love it."

"Good, then you can stay with us as long as you like."

"What time are your guests due in?" Kim asked.

"Early evening… I'm glad you got here sooner."

"As I said, I was pacing the floor, already packed. Spike agreed to check on an earlier flight. They had available seats so we took them."

"What did Spike think about the clothes incident?"

"He was afraid to come in," said Kim. The pair laughed.

"He's used to it, with Mom and the way she teases Dad. He's amused by it. As for those clothes on the lawn, what if your guests showed early?"

"I would've left them there, I was so mad at him." Katrina recounted the story about the press arriving and how she hid Bruce's clothes. "Before long he had another pile started. How do men get that way? Never mind, I already know."

"Where is Bruce, anyway?" asked Kim. "I didn't get to say hello yet."

"Maybe outside," said Katrina.

As Katrina and Kim entered the foyer, the front door opened. Bruce stepped in, toting a washbasket filled with the offending laundry. The two women began to laugh.

"Ha, ha," said Bruce, plunking the basket at the foot of the carpeted staircase.

"Hi, Uncle Bruce. How are you?" Kim went and hugged him.

"Okay, just doing some laundry. Did she tell you how mean she is to me?"

"Yeah."

"Now wouldn't it be easier to use the hamper?"

"Prob'ly." Bruce inched back. "Where is everybody?"

"In the kitchen," said Katrina.

"I'll take my clothes up later." With that, Bruce turned and headed for the kitchen.

The pair watched Bruce walk away. "That worked good," chuckled Kim.

"Someday it'll sink in." Katrina waved her hand, "C'mon. Let's head back and see what's goin' on, then I'll take you both around."

"I just hope I don't have to share Spike with Bruce's dad the whole time we're here," Kim said.

"Don't worry, they'll tire of each other soon enough."

Everyone gathered in the kitchen and the room was abuzz with conversation and laughter. Song was showing off her proficiency in serving. Katrina, being away from kin so long, was content with the family-like atmosphere, Bruce was pumped from the compliments he got for his handiwork, Tim was glad to have someone to talk cop talk with, and Kim was happy just to be on vacation with Spike.

Katrina smiled. Everything, for the moment, was perfect.

"I'll show them around now." Katrina put the last condiment bottle away and closed the refrigerator door.

"You kids go ahead," said Song. "I'll go out and help Tim with the gardening, at least until the guests arrive."

A short while later, as their tour ended, Katrina announced there was "one room left to go." Opening a wooden door and escorting Kim and Spike in, she declared, "And this is Spike's room."

Before Kim could protest, Katrina said, "I promised your mom I would stick to this arrangement. Now, I've caught hell for getting in between you and your parents' wishes before and she was mad at me for weeks. This time I'm going along with what she asks." Katrina didn't agree with Kim's mother on this—after all it was the new millennium—but she understood.

Spike looked at Kim and shook his head to discourage what he knew would be an assertion of her adult rights. "I'll get the rest of the bags and bring them up."

"Thanks. And Kim, please tell Spike about… you know." Katrina turned to the boyfriend. "Maybe you can look around some. I'd sure appreciate it. Try to be discreet. I don't want anyone getting spooked. Well, I got things to do, see you later."

The puzzled look on the young cop's face disappeared as Katrina's footsteps faded down the stairs.

"She's as bad as my mother," pouted Kim. "What are you smiling about?"

"We're alone now," he said.

She went straight into his arms.

Downstairs, Katrina was pacing and fretting. "I wonder what time our guests will get here? What if they stiff us? Maybe I'll check the inn again and make sure it's ready." She sighed. "Oh, relax," she admonished herself. "Even Song's enjoying some free time. Besides, if someone sees me talking to my…" She now thought silently. I just want us to succeed!

Done arguing with herself, Katrina began to relax as she poked through the trinkets in the gift shop which adjoined the library on the first floor.

Bruce did a good job capturing the old-fashioned country look, Katrina thought as she admired the little room. The wooden shelves across the back wall were filled with rows of tropical flavored jellies and candies made from locally grown citrus fruits.

"What's up?" asked Kim, joining her aunt.

"Just playin' around the gift shop."

Kim stood with Katrina and gazed about the tables and bins. "I like the periwinkle blue and white plaid cloths on those tables. They're cute with the matching curtains. I'll have to take some of this peach sachet home with me for Mom." She picked up a bow-tied bundle, closed her eyes and sniffed at the opening. "And these T-shirts are cool. They'll make nice souvenirs." She edged over to the obligatory rack of scenic Florida postcards.

Katrina stood back and smiled as she watched her niece stake claims to nearly everything in the shop. Not much had changed since the days when Kim was a little girl and Katrina took her shopping through the local department store. Now instead of dolls, frilly dresses and little bows, Kim was buying sachet, makeup and souvenirs. Katrina smiled warmly.

The gentle creaking of the wooden floor beneath them reminded Katrina of the present.

"Where's Spike?" Katrina asked.

"Upstairs, lying down for a bit. We're gonna take a ride into town. Wanna come? What's this stuff?"

"Orange blossom perfume. It's the closest thing to what this area smells like during March. The air just fills with the smell of these blossoms... it's one of the draws that brought us here. As for the ride, no thanks. Our guests should be arriving soon."

"Okay. Well, I'm gonna get Spike up so we can go. Oh, Aunty Trina... I didn't get a chance to tell him about you know... when we go for a ride I'll have time."

"Thanks."

"I guess I'll go out for some fresh air too... who knows how much time I'll get in the future?" After Kim left, Katrina turned and saw Bruce. "You're up. I'm going out to join your parents. Wanna come?"

"Yeah... soon as I wake up." He stretched.

Ambling closely behind was a yawning Spike.

"Dazed and Confused," Katrina laughed, eyeing the two men.

"Wiseguy," Spike said.

"Did you sleep?" asked Katrina.

"Yeah, I needed it. After the flight and the drive out here." Spike gazed about the gift shop. "Did Kim see this yet?"

"Afraid so," Bruce said. "There was no stopping–"

"No stopping what?" Kim asked, now joining them. "Oh, I need camera film," she said, scurrying up to a sundries display. She queried the trio when they began to laugh.

The phone rang in the drawing room and Katrina excused herself to answer it.

"Aunty Trina," called Kim, hurrying to the phone, "let me answer it. Maybe it's Mom."

Katrina gave Kim a quick briefing on what to say should it be a paying guest, which it was.

"I'll check," Kim said. "Hold please." While Kim covered the mouthpiece with her hand, Katrina reached over and pressed the hold button. "There's a guy on the line who wants to know if he can book a table for two for breakfast tomorrow if he isn't staying at the inn?"

Katrina gave the go-ahead and Kim confirmed the table for two at the next morning's meal.

"This is fun," Kim said, hanging up the phone. "I want to run an inn."

"It's not all play, there's lots of hard work involved."

"Well, I'd hire help to do all the work and I'd just answer the phone, but first I have to snag my man and go see some sights." In feigned snobbery, the young woman sauntered out the door to do just that.

56

Katrina smiled and shook her head as she scanned the reservation log at the front desk. She was reading Kim's entry when the phone rang. The dial tone buzzed when she picked it up.

"How does your garden grow?" Katrina asked.

"Pretty good," Song replied. She was digging and planting new impatiens–several feet away from the previous site. Eyeing the root system on a purple plant, she then plunked it into the ground. "Did your blueberries arrive yet?" Song asked, looking from her dirty hands to her polo shirt.

"No. I may have to do without them. I hoped to get them in time for the grand opening breakfast or brunch. Guess I'll just make the recipe another day. Oh, we got another booking... for breakfast."

"Good. Did they say where they heard about us from?"

"I forgot to ask Kim. She took the call."

Song became absorbed in her planting and Katrina plopped down on the grass in the middle of the back yard to watch the husband, wife and son. The sun felt good and she tilted her head back as if to catch more rays. The breeze was light on her face and lifted her hair from her neck. Bruce steadied an orange hibiscus bush while Tim reinforced the plant's new spot–under the rear windows–with more soil, water and mulch. Everyone seemed content; even Tim looked like he was enjoying the gardening.

After starting to feel guilty that she was relaxing while the others worked, Katrina rose from her place in the sun, plucked a few weeds from the organic herb garden and announced her plans for organizing some things for tomorrow's breakfast.

"You gonna start on the dough?" Song asked.

"I don't think so. I doubt the shipment gets here today. if it comes later, I'll make the recipe tomorrow and serve them on Monday. It's no big deal."

Song knew better as she watched Katrina shuffle off. "I know how much she wanted to make those blueberry pierogies

57

for tomorrow," she said to Tim. "I told her to use frozen but she said her mom always made them with fresh berries. I wish I could do something about... maybe they'll still get here. What time does Super Express deliver 'til?"

"At the office we get deliveries as late as seven," Tim said. "They also deliver on Sundays."

"Well, good." Song glanced about the yard. "Geez, it's startin' to got dark," she said. "That's it for digging for today. I'll get some things put away and get washed."

Katrina sat alone in the drawing room, stretched out on a couch and sighed in discontent. She thought about her young and carefree niece. "To be in my twenties again," she mumbled. She felt old. "And she's so cute. I wish I could do it all over again."

She envied the fact that Kim could go wherever and whenever she wanted. Kim enjoyed real vacations, lived at home under the security of her parents' roof and just loved her job.

"What's up?" Bruce strode into the room. He knew Katrina by now. "Are you upset over those nasty blueberries?"

"No." She shared her thoughts and feelings.

Bruce sat down beside her and kissed her softly on the cheek.

"Katrina, you're only in your thirties. You're not bad looking and you're considerate of others... well, my dad might argue that one."

She smiled lightly. "I don't want to be good. I want to be beautiful and carefree."

"As I remember, you said you were sick of partying, and hangin' out. You wanted to be more settled."

"I... I'm not sure I meant this settled." Katrina sighed. "Sometimes, I guess, human nature has us wanting something else... wanting everything."

"You're just a little unglued about running this inn. We'll get through it, you'll see."

The answer came to her and she knew that her inner feelings were a gift, not to be quashed. A nudging, that sometimes, when addressed, led to personal growth and fulfillment. She began to feel better and realized she had had these feelings before. "Thanks," she said to him. "Sometimes it helps just to be heard."

She stretched. "Maybe a multi B vitamin will help," she said and recalled how Bs were good for the nervous system.

Katrina went to the kitchen and drew water from the sink's purifying system. Song was sitting at the table looking over a list. "We'll have to set up the patio furniture for the guests' morning coffee," Katrina said, peering over Song's shoulder. "I can't wait till Bruce gets started on that gazebo… or you think a private cottage should go up first?"

"We need a restroom put in on the first floor–" Song was interrupted by the sound of a car pulling up the driveway. "That's either your niece, the delivery man, or our guests." She went to look out.

Katrina chugged down her water, anxious to see who it was. She found herself excited again at the prospect of people arriving and hurried down the corridor after Song.

"It's the guests," Song said. "Katrina, it's them."

The sound of car doors shutting and welcomes being extended made the old place feel alive once more. Even Tim introduced himself to the couple and offered to carry bags. Bruce retrieved a suitcase from his dad and from the woman, and headed up the stairs with them.

Now it was Katrina's turn to make acquaintances with their first official guests, and butterflies flopped about in her trim belly.

Introductions were made and Katrina now could put a face to the anxious voice of Mrs. Konrath. "How nice to have you stay with us." Katrina extended the greeting and noticed the haunting brown eyes that studied her and the apparent nervousness in which one question directed her way could make for an uninterrupted, one-sided conversation. In her late forties, Mindy Konrath was of average height and of above average looks. Smoothing her dark-brown bob, she declared that she wanted to view the rest of the inn and led the way down the corridor.

Song jumped in behind the eager woman and attempted to conduct a tour of the first floor, leaving an apologetic Mr. Konrath behind. "Please excuse my wife, she's so excited about these places," he said. "We've been to so many bed and breakfasts and inns, I could have owned one by now I'm sure."

Katrina laughed and assured her guest that such enthusiasm was refreshing. Just as long as she doesn't get too enthused, Katrina thought.

Bob Konrath, who stood as tall as Katrina, was a handsome, dark-blonde man with blue-grey eyes and an athletic build. He seemed self-assured and patient, and Katrina pondered how often times, opposites did attract. Compared to her husband, Mindy was pale and high-strung.

"If you like, you can follow the tour, or I can just show you to your room."

"I'd just like to run the rest of our things to our room if you don't mind?"

"Sure, it's upstairs, the last suite on the left. Your luggage is already in your room."

"Thank you."

Katrina tried not to stare as Bob Konrath parted and made his way up the wooden stairs.

"Oh Bob," called Mindy, breezing into the room. "You must see this place. Bob, where are you?"

"Mrs. Konrath," said Katrina, "your husband is upstairs. Your room is the last one on the left."

"Oh, I have to see the rest of this place…" and Mindy was up the stairs in a flash with a harried Song following close behind, lest Mrs. Konrath should want to explore the occupied rooms.

Katrina was mildly amused at the diverse personalities she already encountered and found herself looking forward to the future. She waited as Song descended the staircase.

"They're settled in," Song said. "I'm gettin' pooped from those stairs." Song plopped down in the winged-back chair.

"Do they like their room?"

"Yes, she's thrilled with it. He's handsome isn't he?"

"And he's a great dresser."

"Speaking of handsome, where's my Tim?"

"Where else?" Outside," Katrina said. "They're standing out in the dusk. Tim's smoking and Bruce is right there with him. Once the bugs start biting, they'll come in."

"Or when they realize they're hungry."

"Incidentally, any snacks to prepare?" Katrina motioned toward the second floor.

"No, they're goin' out to eat. They'll be in by midnight."

"Why don't we take this time to sneak out and eat? We don't have to go far."

"What about your niece?"

"I gave her a key."

"Good, I'd like a break. Now if Tim will go along–"

"I'll start whining like I do, and he'll go along just to shut me up."

Song laughed. "Yes, that usually works."

"Besides, I haven't picked on him lately. I don't want him to think I don't care."

The women left the drawing room laughing and soon all four were piled in the car, with Tim as driver. As he backed his auto onto the dark street, Tim barely noted the wooded lot opposite the inn. Shifting gears, he pulled away from the estate, voicing his choice of restaurants.

Several yards back, on a path that ran alongside the neglected lot, a car sat in darkness. With an exposed roll of film safe inside his camera, the lone occupant trained his binoculars on the Tudor Grove Inn and scoured the estate one last time. Moments later the driver started up his car, keeping his headlights off. With that, the silver auto crept onto the road, and drove off in the opposite direction.

CHAPTER 8

Song, as usual, was up early, glad to be alone downstairs. She preferred it like that and could work better that way. She had much to do, and once Tim and the others were up she knew she wouldn't accomplish half of what she wanted.

Making her way around the five tables in the elegant Victorian-styled room, Song set the white lace-clothed tables with crystal water and Mimosa glasses, ice pink cloth napkins, and silverware from her own family collection. "I'll die if I lose even one fork from this set," she mused. But it was a special occasion.

While Song aligned each dark cherry high-backed chair, she glanced about the white wallpaper with its embossed satiny ribbon design. Katrina picked it out, leaving the choice of the rose tone carpeting to Song. Stepping back, Song admired the room. It was perfect.

"You've been 'round Katrina too long," said Tim, standing in the doorway. "She talks to herself, too."

"Shh-h. How long have you been standing there?"

"Too long. When are you making coffee?"

"Not just yet. I'm stalling for time. Once they smell coffee brewin', they'll all be down. I've much to do and I don't need others in my way. While you're havin' your smoke, can you start arranging the patio furniture out back? It needs to be ready by eight for our coffee hour. This way, it'll give 'em a chance to wake up, read the paper and allow the rest of the guests to get here."

"Where am I sitting?"

"Well, Katrina's sittin' at the head of the table, nearest the kitchen. I'm to her right... to separate you two. You're on my right, then Spike, her niece, and Bruce is next to Katrina on her left."

"Who's at those other tables?"

"Uh, two other couples," said Song. The third one's a spare. Or we can use it as a sideboard."

"Make some coffee, yeah?"

"Go outside and I'll make instant. You can have brewed later." Song scurried off to the kitchen, avoiding her husband's protests.

Tim grumbled and shuffled out the back door, leaving a trail of smoke in his wake.

In the kitchen, Song was joined by Bruce. "Today's the big day, huh?"

"Oh, mornin', Bruce... yes it is. I'm makin' your father some instant coffee." Song poured boiling water into a cup. "Want some?"

Bruce opted to wait for brewed but offered to take Tim's cup to him. "Well, I'll go help with the patio furniture."

"Okay. If anyone asks, we'll be eatin' around nine," said Song. "I doubt everyone's here before then."

"Yeah," Bruce said, heading for the back door.

"When's Katrina gettin' up?" Song asked.

"She hit the snooze button ten minutes ago. She should be up by now," he said. "What's on the menu anyway?"

"There'll be sausage, eggs and a special French toast. Everything must be perfect," Song said wistfully.

Bruce voiced approval and went outside.

It wasn't much later that Katrina and Kim joined Song in the kitchen.

"Aunty Trina, I put the place cards where you said, but I have two left for that small table and they don't have names on them." Kim lifted her head and inhaled. "Mm-m, food."

"I'll get them later," said Katrina. "Do you want to help out more? Oh, keep the kitchen door closed, okay?"

"Yeah, what else needs to be done?" asked Kim.

"Put this menu on the easel in the foyer. When you come back you can take coffee to the guests and ask if they'd like orange juice. Do some hostessing, you know, chat with the guests... if they want to. Just jump in and entertain."

"Okay." Grabbing a piece of the fresh fruit Katrina was cutting, Kim headed out of the kitchen, reading the menu she was carrying. "I'm having some of this almond crème French toast." Kim looked up in time to see Mindy and Bob exit the front door.

"Well, my prep work is done. What time is it?" asked Song, her back to the clock.

"Almost eight-thirty," said Katrina.

"I guess I'll start cookin' and whoever gets here gets here."

"I'll put the muffins and tea breads out now. Oh Song, who are the other two guests for breakfast? I'd like to add their cards to the table."

"Uhm-m, I forgot the name. Katrina, is someone at the front desk? I thought I heard voices."

"I'll check."

Katrina dashed through the dining room and peeked out at the reception desk. No one was there. She shrugged and went about placing a basket of baked goods on each table.

"No one's out there, Song—"

"Aunty Trina," Kim said, whisking through the kitchen, "that lady wants orange juice but she wants to know if the oranges are pesticide free and if the juice is squeezed fresh."

"The oranges are grown locally and the juice was squeezed here this morning," said Katrina.

"She asked me all kinds of questions about the food," said Kim. "Oh, do we serve egg white omelettes?"

"They're not on the menu, but I suppose we can make one if someone wants. Try not to encourage things that aren't on the menu, Kim. Special orders may be requested ahead of time."

"Okay. Aunty Trina, I think a car just pulled up. Want me to check?"

"I'll do it. Just announce breakfast's being served in fifteen minutes. Oh, and ask Bruce to come in and help now that it's almost time to serve."

A smartly dressed middle-aged couple climbed the three steps up the front porch. Katrina was there to open the door and greet the newly arrived breakfast guests. She was amazed at how much they looked alike, both having dark-brown hair and similar features. Brief introductions to the inn and menu were made, and she escorted them to the backyard for coffee and conversation.

"Breakfast is being served in about ten minutes," Katrina said, as she escorted them to a striped shaded table and chair ensemble. "Please join the rest of our staff and guests. Would you prefer coffee, tea or freshly squeezed orange juice?" Katrina addressed the gentleman, but he didn't seem to hear. He was staring at something.

"Wren darling, she's talking to you," said the woman.

A light smile came over his face and Katrina turned to see what was so interesting.

"Sorry, I'll have juice. Thanks."

"Same for me."

Katrina couldn't help notice that Tim had ceased his discussion and knocked over his coffee cup as he rose rather hastily and headed for the inn. She wondered what was going on. She looked back at the couple as she tried to appear casual, then glanced at the small gathering. Everyone seemed to be enjoying conversation, including the newly arrived Mr. and Mrs. Wren Dukette.

Katrina returned to the kitchen, curious about Tim's behavior.

"I don't know who they are, Tim." Katrina heard Tim grilling Song as she entered the kitchen.

"Katrina," he turned to her, "who is that guy... what's his name?"

Before Katrina could speak, another car was heard advancing toward the inn. "Oh God, the other guests," she said. "Song, who are they so I can address them?"

Song and Tim just stared back at her and looked as though they lost their tongues. "I don't know what's going on here but I have a door to answer," Katrina said. "Breakfast should be served."

Katrina, slightly confused, headed for the front door. Passing her niece in the hall, the young woman offered to greet the guests while Katrina announced the commencement of breakfast.

"Yeah, thanks," said Katrina. As she turned and headed down the hall, she noticed Bob Konrath. When he saw her, he smiled at her then made his way to the gift shop. A hint of his cologne lingered in the air. Lucky for him I'm real busy, she mused.

Katrina cut back through the kitchen and caught the tail end of Tim and Song's conversation. He was now smoking.

"Is everything okay?" asked Katrina.

"Yes, I'll tell you later. Tim, put out the cigarette and go sit down at the table," Song said.

Katrina rounded up the guests and remembered that she'd left Kim at the front door. She ran up the stairs, and through the back kitchen door just in time to hear Kim making small talk with the recently arrived guests. The voices sounded familiar, and the female's voice sounded uncomfortably familiar. Katrina rounded the corner to the dining room in time to see Song pulling a chair out for none other than Jessie Hodgkins. A look of discomfort shot across Song's face and she turned to avoid Katrina's scowl.

"Song, I'll help you serve now," Katrina said, and followed the older woman into the kitchen. "Who invited her?" she demanded.

"Sh-h, they'll hear you."

"It must've been Tim 'cause you wouldn't have been so stupid."

Song avoided Katrina's eyes while she loaded a plate with sizzling hot sausage and bacon.

"Don't tell me it was Bruce?"

"No, Katrina... " Song quickened her pace as she headed for the dining room. The sausages, bacon and Song disappeared around the corner.

"Nice time for surprises," said Katrina. She leaned against the counter, shaking her head.

"Aunty Trina, are you all right?" asked Kim, coming into the kitchen. "Do you need help?"

"Yeah lots... Just kidding. It's just that someone invited the last woman I need to my bed and breakfast's grand opening, that's all. Do we have everything out there?"

"Everything but you. We'll talk later. Don't let her spoil your day. If you want, I'll spill coffee on her."

"No, she'll just melt," said Katrina. "Besides, I'm not sure how to get melted witch out of the carpet." Katrina smiled and followed Kim into the dining room.

The dining room bustled with the sounds of silverware clicking against china, conversation, and compliments bestowed on the innkeepers. Katrina looked up at Bruce and received his encouraging smile.

"Aunty Trina, how about a toast?" said Kim.

The gathering offered up cheers for the health of the innkeepers and for the success of the inn. The staff reciprocated in like manner.

Katrina's eyes roved the dining room occupants. The sexy Jessie Hodgkins had most of the male attention as she gushed about all the handsome men in the room and her fabulous career. Mindy Konrath went through her packet of vitamins and gave a synopsis of the benefits of each pill contained in the pouch. Tim said little but ate a lot, making sure not to glance over at the Dukettes. Song was chatting with Jessie, and jumped up several times to personally fetch things for the young woman. Kim, Katrina noticed, kicked Spike under the table when she felt he may have been smiling too long at Jessie. Bob Konrath, cool and sophisticated, talked mostly with Jessie, ignoring the sour looks from his wife. Lou Smagatino, who had accompanied Jessie, and who Katrina noticed for the first time, wasn't bad looking and seemed a bit annoyed at his breakfast date and cohort for ignoring his attempts at conversation. Mr. and Mrs. Dukette stayed off by themselves in the far right corner of the room where they engaged in heavy interchange, and often looked in Tim's direction. Bruce made casual conversation with Jessie, but squeezed Katrina's hand affectionately under the table several times.

What a motley crew, Katrina mused, and started to calm down enough to enjoy herself. She tried a little of everything and openly complimented Song for doing such a good job cooking.

"You must give me the recipe for this French toast... did you use fertile eggs? The fruit cup, Song, is this fruit chemical-free?"

Song was about to answer when Tim rose from the table. She knew it was time for his cigarette break and wished he sat and talked some more. He left out the back, taking care not to pass the dark-haired Mr. Dukette. Chit-chat continued and Mindy, not about to miss an opportunity for a larger audience, promptly jumped up and took over Tim's seat.

"You don't mind do you, Honey?" she said to her husband. "I want to sit next to the ladies and find out more about this wonderful inn." Katrina noticed that Bob merely nodded.

"Song, whose idea was this bed and breakfast?" Mindy Konrath asked. "I think it's a wonderful idea and I wish I could someday take on a venture of this sort."

The others turned to Mindy, and Katrina wondered when she would let Song actually answer. Mindy quickly sipped her water and barely swallowed before she started to talk once more. Sensing a tickle in her throat, Mindy reached for her glass, this time knocking it over. She started to cough and gag.

"Slap her on her back, she's got water down the wrong pipe," Katrina said. She didn't think the condition was serious. But Mindy didn't stop choking. Her frantic eyes bulged and she clutched at her throat.

"Raise her arms above her head," said Song.

Spike hurried to the woman who tried to stand up and knocked over her chair. Gasping for air, she fell to the floor.

"She's turning blue!" cried Katrina.

Quickly, Spike grabbed Mindy and gave several fist thrusts to her abdomen.

"Mindy, Mindy!" Bob Konrath called, attempting to run to her side.

"Stay back, give her air!" Spike ordered. Laying her down, he began mouth-to-mouth breathing. "Somebody call emergency."

It was Wren Dukette who dashed to the phone, dialed and gave the dispatcher directions to the inn. Everyone was in shock. Katrina prayed and Song appeared stricken as the young cop pumped on the woman's chest.

"I'm losing her," Spike said, desperately trying to save her.

Finally, he stopped. He moved back and Bob Konrath knelt and grabbed the lifeless body of his wife into his arms and sobbed heavily.

"I'm sorry. I did all I could." Spike's hand rested on Bob's shoulder. A dead silence enveloped the room; life felt as though it stood still in time. The only sound was the soft weeping of Bob Konrath.

A gentle movement came forth from the group.

"I'll have to cover this," Jessie said. "I hope you folks understand."

"Jessie, can't you wait?" Lou protested.

"Have you no respect?" said Bob. "My wife is dead and you're worried about some damn story."

Spike moved to calm the man and ordered everyone into the drawing room.

"I'll get us all some brandy…" Song offered.

"I'll get Dad," said Bruce. He walked to the front window and looked out. "Hey, Katrina, there's a box out on the front porch. I think your blueberries are here."

"Please bring them in," Katrina said.

"Yeah, round everyone up, pass out some brandy or something," said Spike. "Make sure no one leaves till emergency gets here. Bob, you gonna be all right?"

"Yeah..."

Spike left Bob sitting at the empty table while the grieving man collected himself. "Katrina, keep an eye on him and this room. Don't let anyone touch anything. I'll go get the rest of them in here."

"What's going on? Didn't she just choke?"

"I'm not sure. She was drinking water. Maybe a vitamin got stuck."

"You'd think it would've dislodged."

"I know," said Spike. He left Katrina contemplating his remarks.

Katrina turned. "Uh-oh," she said, seeing Jessie talking to the others, a pen and pad in hand. Katrina approached the reporter ready to address her when she glanced at the woman's notepad. At the top of the page Katrina read the words, "Country Inn, Dead and Breakfast."

"Spike, how about me goin' outside for a smoke?" said Tim. He had the young cop off to the side out of earshot of the others. "The paramedics are gone, the ol' girl was pronounced dead..."

"Tim, I'm now talking on a professional level. It'd be best if you went back in there with the rest, have a beer or something and wait for the police to get here. If they see you outside, they'll want to roam around and I can't chance that right now. You've been there. You understand."

"Yeah... so you think she was iced?"

"I'm not ruling anything out, but what I think and what the paramedics just told me... well, it doesn't look good."

"Too bad... I just wish they'd let me smoke in this damn place." Tim walked away grumbling and parked himself on the couch next to his wife. Song was engrossed in conversation with Jessie and Kim, who sat on the opposite sofa.

71

While Tim tried to make himself comfortable on the couch, he scanned the room in effort to keep his mind off cigarettes, and to amuse himself by contemplating the beauty Jessie's naked body.

Tim chuckled, then mumbled, "Bruce's sitting there at the desk reading the Sunday cartoons and there's a dead body in the other room." Tim's gaze roamed toward the chess table. His smirk vanished as he looked at Wren Dukette and his wife half-heartedly engaged in discussion over their strategies.

"What?" asked Song.

"Nothing," Tim grunted.

Spike stood vigilantly over the assemblage in the large drawing room and eyed every person; he knew choking wasn't the cause. He wondered who could've done it, because someone killed Mindy Konrath. The young cop glanced about the room. Just then Spike noticed Tim's expression change dramatically when the man's gaze fell upon the couple sitting across from him at the chessboard, Mr. and Mrs. Dukette. As Spike decided to take notes, he saw that the Dukettes had ceased playing their game, and had come together in a whispered conversation, occasionally glancing at the edgy Tim sitting across the room on the couch. Mrs. Dukette nodded in agreement, and it appeared that Wren was about to make a move when a car was heard pulling up the drive toward the inn.

"I think they're here," announced Katrina.

Wren Dukette sat back down and Spike made his way to the reception desk in time to hear Katrina whisper to Bruce that she couldn't wait for the body to be removed.

Spike opened the front door and quickly closed it behind him. He introduced himself to the two arriving officers and asked for discretion when dealing with the incident since some of the occupants were unaware of his suspicions. "There's some excitable types in there... you know what I mean," he said.

Spike opened the front door and found Katrina standing there. He almost ran into her as he led the uniformed men through the drawing room, passing the front desk, occupied couches, chess table and into the dining room where Mindy Konrath lay covered by a white sheet.

All eyes were focused on the investigation being conducted in the dining area. Spike took his place in the doorway, almost blocking the entire entry. A uniformed policeman ushered Bob Konrath into the room and the door was ordered closed behind him.

"I'll be out here if you need me," Spike offered and left the dining room, leaving the door slightly ajar. "This is turning out to be some vacation," he sighed as he plopped into the vacated wing-backed chair.

"Spike, before you get too comfortable, let me sit there," said Tim. "This couch is too damn soft for me."

"Yeah."

"What's going on?" Katrina asked. "Why all the cloak and dagger bull?"

"It's procedure, Katrina."

"It's a homicide, isn't it?" asked Jessie Hodgkins.

"We're professionals," said Lou, "we have a right to know."

Spike eyed Lou with annoyance, until he noted the photographer appeared concerned for matters other than photography.

"Look guys, I really don't know. I'm not on duty and this is not my jurisdiction. They'll let us know soon enough. Song, is there any brandy left? I could use some about now."

"Sure, I'll go get it."

"Spike, I have to go to the bathroom," Kim said.

"Can you hold on a minute? They should be done soon."

"Well you can't stop us from stretching," Wren Dukette declared. He got up from the chessboard, reached his arms skyward then went to the reception desk. "May I see the paper?" he asked Bruce, who was leaning on the folded morning edition.

"It's all yours."

"Oh that's right, I never got to see our article," chirped Song as she handed the weary Spike a snifter of brandy. "I'd like to see that when you're through, Mr. Dukette."

"Geez, what's taking so long?" Jessie blurted, breaking from the chat she was having with Kim. "What time is it, Lou?"

The dining room door opened and the two officers and an ashen Mr. Konrath exited and joined the others in the drawing room.

"The coroner should be here soon," a stout white-haired cop by the name of Officer Casey said.

"Hold on, I think they're here," Wren Dukette said, pulling the drape aside and peering out at the drive. "Is it okay to draw these back some? It feels like a morgue... Excuse me," Wren stammered, "that was a careless thing to say." With paper in hand, Wren Dukette took his seat at the chess table.

Katrina's spirits crashed as their serene bed and breakfast hummed with the activity of uniformed police officers, medical examiners and authorities conducting what was now obviously a murder investigation.

The unwelcome flashback of a similar episode flooded her mind with the memory of her own father's death. Even though it was natural causes that took his life, she recollected how her mother screamed for Katrina to call emergency and how, dazed, she gave directions to the dispatcher as she heard her own voice quivering into the phone, "My father is dying, please come quickly." The doctor, the cops, the "meat wagon," as her brother had called it–the ugliness of that black, zippered body bag came flooding into her mind. She gasped when she realized it was happening once again, this time not in a unwanted memory but right here in the present, right now... in her supposed-to-be dream-come-true establishment.

"Excuse me, Katrina, are you okay?" Lou asked.

Katrina looked at the photographer. How nice of him to ask. "Yeah, I'm okay. This is a little unsettling, that's all." Katrina watched as the men carrying the body loaded up the vehicle. She wanted to look away but found she couldn't break her stare.

A man who announced himself as being with homicide asked everyone to be seated, and waited for Katrina and Lou to come away from the window.

"My name is Lieutenant Klonski." He was a tall, average-built man, whose manner indicated he was a veteran of many investigations. "I'll be heading an investigation of the death of Mrs. Konrath. There's no easy way to say this but... well... let's just say we can't say for certain that she died of choking."

"Plain and simple, it's murder, huh, Lieutenant?" said Jessie, her pleased expression showing that she knew it all along.

"How were you so sure, Ms. Hodgkins?" Katrina asked sarcastically.

"Excuse me, ladies, this is my investigation," said Klonski.

Both females sat back in their chairs and quieted. To Katrina's further dismay she was reminded of the seriousness of the situation as she looked towards the half-opened dining room door exposing flashing cameras, men examining the vacated tables, and finally the sealing off of the room with the standard yellow tape, signifying "Police Line Do Not Cross."

"Excuse me, sir... but I have to go to the bathroom." Kim never waited for permission, but got up from the sofa and headed for the drawing room exit.

"Don't be long," said Klonski. "I need you back here before I can begin questioning."

"While she's gone, may I use the phone to call my mother?" asked Theresa Dukette. "We were supposed to visit with her this afternoon. She'll be worried."

"Sure, but keep it short."

"While they're doing that I'm having a cigarette out on the front porch, Lieutenant, if you don't mind?" said Tim.

"Jesus... go ahead, make it a quick one."

Five minutes passed and Kim had not returned.

"Scotty, go upstairs and see what the hell she's doing up there, will ya," Klonski ordered one of his men.

"Knowing my girlfriend, she's putting on makeup and singing to herself in the mirror," said Spike.

Minutes later Kim returned and joined an impatient Klonski.

"Thank you for your cooperation, Miss," he grunted.

"You're welcome."

Tim snickered and shook his head.

"Now, the better you work with me, the sooner I can get you out of here. I'll begin by questioning you collectively and we'll see where that gets us." He eyed each of them in turn. "Did anyone notice anything suspicious or out of the ordinary... anything you feel you should report that would help our investigation?" Klonski scanned the room and caught Katrina and Song looking at each other uneasily.

"Yes, ladies, something you want to say?" Klonski's voiced boomed as he moved in closer to the couches and looked squarely at Katrina leaning against the fireplace mantle. She began to pace again and Song shifted in her seat.

"Song, you need to tell him about last night, but in private... for obvious reasons."

"Okay, in private then." The lieutenant's pen flew across a black note pad and he looked back at the group for more questioning. "Anyone else have something to say?"

Theresa Dukette raised her fingers indicating she wished to speak.

"Go ahead, Mrs..."

"Theresa, Theresa Dukette. Well, I noticed that the deceased appeared nervous... rather talkative. Was this typical of her? Or perhaps was she sick, upset or on drugs?"

"No," said Bob Konrath. "My wife is... was hyper that's all. She's always been the nervous type. That was just her nature."

"Lieutenant, maybe you should ask Tim why he got up from the table and went outside," said Jessie.

"What do you mean?" Song said quickly. "Are you pointing blame at my husband?"

"If you had noticed," Katrina said, "you'd have realized he always has a cigarette after he eats. Anyone could figure that one out." Katrina frowned at Tim who sat in his chair obviously enjoying being the center of controversy between the two women.

Klonski scratched his grey-brown sideburn and proceeded to scribble in his notebook. He liked to hear suspects argue among themselves. Sometimes they would inadvertently supply him with clues.

"Katrina, it's obvious they all know what's going on here," said Klonski, "so I cannot remain discreet. I hope you understand."

"I guess."

"Suppose Mrs. Konrath wasn't the intended victim but Tim was," Spike said.

"But who would want to kill Tim?" asked Song.

"Katrina doesn't seem to like him too much," Jessie said.

"For assuming to be an intelligent person, you disappoint me," said Katrina. "Do you think for a moment that I would risk jail over his droopy butt?" She glared at the blonde reporter.

Song gasped in humiliation, but Tim chuckled while suppressing a cough.

"I apologize, Song," said Katrina. "I mean no disrespect. I'm merely trying to prove a point." She felt oppressed by all this. She stared at Jessie, wondering why she was even here.

"You insult me but apologize to her," Jessie said. "Where's my apology?"

"You don't deserve one," said Katrina, dismissing her with a wave of her hand. "But what about you? What business did you have coming here today? No one invited you for breakfast."

"That's where you're wrong," said Jessie. "Song invited me and Lou."

"What?" Katrina flashed a horrified look in Song's direction, and the older woman looked as though she wanted to hide in safety under the sofa pillow.

"Song, are you crazy?" said Katrina. "She hits on your husband and you invite her to our inn. Why don't you just pack his overnight case for him and tell him to have a nice time?"

"Because!"

"Because what?"

Song shrank back into her place in the sofa and wrapped her arms around herself in defense and resignation. "She told me that if I invited her to the inn for breakfast she would do an article on me in today's morning paper. It was to be titled, she said, 'The Manor and Her Matriarch.' " Tim laughed hoarsely and most of the group chuckled.

"Well, let's take a look at the newspaper right now and see this article on you, Song," Katrina said. "Mr. Dukette, may I have it please?" She walked over to him and nearly grabbed the paper from his hand.

While Katrina flipped through the pages, Jessie retorted with a shrug, "It isn't in there. I didn't get a chance to finish it."

"I can't believe you," said Lou. "I've seen you manipulate a free invite before, but this is a new low for you."

"Well, Lou, you did come along now, didn't you? Why did you show anyway? I thought you had a golf game this morning? Everyone knows you'd never cancel a game for anything or anyone."

"Answer the question, Lou," said Klonski. "Why did you come here today?"

"Lieutenant, I'd rather discuss that with you in private, if you don't mind?"

Klonski studied Lou, grunted, and then eyed the others. "That's enough for now. I want to talk to each of you individually. That shouldn't take too long if I get everyone's cooperation. Detective Lewis will assist me in the investigation and we'll conduct the questioning in the library and gift shop. Officers Casey and Scotty will stay here with the rest of you.

"In the meantime, go over this morning's events and try to recall if there is anything you may have observed that you feel will help in this investigation." Klonski started to back away from the group toward the exit. He stopped. "Please cooperate with the officers. They are here for your protection; unpleasant as it may sound, the person sitting next to you may be Mindy Konrath's murderer. Thank you."

CHAPTER 9

Song stood in the doorway of the dimly lit library waiting for Lieutenant Klonski to look up from his pad into which he was writing notes. Not wanting to interrupt him, she glanced at the book-lined wall to her right and realized that she hardly ever got the time to browse through any of the volumes that filled the shelves.

She was nervous and wished for this to be done. Song's thoughts were interrupted as the homicide detective belched, and Song flushed as he looked up and discovered her standing there.

"Oh, come in. Darn indigestion," he said. "I ate at that greasy spoon in town this morning and I'm beginning to get heartburn. Have a seat." As Song approached the tartan plaid couch, Klonski noticed her awkwardness. Hoping to make her more relaxed–relaxed people always revealed more during interviews, Klonski said, "This is some place you got here."

"Thank you, Lieutenant."

"I heard you're a good cook."

Song blushed again and he sensed she was calming. "Maybe I can get to judge for myself sometime. Anyway," he said mildly, though he now sat up straight in the dark leather chair he occupied, "Mrs. Versay, you requested to be interviewed first. Is there a particular reason why?"

"Well, it's nearly lunchtime and I've got to get something started to eat. I do have guests to take care of, you know, and well, Tim likes his meals on time."

"You mentioned earlier that there was something you thought you should tell me. What was that?" Klonski referred to his previously written notes.

Song's face paled as she recounted the incident in the kitchen window last night and answered a battery of questions

Tina Czarnota

surrounding the event. "As I said before, he had a stocking over his face. At least that's what it looked like to me."

"How can you be sure it was a man?"

"Like I said, the person was tall and when he noticed I saw him, he turned to run and I could see what looked like a shaved neckline, as though in a man's haircut. Of course it was a quick look, for I ran and screamed, or screamed and ran. I can't remember which came first."

"Is that your husband out there, the guy that likes to smoke?"

"Yes, it is. I know he smokes way too much but he'll never quit. He'll probably die with a cigarette in his hand. Oh garsch, I shouldn't talk like that."

"You've been with him a long time now, probably had his kids, gone through some ups and downs. What kind of man would you say he is?"

"He's my husband, why?"

"I was just wondering. I've been married for a while myself, and I just like to see what makes other couples tick."

"Well, Tim was the only breadwinner for the most part up until I went to work part-time cooking. He manages the money and he always paid the bills. I took care of the home and kids and now they're both on their own. My son is the tall one out there. He built these bookshelves. He is living with Katrina, the tall girl... well, she's hardly a girl anymore. I still call them kids, you know. They are still kids compared to Tim and me."

"How do you and your husband feel about your son's girlfriend? Are you happy with his choice?"

"I don't butt into his affairs. Although, she and Tim go at it a bit too much. Sometimes it makes me nervous and sometimes she makes him mad, especially when she gets after him about smoking. She says he's a chauvinist."

"Do you think he is?"

"Tim is Tim. He'll never change."

Klonski continued with his questioning and directed various questions her way regarding acquisition of the inn, the guests and routine questions surrounding the case.

"Thank you, Mrs. Versay," Klonski finally said. "That will be all for now." Song left the room as the detective completed his notes. Before calling in his next subject he walked over to the closed door adjacent to the bookstore, knocked and opened it.

"Excuse me, Lewis." Klonski walked in and was formally introduced to Theresa Dukette. "Please proceed, I just want to look around here a bit."

Lewis already knew his boss' technique and proceeded with questioning so the lieutenant could watch reactions to questions posed to witnesses. Catching the last portion of the interview, Klonski made a quick note in his book to remind himself to go over Detective Lewis's notes and to re-question the woman if he found it necessary. He was beginning to think this was going to be a long day.

After Klonski had interviewed Song, Tim requested to go with Detective Lewis. Being denied, Tim cursed to himself as Lewis escorted Theresa Dukette out of the room. "Right this way, Ma'am, and down the hall to the left please."

"Right this way and up your ass please," grumbled Tim.

"What did you say?" Katrina couldn't help but laugh.

"Nothing."

Katrina plopped down on the couch in the spot vacated by Song and sighed. "Whatta drag."

"How the hell did the broad get herself poisoned anyway?" Tim said.

"I don't think she set out to get poisoned, do you? Wait a minute—what if she committed suicide?"

"Naw, you watch too many movies, Katrina."

"What if it really was meant for you then?"

"Then I know who would've been behind that one," Tim said, wryly.

"Doesn't it bother you at all? I mean, what if it was? You can't tell me that wouldn't bother you." Katrina paused. "Wait a minute. Who would've been behind that one?" She peered at him closely, wondering what he meant by the comment.

"Never mind."

"Hey, that Dukette guy's heading our way."

"I'm going for a cigarette."

"Too late," said Katrina. She looked up at Wren Dukette. "How are you holding up?"

"Fine, thanks," he said. "You know, I've been wanting to talk to you for the last few hours." Wren eyed Tim. "You're Tim Versay, aren't you?"

"Yes he is."

Wren offered his hand and Tim took it, slowly.

"You look familiar and the name has a ring to it, but I can't place it."

"Wren Dukette," the man said his own name as if to jog Tim's memory. "I never thought you'd forget me. Well, it has been a long time."

"If it's privacy you want, I'll leave," Katrina offered.

"Oh no, that's quite all right," said Wren.

Tim sat still, but gazed about the drawing room for an escape route.

"Care to sit down, Mr. Dukette?" said Katrina.

"No, thank you, and call me Wren, please."

"Mr. Dukette, you're next," Lieutenant Klonski said, approaching the trio. "Please follow me. We'll interview in the library."

"Excuse me, we can talk later," said Wren.

Tim sighed, relieved, as Wren Dukette followed Klonski out of the drawing room.

"That was close," mumbled Tim.

"What's the matter with you?" said Katrina. Her brows narrowed in suspicion. "What's going on with this guy and you anyway? I would think you'd like to face him and get it over with."

"I'm going for a cigarette."

"You stole his girlfriend? You stole his mother away from his father? Tim, what did you do to the guy?"

"What makes you think I did something to him anyway?"

"I know you. You sat through a hurricane barely locking the front door. You stared down the grim reaper and laughed in his face. But this guy, this guy just buckles your butt."

"Katrina, you're bored." Tim got up and started digging in his pocket for a cigarette.

"I still want to know." Seeing she would not get her answer, she said, "Oh, go outside already."

Klonski shut the door behind him and settled into the mahogany chair once more. He smiled pleasantly at Wren. With pen in hand and tape recorder engaged, Klonski proceeded with small talk. "So how's the food here anyway?"

"Quite good actually, although breakfast was a little too exciting for my tastes."

"Yeah, I'll bet," said Klonski.

Routine questioning ensued and Wren asked whether he and his wife could be excused soon. "We were due at my mother-in-law's house for dinner and she is waiting for us."

"Well, I can't be certain that you'll make dinner. We'll just have to see how things proceed. I would like your in-law's address and number before you leave."

"That will be no problem."

"Mr. Dukette, you say you came out this way to visit your wife's mother who lives in the area."

"That's correct."

"You reside in Tampa, isn't that so?"

"Yes."

"I'll get right to the point." Klonski's eyes were sharp and penetrating. "What's your connection to Tim Versay?"

"What do you mean by connection?"

"I've noticed you've been watching him, pursuing him, if you will, and any time you get near him, he looks as if he wants to bolt out of the room."

"I hope you're not going to blow this out of proportion."

"Tell me what's going on between you and Versay."

Wren Dukette's usual composure gave way to a simmering anger as he proceeded to tell his story. "You see, many years ago, I was employed by a large Tampa-based insurance company, working as a mail clerk. I busted my butt for that company but I didn't care. I wanted to get up that corporate ladder so bad, I could taste it. Well, the big chance came. There was an opening for an adjuster trainee. My supervisor felt I showed great promise, and though I was only nineteen years old he urged me to bid for that job. I was refused. Even though my record was impeccable, I learned that the final decision rested with the branch manager. He's the one who turned me down. I forget for what reason exactly, but it was something to do with lack of experience. I was crushed. I quit that same day and my life has never been the same."

"Let me guess, that branch manager was Tim Versay. Is that correct?"

As though admitting sins to a priest, Wren nodded.

"So you've been carrying this inside of you for all these years and now you're going to let him have it."

"Wait a minute, you've got it all wrong. Sure I hated him at first and for a long time after that, but that's not why I came to talk to him. Actually I came to thank him."

"Thank him? For what?"

"I'll make a long story short. I am now CEO of the southern division of one of the largest auto parts distributorships in the United States. If I had stayed at that insurance company, God knows where I would have wound up. A few years after I left, that insurance group became defunct."

"How did you know Versay was going to be here?"

"Lieutenant, I read the papers and then there's talk within the Tampa circles. It's my business to know what's going on in business if you know what I mean."

Klonski frowned. He was skeptical. "Why come all the way out here to do it? Why not just call him at the office?"

"Well, I guess this is where I get to 'rub a little salt,' Lieutenant. Confronting Versay at a frilly B and B would knock him down a few pegs, that's all. I just wanted to have a little fun with it. Besides, I already told you, my mother-in-law lives a short drive from here."

"Are you sure you haven't carried a little burn over the years that you may have wanted to avenge?"

"You mean kill Versay, don't you? Not a chance, Lieutenant, not a chance. He's not worth killing."

Dismissing Wren Dukette, Klonski rose, stretched and made for the door leading to the gift shop. He was curious to learn if Lewis found anything.

After the trademark, knock once and open, Klonski entered just in time to catch Lewis dismiss the young, attractive woman whom he remembered to be the niece of one of the owners.

"Thank you," Kim said to Lewis as she left the room.

"What did you get out of her, Lewis, besides her phone number?" Klonski smirked.

Ignoring that remark, Lewis flipped back a few pages in his note pad and read over the jottings he scribbled during the latest interview.

"She's here with a boyfriend who happens to be a cop. They just got in town yesterday. Says her aunt was upset over incident regarding a man's face in the window. She hasn't seen anything out of the ordinary. Says her aunt's dislike for Tim Versay is just a put-on, but she admits the guy is hard to like. Her boyfriend, the cop, wants to get on with their vacation and is thinking of leaving as soon as he can. She, the niece, says that Hodgkins promised to do some sort of a story on her also, but she likes Hodgkins. She says Hodgkins confided in her that she has the hots for Lou, you know, the photographer, and that Spike has his own opinion of what happened and that I'd have to ask him what it was. And that's about it."

"Did she say anything about the relationship of the aunt and boyfriend?" Klonski asked. He scratched his sideburn, annoyed that the investigation seemed to be going nowhere.

"Not really."

The two men continued discussing the notes and their conjectures.

"Who's next?" Lewis asked. Younger and thinner than Klonski, his eyes showed the enthusiasm his superior lacked.

Klonski mumbled as he headed for the door and was confronted in the hallway by an excited Lou Smagatino.

"Lieutenant," Lou said, "I just got a call to cover a breaking story. You know where my office is. Can you just catch me there for questioning? Or, I'll find you at the station."

"Just answer me a few questions on your way out," Klonski said. He opened the front door onto the porch and squinted at the afternoon sun. "Damn that's bright." Shielding his eyes from the sun he walked down the short flight of stairs with Lou. "Did you see anything that might help me out here?"

"I didn't see anything that looked unusual. Jessie and I arrived late, pretty much just in time to be seated. I thought she was invited, but I should have known, she conned her way in. She's pulled some shit before just to get an in to parties and functions. Yeah, if there's something there in pants that she likes, she's after it, no matter who he may belong to."

"I understand she has a thing for you," said Klonski.

Lou stopped and looked at the lieutenant squarely.

"Yeah, me and every other guy in the state of Florida."

"She's engaged, right?" Klonski watched for Lou's response.

"Was," said Lou. "As I said, she wants everything she sees. So we've had some fun together. So what? It was nothing serious."

"Why did you come today then?"

The photographer hesitated as he thought about his answer. "Well, off the record, I guess I just wanted to see what was going on with the tall one."

"You mean Katrina?"

"Yeah, I guess she's tied up with that Bruce dude though. There didn't seem to be much there so I thought–you know–I just think she could get a modeling gig in Tampa," Lou stammered. "I thought I could do her head shot 'cause I heard her say she was interested. Anyway, that's about it."

"Give me your card in case I need to call you."

Lou dug into his wallet, produced a calling card and handed it to Klonski. "Oh, Jessie will need a ride to–"

"I've got it covered." Klonski turned his back and headed toward the stairs, eager to return inside and escape the blinding sun. Off the record, thought Klonski. He should know better than that.

CHAPTER 10

Lieutenant Klonski entered the library, walked quietly across the Oriental rug and stopped to listen to Lewis question Jessie.

"Why, Lieutenant, do your men always drag their interviewees through the mud?" Jessie said. "Come watch, you may enjoy the show."

"Just answer the questions." Klonski looked over Lewis's shoulder at his notes and then at Jessie Hodgkins.

"Now what was the question? Oh yes, my involvement with Lou. Since he always seems to be so damn busy, I figured at least on assignments I wouldn't need an appointment to see him. I'd see him at work."

"Then why hit on other men?" asked Lewis.

"What do you mean by that?"

"You know what I mean," said Lewis. "You have a reputation for being a... flirt."

Jessie smiled. "What's wrong with that? A li'l flirting doesn't hurt. Besides, I thought I could make Lou jealous, maybe even appear more desirable."

"How long have you been on staff with the paper now?" Klonski asked.

"About a year and a half or so."

"Do you like your job?"

"I love it. I'd sell my... Yes, very much, why?"

"I heard your employer may be looking at some cutbacks, especially in your department. How do you feel about that?"

"Pardon the pun but that's news to me."

Standing across from the attractive reporter, Klonski folded his arms and with a cavalier delivery asked the woman, "Would you consider sensationalism to further your career?"

"Lieutenant, pu-leese, it happens all the time."

"What do you think about creating an incident so you could be there just in time to cover it?"

Jessie sat up straight. "Wait a minute, you're just grabbing at straws."

"Am I? Isn't it a strange coincidence, Ms. Hodgkins, that you fabricated stories on naive women, to gain an invite to breakfast where one of the guests just so happens to drop dead?"

Jessie stood up, her pale complexion turning a sunburned pink. "That's a lousy accusation, and you're off base."

The knock at the door ended the harsh words.

"Lieutenant, it's me, Mrs. Versay," came the tiny voice.

"I'll be right there. Lewis, see what she wants."

"As for us," Klonski faced Jessie, "we're through for now, but if I need to, I know where to find you."

"You just go ahead and do that, Lieutenant," she said. "I'll be waiting."

As Jessie left the library, young Lewis opened the hallway door revealing a timid Song holding a tray of tea sandwiches.

"Did I come at a bad time?" she asked.

"Oh Mrs. Versay, your timing couldn't be better." Klonski flashed an automatic smile and walked over to the door and accepted the offering.

"I'm serving tea right now. That is to hold us over till lunchtime. I do hope you'll dine with us when you're done with your questioning."

"It would be our pleasure, isn't that right, Lewis?"

"Oh sure."

"Well, I won't keep you. I'll stop by later to remove your tray, gentlemen."

"Thank you, Ma'am."

Jessie hurried out of the library into the hallway where she found Bob Konrath assisting Katrina's misguided attempt to push a food-laden tea cart into the drawing room.

"Where's Lou?" Jessie demanded.

"He left about fifteen minutes ago," said Katrina.

"Oh great. Did he say where he was going?"

Katrina ignored the woman. "Thanks for the hand, Mr. Konrath, but you really don't have to do this."

"I need to keep busy," he said. "It helps to keep my mind off things."

Not appreciating being ignored, the reporter pushed past the struggling pair and searched the drawing room for an ally. Stomping over to the floral couch where Kim and Spike were resting with eyes closed, she shook the young woman by the shoulder, startling her and waking Spike.

"Oh, you scared me," said Kim. "I was starting to drop off."

"Never mind that, Kim," said Jessie. "Where did Lou say he was going?"

Spike rubbed his eyes and grimaced at the pretty blonde.

"I didn't pay attention. Spike, did you?" said Kim. Not wanting to betray a male counterpart, he denied having any information.

"Well, I need a ride," said Jessie, glancing at her watch. "Spike, you're not busy."

"Why don't you hang for a while?" said Kim. "My aunt will be serving tea and sandwiches. Besides, you never got to tell me about the clothes stores in town. You can't go now, here comes food."

"Kim, if she has to go, I'm sure we can find her a ride," said Katrina.

Jessie smiled at Kim. "You talked me into it. I'll stay."

Katrina grimaced at her niece as she set a tray of food on the coffee table situated between the two couches. She turned and walked away. Jessie pleased with herself, plopped down on the vacated sofa and smugly helped herself to a sandwich.

"Katrina, Klonski's calling you. You're next," Bruce said.

"Damn, I was just going to eat. Grab me a couple sandwiches before they're gone and save them for me, okay?"

"Yeah, go–he's waiting for you."

"I'm scared, I don't know what to say," Katrina said suddenly.

"Just don't get wise with him," said Bruce. He reached for her hand and squeezed it. "I notice he doesn't like a smart ass."

"Thanks, wish me luck. By the way, where's your father?"

With a sandwich in hand, Bruce motioned toward the front porch. Stealing a moment, Katrina hurried to the front door, opened it and called out to Tim while he stood engrossed in a cigarette. "Hey, Tim, food's on and Jessie's saving a place on the couch for you. She said she wanted to talk to you."

Tim quickly tossed the lit butt aside, pulled up his baggy-pant waist under his ample belly, and grabbed the door Katrina let slam shut.

Katrina got in line behind Lewis as he escorted Bob Konrath down the hall to the gift shop. Making a quick left she entered the library just in time to hear Klonski belch. "Should I close the door?"

"Oh excuse me. Yeah go ahead. Damn indigestion."

Closing the library door behind her, Katrina walked over to the mahogany club chair. Klonski stood with his back to her as he looked over his notes and fished in his pants pocket with his free hand. Fumbling, he tossed his notebook onto the plaid couch and noticed Katrina was still standing.

"Go ahead, sit down," Klonski said, twisting the cap off a prescription bottle. He tipped his head back and tossed a capsule into his mouth. He chased it down with a sip of water.

"Did you ever try a digestive enzyme for your stomach?" Katrina asked as she sat.

"A what?"

"A digestive enzyme. It's a natural formula that helps break down your meal. It aids digestion. I have some if you'd like."

"Thank you, but right now you're here to answer some questions." Klonski moved to the front of the plaid couch and sat down. He shifted his weight, trying to ease his stomach. He noted Katrina's nervousness, and his suspicions were aroused.

When Katrina saw him writing in his notebook before he asked her any questions, she became even more upset. She was convinced Klonski thought she killed Mindy.

"Katrina, how well did you know Mrs. Konrath?" Klonski finally asked.

"Not very. I spoke with her on the phone when she called for reservations." Katrina concentrated on keeping her voice calm. "I met her in person when she and husband arrived, and I saw her briefly in the backyard before breakfast, during breakfast and then–and then I watched her die."

"What did you observe about her, if anything?" Klonski studied her reactions.

"Well, she seemed to be a nervous woman. She talked fast, sorta overwhelming people while she spoke."

"You mean somewhat annoying?"

"Yes, I guess you could say."

"Did she annoy you, Katrina?"

"A little." Katrina stopped. "Wait a minute. Are you implying that she annoyed me so much that I was driven to poison her?"

"Who said she was poisoned?" Klonski's voice was mild but his eyes were hard.

"Oh brother. She wasn't exactly shot now was she?" Katrina remembered Bruce's advice and calmed down.

"We don't know that," said Klonski. "I'm just trying to find out some information. What kind of couple would you say Bob and Mindy were?"

"Well, he seemed kind toward her–you know, patient. He appears to be–a gentleman. Anyway, he's been nice to me. Other than that, I don't know what to say."

"Would you say he's good-looking?"

"Yes so?"

As the lieutenant's pen flew across the page in his notebook, Katrina became worried that she might be accused of murdering Mindy. She forced her mind to slow down.

"What kind of relationship do you have with Tim Versay?"

"He's okay. He's my boyfriend's father and though he's a bit chauvinistic for my tastes, he's okay."

"Your not too crazy about him," said Klonski, baiting her. "In fact you really don't like him much do you?"

"Look, he's the last person I'd land up with but that's not my problem. I like him but I don't. I hate him but I don't, get it?"

"There's speculation that he was the intended victim and not Mrs. Konrath. What do you think about that?"

"I'll put it this way, Lieutenant," Katrina said tersely. "Do you think for a moment I'd risk sitting in jail over his fat ass?"

"What do you think about Lou, the photographer?"

"He seems like a nice guy. Why?"

"Just wondering. One of the guests made this observation, Katrina. Let's see." Flipping through his notes, he came upon the quotation given to him earlier by Lewis. "Here it is. It says, 'Her dislike for Tim Versay is just a put on...'"

"Yeah, it's like a game."

"Katrina, is it possible that your game is only for show, and that you are secretly conducting an affair with him on the side?"

A silence fell over the others in the drawing room and all ears perked in the direction of the library.

"What was that?" Song asked. "It sounded like a shriek."

"It sounded like a wail," said Dukette.

"It was neither," said Bruce. "That was Katrina bursting out laughing. Klonski must have told her a joke."

"Well, that's done," Klonski said to Lewis after the interviews were finished. Klonski stood up and stretched. "And Spike gave his statement at the station when he drove Jessie downtown?"

Lewis nodded.

"Get your notes out. I just want to stretch my legs and see what's going on out there. When I return, we can see what we've got together. If it checks, I'll let some of the boys go. I'll be right back."

If he'd occasionally trust some of the cops with questioning we'd be out of here a long time ago. But Klonski knows what he wants, mused the sergeant as he watched his superior open the library door and exit. Judging his boss to be a safe distance away, the younger detective laughed to himself. For his next birthday, the department has to take up a collection for a case of antacids and a crystal ball for that guy.

The aroma of home cooking beckoned and Klonski gladly followed it into the kitchen where he found a harried Song.

"That smells great, Mrs. Versay."

"Oh Lieutenant, I didn't hear you... we'll have lunch, but it'll be a late one. I sure hope you're able to figure out who did this terrible thing. I'm afraid I'll never feel quite right about this place again."

"We're doing all we can. Where is everyone?"

"Some of 'em are out in the yard, some of 'em are still in the drawing room, and a few went upstairs to lie down. I hope Katrina's setting up a table in the drawing room."

"Right. The dining room is off limits till further notice." Drawing a glass of water from the sink purifier, the detective walked past Song at the island range, parted the white curtain, and peered out the back window observing the small assemblage out in the yard. Spike, he noticed, had returned and was in deep conversation with Tim Versay. "The Dukettes haven't left yet, I see."

"No, they said something about her mother getting tired of waiting for 'em and making other plans for the afternoon. I persuaded them to stay for lunch. I figured it's the least thing I can do to make up for this mess," explained Song.

"Did you happen to see where Bruce and Mr. Konrath went to?"

"Oh, it's warm in here," Song said while stirring gravy in a pot. "Lieutenant, can you lower the air conditioning a notch? It's on the sidewall near the phone. I wonder if Katrina called service. Well, let's see–Mr. Konrath was sittin' with the Dukettes a bit ago. Kim, last I heard was upstairs with Jessie.

95

Garsch, I don't know where everyone else is." Song turned and noticed she was talking to the walls. She hadn't heard the detective leave.

Klonski met Lewis back in the library. "I looked around some," Klonski said. "Nothing much going on. So, where were we?" He looked at the notes laid out on the library coffee table. "Let's start with Bruce. What did you come up with on him?"

"Well, this one seems the quiet type. I don't know if he didn't have too much or didn't want to say too much. He just pretty much clammed up. I had to draw him out."

"Yeah and–?"

"I'd plant things to piss him off and he'd just answer with a yes or a no. Like I asked him if he thought his girlfriend hated his father enough to maybe want him dead and he'd just answer no. I questioned him about the window incident and he just confirmed that it did happen.

"I hope we get good prints off that back window," Klonski interrupted the younger detective. "Go ahead, what else did you get from him?"

"He never offered anything on the bricks falling. I had to remind him that it happened and he just agreed that 'yes they fell on Tim and Katrina.' He said they could've fallen anytime. Oh, one thing he did say was that Katrina doesn't like women much, that there are very few women she trusts or likes. And he said that Katrina didn't think Mindy Konrath fit her husband because he was cool and secure and she was nervous."

"Did he have an opinion on whether it was murder, suicide, or a botched attempt on his father?"

"Where was... here it is," Lewis said, looking through his notes. "When I asked him he just said that he wondered if an attempt was really made on his father or if it was made to look that way. Never really stated his opinion, he just wondered if." Lewis paused, then said, "So, what did you get on Konrath?"

"That's the pisser. I didn't get much from him." Klonski sat back in the leather club chair, and rested the back of his head in his intertwined cupped hands. He closed his eyes for a moment.

"Man, I'm tired, Lewis, I'm due for a vacation. Anyway, Konrath struggled with tears a few times, I could see that. He seems in shock over this. He kept repeating that he couldn't believe this happened." Klonski shook his head, frowning. "He claims his marriage was intact. Sometimes she was given to mild depression but was happy enough. She used to take anti-depressants but was off them now. She was looking forward to staying at this place. One thing he said that throws me was that she made a comment that she'd like to die in a place like this–when it was her turn, that is."

"Sounds like depression, or–"

"Or…?"

"Or it's a good bullshit story."

"Yeah, maybe..." Klonski thought for a moment all the homicides he had investigated during his twenty-three years as a detective. There had been many. He had learned a trick from every one of them.

"But I won't rule anything out yet," he said, "no matter how bizarre. I just wish it was suicide–nice and cut and dry. Anyway, at the end Konrath was saying things like, he wondered why Tim got up and rushed outside for a cigarette. Most people linger some or at least say they are going out, but Versay just shot out of his chair and hurried out. Bob then speculated that maybe Song put poison in the food and for some reason targeted his wife. I sure could use those lab reports now."

"Did he or she know any of these people before they came here this weekend?" asked Lewis.

"Konrath claims no. Other than this, he saw nothing suspicious and that's about all I got from him." Klonski glanced at his watch and frowned lightly. "Damn, it's getting late." Thumbing through his tattered notebook, the elder detective folded over excess pages. "This guy–Versay–is a character. When asked if he thought poison was meant for him, he laughed. I asked him if he could think of anyone that wanted him dead, he answered, 'probably' and started to laugh again. The story about Wren Dukette checks. He claims he did let him go because, get

97

this, his first name reminded Versay of a bird. And he thinks Katrina probably wouldn't be capable of doing him in, though she'd like to. He claims she's a ditsy broad but entertaining at times. She pisses him off when she gets on him about smoking, or puts 'women's libber ideas' in his wife's head."

"Klonski, did you ask him if maybe his wife wanted him dead for being a pain in the ass all these years?"

"Yeah, but he doesn't believe it."

"Did you ask him about Hodgkins?" asked Lewis.

"He thinks she's a hot, conniving bitch, qualities he likes in a woman. As long as it isn't his wife. His parting words were, 'Ain't it ironic that Katrina's always warning me about my smoking and it may be that smoking saved my life.' Then he laughed and went outside for a cigarette."

Klonski shook his head and inhaled deeply. He was tired.

"You staying for lunch, Lewis?" Klonski asked. "It'll give us a chance to see this bunch in action."

The younger detective smiled. "Sure. I could use a decent cup of coffee and some food."

Klonski nodded. "Tell the boys to wrap it up and leave. See you at the trough."

Kim closed the front porch door behind her and shut her eyes as they adjusted to the dim hallway.

"Sun is sure strong, isn't it?"

"Lieutenant Klonski, is that you?" Kim feigned blindness. Oh I'm to tell everyone that lunch is on in ten minutes, in the drawing room. Will you be staying?"

"Yes. Do you know who else is staying for lunch?"

"Well, Jessie left. I guess she had some plans. Spike is back. Mr. Konrath was out in his car making a phone call, so I guess he's staying. The Dukette's are–"

"Aren't the phones working in the inn?" Klonski asked, curious why Konrath would use a car phone for a call.

"I think they are," said Kim. "Check with my aunt."

"Thanks. See you at lunch."

CHAPTER 11

Song arrived with a huge bowl of mashed potatoes and requested that they be passed around the table with the rest of the food. The cook was lavished with praise as she took her place at the head of the table nearest the kitchen.

Katrina, sitting at the opposite end across from Song, was only too pleased to get up and remove the place setting and chair that would have been occupied by Jessie had she stayed.

"Sorry lunch took so long, folks, but with all that was going on…" Song said.

"No need to apologize, Song," said Theresa Dukette. "We all had a chance to socialize and acquaint ourselves with one another. In spite of all that occurred today, I have no doubt your inn will be a great success."

"Thank you."

"Bruce, pass me the roast beef, would you?" said Tim. "Say, where did you go earlier? Spike and I waited for you to come back out. What the hell are you, antisocial?"

"I was tired, Dad. I went to lay down."

"Hey, where did Jessie go anyway?" said Tim. "I knew something was missing."

"She told me to tell you she couldn't control herself around you so she had to leave," Katrina said, passing the salad bowl.

"Who's asking you?"

"She had to go someplace," said Kim. "She placed a call to a friend and made some plans to go out."

"You mean she wasn't going to interview the Pope?" Katrina said. "Maybe she had backstage passes to an Elvis concert."

The diners chuckled, except for Kim. "I think she's cool, Aunty Trina. Why don't you like her?"

99

"Your aunt resents women who are more beautiful than she is, Kim," said Tim.

"What good is her beauty when she uses everyone?" Katrina shot back. "She tells people a bunch of shit, they believe her and she uses that to her advantage–except some of us aren't intelligent enough to see that, Tim."

"Tim, Katrina, we have guests at the table, please," said Song. She looked anxiously at her guests.

"Lieutenant, what do you think?" asked Katrina. "You're trained for that sort of thing, right?"

Klonski finished chewing and swallowed before he answered. "Let's put it this way. Sometimes we see it, sometimes we don't. Sometimes we see it and we pretend that we don't, understand?" An uncomfortable silence fell over the diners as the seasoned detective gnawed off the end of his dinner roll all the while watching for reactions.

"Well, would anyone like coffee?" asked Song, hoping to change the subject. There were several takers and Song left, welcoming the chance to retreat to her kitchen.

"All this talk upsets my wife, Klonski, so just excuse her," said Tim. "So how's the investigation progressing? You have any idea who did it?"

"Mr. Versay," Lewis said, "you know we're not allowed to divulge any information. So for now, just leave the questioning to us. We'll let you know if anything comes up."

Tim smiled, but said to himself, "Smart ass rookie."

Light table conversation returned and so did Song, confirming that coffee was brewing in the kitchen.

"Mr. Konrath," Song said, "I'm glad you've decided to stay for lunch. You'll need to keep your strength up with all–"

"Thank you, but what I should be doing is packing to get back to my family." Bob laid his fork down and sighed deeply.

"Are you able to drive? You're welcome to rest upstairs before you leave," Song said gently.

Klonski cleared his throat. "You'll need to stop by the office and sign a few papers, Bob. I'll let you know when they've been processed."

Song offered seconds to everyone and half-empty platters were passed around once more. "Katrina, will you get the coffee?"

"Yeah." Normally Katrina would have playfully snatched Tim's plate away from him while he was still eating, but the mood being somber, she left without any high jinks.

In the kitchen, Katrina transferred the steaming brew into white carafes and half-heartedly inhaled the enticing aroma. "Song, you need help with those dishes?"

"I can manage."

"I got to thinking. I'm kinda bummed over this mess, and I thought maybe we should close for a few days, drive up to Tampa, hang there for a bit and clear our heads. This place is giving me the creeps and I need to get away from it, just to–say, get back in bed and start the whole day over again, if you know what I mean?"

"I do, but shouldn't we keep the inn manned?" said Song. She thought a moment. "I'll ask Tim and see what he thinks."

"Well, don't mind if Bruce and I decide to go should you want to stay," Katrina said, lifting the tray with coffee. She left the kitchen for the drawing room.

"Song, I'd love the recipe for that pie," exclaimed Theresa after a dessert of German chocolate pie had been finished. "Of course if it's a Tudor Grove secret, then I won't pry."

"Theresa, why don't you see if your mother's back yet?" said Wren. "We need to finish our coffee and get going soon."

"I know you're eager to be on your way but please don't rush on our account," said Song.

"Thank you, but we should get going. However, I'd appreciate another cup of your coffee."

"Absolutely." Song got up and began to make her way around the table refilling cups.

101

"Mrs. Versay, I also need to make a phone call... in the library," Klonski said. "I'll take another regular, please. I'll be right back." He rose from the table and headed out the drawing room door.

Noting that his wife was enjoying conversation and coffee, Wren excused himself from the table, informing Theresa of his intentions to make the call for her. "You finish your coffee, I'll be right back."

"So sweet of you, darling. Thanks." As he stood, Theresa smiled up at her husband, then noticed a wet spot on his left jacket pocket. Still standing, a look of annoyance came over Wren's face as he looked down at the soiled fabric.

"It looks like something leaked in you pocket, dear."

"Take it off, Mr. Dukette, and I'll soak it for you," Song offered as she put down the carafe.

Theresa reached out and felt the fabric, then slipped her hand into the pocket. Lewis looked over to his right, just beyond Theresa and observed the activity. Klonski returned and walked over to his empty chair next to Mrs. Dukette.

"What is this, Wren?" Theresa held up a clear glass vial and started to examine it. The lid, barely screwed on, fell off and landed in Theresa's half-filled coffee cup.

A look of surprise came over Wren as he began to remove the offending jacket.

"Mrs. Dukette, put the bottle down and don't tip it," Klonski sternly ordered. "Mr. Dukette, drape your jacket over the chair."

With a single, stiff movement, Theresa set the nearly empty bottle down on the table next to her dessert dish. Wren inched back.

"Please move your chair, Mrs. Dukette, and let me get in there," said Klonski. "Lewis, bag this." After examining Wren's jacket and handing it over to Lewis, Klonski leaned over and sniffed lightly at the small container. He asked his sergeant to do the same.

"Cyanide?" Klonski muttered. Lewis nodded, then gently deposited the jacket and vial into separate evidence bags.

"Not again," cried Song.

"It can't be," protested Wren.

A murmur rose from the shocked diners as Klonski informed Wren that he should willingly accompany him down to headquarters for some further questioning.

"Does my husband have to go, Lieutenant?"

"If he doesn't," said Klonski flatly, "I would have to arrest him on suspicion for the murder of Mindy Konrath. He was found with cyanide on his person and–"

"And what, Klonski?" Bob Konrath said suddenly. "You mean this scumbag killed my wife? Why you…" Konrath lunged at Wren with his hands aiming for the suspect's throat, but was restrained by Spike and Lewis.

"Stop it! My husband's innocent!" shouted Theresa. Katrina and Song, forgetting their own shock, ran to Theresa's side and tried to calm the woman down.

Lieutenant Klonski ordered everyone to be quiet, to step away from the table, and to sit down.

* * *

The police car carrying a glum Wren backed out of the inn's driveway onto the quiet road. Theresa insisted she be with her husband.

"Spike, thank you for offering me a ride to the station. I'm just too upset to drive," said Theresa. "You can leave me there." She turned to Song. "If it's not too much of a bother, may I leave our car here? I'll be back as soon–"

"Theresa, I'll hear nothing of the sort. When you're ready to go to your mom's, one of us can take you there. Leave your car here as long as need be. Good luck."

"Thank's Song, we'll need it."

"Kim, you comin' for the ride?" Spike asked.

"No, I'll stay and help clean up."

As the proprietors escorted the forlorn woman out the front door, the front desk phone rang. Kim quickly answered it.

Minutes later, Katrina shuffled up the steps to the front porch. Hearing her, Kim lowered her voice.

"I have to hang up, someone's coming," she whispered into the phone. "Bye."

Kim quickly hung up the receiver. She looked up. "You want me to start folding up these chairs?"

"Were you just on the phone?" Katrina asked.

"Uh, yeah. It was another hang up," said Kim.

"Damn. I forgot–"

"Didn't you call for service?"

"Not that," said Katrina. "I forgot to tell Klonski about the hang-ups."

Katrina walked past her niece, tossed a pillow aside on the couch and lay down. Closing her eyes she cradled her hands behind her head and heaved a weary sigh. "I can't believe this mess. I keep thinking this is all a sick joke being played on me and that Tim will come in here joking with Mrs. Konrath at his side, pointing at me and laughing at how I fell for it."

"Aunty Trina, I don't think that will happen. I'm afraid this is all too real." Kim scraped a plate, then looked at her watch.

"I'm sorry this happened on your vacation, Kim. I wouldn't blame you if you wanted to leave. Maybe you can still salvage the rest of your time off." Katrina felt drained. "What does Spike think about this fiasco? Here the guy thinks he's gonna get away from work and he's faced with more police procedure."

"Don't worry, Aunty Trina. It's not your fault."

Katrina sat up. "Look, Kim, we may get out of here for a few days. You know, close up and go to Tampa. It's a jumpin' town. Why don't you think about it? We can stay in a nice hotel and get away from this gloom and doom."

"We'll see, Aunty Trina. I don't know what we'll do."

Katrina barely heard her niece as her thoughts turned to the latest events in her nightmare.

"I can't believe Dukette was found with cyanide on him. He seemed like such a nice guy."

"Aunty Trina, they all seem like nice guys at first, then they show you their true colors."

"Do you think he really did it? If you had to point a finger at someone, would it be him?"

"I don't know, Aunty Trina. I guess it could be any one of us."

"I know. That's the creepy part. It's probably someone really remote, like–like Bruce's mother."

Katrina looked up at the doorway, startled to see Tim standing in the hall listening.

"How long have you been there, Tim?"

With her back to the door, Kim whirled around to see Tim standing in the doorway with a sly grin on his face. She shuddered and was relieved when Tim and Katrina started tossing barbs at each other.

"Not only does your aunt try to kill me, but she makes you do all the cleaning."

"I was just getting up to help her. Besides, if it was me, I would have done it right the first time."

"What do you mean the first time, Katrina?" Tim chuckled then coughed, thus drowning out her response.

"Go ahead and cough," said Katrina. "Strange how you manage to remain quiet when it serves you."

Tim walked over and sat in his high-backed chair, staring at the empty fireplace before him. While finishing clearing the table, Katrina picked up a butter knife, stepped behind Tim and in mock exaggeration pretend to lower it into the unsuspecting man's back. Soft footsteps broke up Kim's giggling as Katrina wheeled around to see Song approach the drawing room doorway. Hoping the woman hadn't seen her "weapon," Katrina hid it behind her back, embarrassed at her own tasteless prank.

"That poor woman," Song said. "I feel so sorry for her. Oh girls, thank you for cleaning up." Song passed the half disassembled table and sat down on the couch next to Tim.

"Where's Bruce?"

"After Aunty Trina came in, I noticed him go upstairs," answered Kim.

"He sure spends a lot of time by himself," Katrina said. "How did you raise him that he's such a hermit?"

"At least he's not playing with a butter knife behind my back," Tim said lightly.

Kim and Katrina looked at each other and started to giggle.

"What?" asked Song.

"Never mind," said Tim. "Anyway, what now? What do we do now?"

"I say, in respect for the deceased, we close the inn for a few days," said Katrina. "What do you guys think?"

"I think Katrina's right," said Song. "We should close for a few days. What do you say, Tim?"

"Whatever you two want to do. This is your deal, not mine."

"I still want to get out of here for a few days," said Katrina. "I'm gonna check with Klonski and see if we can blow this place for a day or two. It's giving me the creeps."

"Do you think that's such a good idea?" Bruce said, joining them. "It may look like we're running from something."

"Well, let's see what the lieutenant has to say," said Song. "He's such a nice man." Song motioned for Bruce to sit next to her on the couch.

"Yeah, Dukette seemed like such a nice guy and he was found with poison on him!" said Katrina. "I wonder what Spike will have to say when he gets back? I'd like to hear what he thinks about all this."

"Why, Katrina, don't you think Mr. Dukette did it?" Song asked.

Katrina folded the last tablecloth, put it aside, and walked over to the remaining unoccupied sofa. Sitting down, she encouraged her niece to do the same, noticing that Kim seemed preoccupied and unusually willing to perform domestic chores.

"Song, I don't know what to think. Come on, Kim. Join us. The rest can wait."

"Okay." Kim finished folding the last chair, propped it against the wall, glanced at her watch and joined the others.

"It just all hit so hard," said Katrina. "I'm afraid I'm still numb. I hate to think it was any of us, and in my own way I'm refusing to believe that any of this happened."

"Katrina," Tim said, shaking his head and smirking, "what part of 'she's dead' don't you understand?"

"I can't believe this happened to us. I can't believe this happened at our inn. Maybe this sounds selfish, but we worked so hard to make our dream come true and before you know it, wham, there's a murder committed in our dining room. Can't you understand how I feel?"

"Well, who's it s'posed to happen to?" said Tim. "The guy next door?"

"Tim, your so comforting, I could barf," said Katrina.

"That's enough," said Song. "Arguing won't bring Mrs. Konrath back. I feel bad, too."

"Well, Song, we each have our own way of coping and this is mine." Katrina sulked and glanced at her niece who looked back with sorrow in her eyes. Katrina chided herself for upsetting Kim and the others, and realized she needed to put on a strong front. Katrina hugged her niece sitting next to her, smiled and dropped the subject.

It was Bruce who broke the lull. "Well, I'll tell you what concerns me."

"What?" Tim asked.

"Dad, what if that poison was meant for you? I mean what if Mindy got it instead of you? If an attempt was made on your life and it failed–well, what if someone tries again?"

"Oh garsch, but Mr. Dukette may be in jail," said Song.

"That's if he's the one who did it," said Katrina.

"Thanks, Katrina!" said Tim, looking away from Song as she wrung her hands in her lap. "Yes, he's the one that did it. He was found with the poison, case closed." He shot Katrina a look of annoyance.

"Well, if you want to deal in reality, then we will, Tim. If not let's just forget it." Katrina was just as annoyed with him.

"She's right, Dad," said Bruce. "We should discuss this. We'll all feel better if we understand what's really goin' on."

Bruce took the initiative and gave anyone the option to leave if they didn't want to hash over the incidents of the day.

No one left the room.

"Why talk about it at all?" asked Tim.

"Because its not healthy to sweep things under a rug," said Katrina. It's better to discuss things openly than to pretend nothing happened." With all this stress, Katrina figured she'd need lots more than vitamins.

"Okay, Katrina, psychologist, have it your way," said Tim.

Bruce spoke up. "Okay, we have two possibilities. It could've been meant for Dad, or it could've been meant for someone else, namely Mrs. Konrath."

"Tim," said Katrina, "remember asking me in the kitchen, when everyone was arriving, 'Who is that guy?' referring to Wren Dukette?"

"Yeah?"

"When did you realize Wren was who you thought it was?" asked Katrina.

"I'm not sure what you mean?" Tim said, squirming.

"Dad, when did you figure Dukette was the guy you fired years ago?" asked Bruce.

"Let me see. Give me a minute to think." Tim finally decided to cooperate.

"What about the poison found in Mr. Dukette's pocket?" said Song. "I hate to think it, as he seem's nice and all, but you did fire him, Tim." Song looked at her husband and received the dirty look he passed to her.

Katrina affirmed Song's comment by giving Tim a smug look and then looked away.

"Okay," said Katrina, leaning forward on the couch. "Why don't we list everyone who was here and mark next to their names possible motives for each person."

Song obliged by getting paper and pencils from the reception desk. She promptly passed them around. There was an awkward silence as the group got started on their lists.

CHAPTER 12

Wren Dukette sat forward in the old, grey office chair and pounded his fist on the table. "You've got to believe me, I don't know how that vial got in my pocket. It's not mine. I've never seen the damn thing before in my life." The interrogation room was gray and bare.

Klonski fired back at Wren, countering that he had an adequate motive for wanting Tim Versay dead. "It was payback time, right?"

"Yeah, it was payback, but I wouldn't kill him. Lieutenant, haven't you heard that 'living well is the best revenge?' That's compensation for me. Besides, why are you assuming it wasn't his wife or the other one–Katrina? They had motives. Or maybe it was just meant for Mrs. Konrath. Are you exploring those options?"

"You were found with poison on your person–" the door to the small room opened and Lewis came in. Klonski's look of irritation soon was replaced by stern approval as his assistant waved a folder in front of him.

"I have something for you," Lewis said.

"I hope so. Excuse me for a few minutes, Mr. Dukette. Remain seated and I'll be right back."

"How long before I'm free to go?"

"We first have to see if you are," Klonski retorted. Rising, he began leafing through the file contents as he left the stark interrogation room.

The two detectives walked down a tiny corridor as the elder man continued to shuffle through the information. Klonski led Lewis to a small office. "Jesus, this door creaks worse than I do. What did Casey find out from the neighbor, Lewis?"

"Nothing, no one was home. You gonna hold Dukette?"

"Let me see what we have in here first." He sat behind the desk, still looking at the information in the folder. "Good, we got some clear prints off the rear window. Yep, Cyanide did it to her."

"Was there ever any doubt?"

"I just had a hunch, that's all. Well, I think I'll have to let Dukette go."

"What? You don't have enough to hold him?"

"Maybe..." Klonski was following another gut feeling and for now, was holding his cards close to his vest. "The hitch is, he's not to leave town till I say so."

"You're the boss."

"Thank you for noticing."

"Sorry, Spike, we could barely hear you knock," said Song, opening the door. "Why didn't you ring the bell?"

"I did. I guess it's not working or you didn't hear it. What's going on?"

"We're all in the drawing room. Would you like an iced tea or something?"

"Not right now, Song, thanks."

Spike joined the others and recounted the tale of his trip to police headquarters.

"I'll never again complain about our place back home," he said. "Their station is such a dump. Must have a small budget. Anyway, when Mrs. Dukette and I got there, Klonski already had Wren inside for questioning. There was no place to sit except for an old wooden bench that looks like it was rescued from the dump. That place smelled so moldy that Mrs. Dukette sat outside and waited for Wren out there. I offered to keep her company for a few minutes and we sat in the car and talked some."

"Did you find anything out?" Kim asked.

"Not much. I heard Klonski and Dukette yelling at each other at one point, but Theresa and I were on our way out and I couldn't make out what they were saying. Lewis was standing right there at the front desk and would have seen me if I tried to stop and listen."

"I'm going for a cigarette," said Tim.

"Don't you want to hear what happened?" Song wished her husband would stay. "You always miss so much."

"Shhh," hissed Katrina, "let him finish."

"There's not much to tell. Theresa confirmed the story about Tim firing Wren years ago. She thought it was a little immature about how her husband wanted to cast it up in Tim's face, but when Dukette insisted she figured she'd go along with him; at least she would get a visit to her mother's out of the deal."

"That's it?" Kim was disappointed.

"Yep, Theresa said she had kept me long enough and insisted that I leave her at the station. I walked her back in, she thanked me and that was it."

Faint footsteps could be heard above and Spike asked about them.

"It's Mr. Konrath," said Song. "He's staying the night. Poor man. Garsch, kids, it's going to be dark soon. I should get a dinner on."

"Song, we just got away from the table," said Katrina. "Sit and relax."

"Oh, Tim likes to eat on time—"

"Don't fix anything for us, Mrs. Versay," said Kim. "Spike and I are going out for dinner. Aren't we?"

"Yeah."

"You know, we should get a wreath or something for the front door," said Katrina softly. "I think it would only be right to get a floral piece sent to the parlor where his wife is laid out, too." Katrina grimaced. "Although that's a puny offering considering his wife died at our inn."

"It's a wonder the guy's even talking to any of us," Bruce whispered. "He's probably sticking around to do a bit of his own snooping. I'm sure he'd like to get his hands on the killer himself."

"Yeah, and seek revenge on his own," said Kim.

Tim returned to the room and immediately Song changed the subject. "What time do you want to eat, Tim?"

Katrina didn't wait for Tim's answer before she started making plans with Kim, Spike and Bruce to go into town for their evening meal.

"Let's get out of this place. Be ready in about an hour, you guys? That's if it's okay if we join you and Spike," said Katrina.

"Yeah," said Kim. "Maybe we could hit a nightspot after dinner. Well, I'll go up and get ready though I'll need more than an hour."

The two couples agreed on a time and parted. Katrina and Bruce sat and talked with Tim and Song, inviting them along for dinner.

"You kids go ahead," Song said. "Tim and I will eat here and keep an eye on the place. Besides, someone should be home in case Lieutenant Klonski calls with any news."

"Well, if you change your mind, you're welcome," said Katrina. "And I've got to get ready."

Katrina climbed the stairs to the second floor, anticipating a shower and a night out in town. Ahead of her, she could hear the soft creaking of floorboards and approaching footsteps.

"Oh hi, Mr. Konrath." Bob Konrath stood to the side waiting for Katrina to reach the top step before descending. "How are you doing?"

"Well, I'm going a bit crazy up there by myself," he said. "And Klonski doesn't think my paperwork will be ready till morning. I thought I'd go for a ride and get some fresh air and do some thinking. I've been on the phone all afternoon breaking the bad news to family and making funeral arrangements. I just need to get out for a while and face adjusting to..." He stopped talking.

"I understand, Mr. Konrath," Katrina said, searching for something to say. "I hear Klonski's great at what he does and I've no doubt that–well, I'm sure he'll have some good results in no time."

"I appreciate that, Katrina, thanks. Now I should talk to Song about getting back in tonight. See you later." Bob Konrath turned and proceeded down the staircase.

Occupying the same table at the steak house, Bruce assured Spike and Kim that they wouldn't be disappointed with their meal. He steered the conversation back to the murder. "I couldn't say too much back at the inn. My mom was getting spooked. Anyway, my question is, why did Konrath make a call on his car phone when he could've used the inn's phone. Katrina, didn't you say Bob told you, in the hall, that he was on the phone all afternoon?"

"He did, I know, so why use the car phone earlier? Unless Bob, on the spur of the moment, decided to call someone quick and made the rest of his calls from his room later. The reception would be better. Cell phone coverage is still sketchy around this area."

"That's possible," said Bruce. "I'd sure like to get in his car and redial that number. I wonder who'd be on the other end?"

"You guys think he did it?" asked Kim.

"Well, I'd like to think we could all be ruled out," Bruce said. "I'd hate to learn that my girlfriend's trying to bump off my father. So assuming we're all clean, I'll focus on Dukette and Konrath."

"Wouldn't it be great if Jessie was having an affair with Bob or Wren and that she's tied in?" said Katrina.

"You'd like that, huh?" said Bruce.

Katrina smiled. "As long as she'd be hauled off."

Bruce scratched his head. "Dukette had motive and the poison. But was the poison planted? If it wasn't, why didn't he ditch the vial?"

"He didn't have the opportunity?" said Katrina. "Or maybe he feared it would be located so he kept it on himself. This way he'd know where it was at all times. That is until he left the area and disposed of it for good."

Spike spoke up. "I know I'm going to sound like a cop, but we're all still suspects. Like Bruce, I'll assume all of us at this table are innocent." Spike shifted in his seat. "So, let's go over suspects. There's Lou, the photog, Jessie and Theresa. And we've already mentioned Wren and Bob. Just to confuse things, I have to throw in Mindy Konrath too."

"What?" Katrina said.

"That's a possibility. The poison could have been for someone else and she just happened to be the recipient. Or she may have been the one that planted it and her scheme backfired."

"You mean that someone knew what she was up to and switched things at the table so she'd get it instead?" said Kim.

"It's possible. I know this confuses things, but we have to consider all angles. Anyway, I'm sure Klonski thought of taking a saliva print off Konrath's car phone. If not, I probably should remind him before Bob leaves the area."

Katrina barely heard Spike's last comment. "If she was poisoned," said Katrina, "is it possible she was administered the dose before she got into the dining room, and it affected her at the table? Maybe she was supposed to die upstairs in her room or outside and not at the table. Maybe the killer miscalculated and it took at breakfast instead of earlier or later."

"What's your point?" Bruce asked Katrina.

"Well, that may expose the killer as a novice who really didn't know what he or she was doing? I mean the timing doesn't seem right. Why have someone die at a busy breakfast table?"

"Why not?" Bruce said. "It would make things all that more confusing like they've become. Quiet, the waitress is bringing our food."

The foursome gingerly attacked their dinner and the conversation took on a more cheerful tone, however, briefly returning to musings of clues and murder.

"Where do you want to go from here?" Kim asked.

"If it's okay, I'd rather not go to a club that's real crazy," said Katrina. "There's a place in the boonies that's suppose to be good. They play a lot of mellow rock. Is that okay?"

"Yeah," said Kim.

"Spike?"

He nodded, remembering he'd heard about the club at breakfast but couldn't remember from whom.

"I'm just not in a mood for a jumpin' crowd," said Katrina. "I had enough excitement to last a decade."

"There's an empty table," said Spike. "Let's grab it." Spike led the way through the crowded bar to a high backed, cushioned booth. There was a break between music sets and making conversation was not hard. Kim was surveying the tropical mixed drink list as Bruce was eyeing the place, hoping to wave down a waitress.

Bruce lowered his arm and took another look around the busy club. His gaze backed toward the entrance. "Hey, know who just walked in?" Bruce said. "Don't turn around... It's Hodgkins."

"Great. I'm gonna love living in a small town," Katrina said, grabbing a menu to hide behind. "Don't invite her to this table... Where did she go?"

"Aunty Trina, I don't think she saw us 'cause she went straight to the bar. Why are you hiding anyway?"

Katrina peered around her menu in time to catch Jessie elbow her way through the crowd, conveniently squeezing herself between two men sitting at the bar.

A young, suntanned waiter blocked Katrina's view as he approached their booth to take the foursome's drink order. It was Bruce's turn to kick Katrina under the table as she had done many times, when she felt he had looked too long at an attractive waitress.

"Well," she muttered, "now you know how it feels."

"She's gone." Spike was the first to notice.

"So?" Kim said.

"I know you like her, Kim," said Katrina, "but we have to look at her in a different light. She's not just a bitch, she's a suspect."

"You read too many mysteries, Aunty Trina," said Kim.

"No such thing. Besides, it wouldn't hurt to see what she's up to," said Katrina.

"Where's the ladies' room?" Kim asked.

Spike pointed to the right of the crowded bar, and Kim got up and left the table. Katrina hoped her niece wasn't going to approach the blonde, but noticed that after Kim passed the bar she went in the opposite direction. Curious at first, Katrina dismissed her thoughts guessing that Kim went to make a phone call.

Katrina and Bruce bounced some as they felt the occupants of the booth behind them shift about in their seats. Bruce looked at Katrina and rolled his eyes, mimicking a seasick expression. Katrina was about to whisper a protest when she heard the occupants of the adjacent booth began to converse.

"Busy here tonight," said a male voice.

"Leave it to me to get us a nice booth. So private and cozy," came a female response. Giggling and cooing ensued.

"So what else were you up to today?" the man soon asked.

"That's enough don't you think?" she purred

Bruce noticed Kim heading back to their table, leaned across Katrina and whispered something to Spike. As Kim neared their table, Spike held a finger vertical to his lips. The young woman shot him a look of confusion.

"...so the groundwork was laid and... and now this colossal story gets dropped right into my lap."

"That's Jessie Hodgkins!" Kim whispered to Spike. He responded with a grimace and a gentle hand over her mouth.

"...besides, I'll get tons of mileage out of this one and when the murder story runs dry–well, let's say more strange things will be happening at that inn and I'll have material for weeks. The fun's just starting."

"That may put 'em out," Jessie's companion said.

118

"Oh well!"

"You're such a bad girl. Come home with me."

Jessie and her friend giggled and drank, then left for his apartment. As they rose, the foursome looked down.

"They're gone," said Bruce. "You can put the menu down."

"Think she saw us?" Katrina laid her drink list on the table and looked toward the exit.

"No. They were too busy giggling and groping," said Bruce. "Here come our drinks."

Katrina barely noticed Mr. Hardbody set their drinks on their table and barely heard him apologize for the delay. A love song by a famous bespectacled, British piano player reverberated throughout the nightclub, matching the club's tropical decor.

Kim waved a hand in front of her aunt's crestfallen expression, looking for an eyelash to flutter. "Is there anybody in there?" sang Kim.

"I can't believe her," Katrina finally said. "She's trying to put us out of business."

"Aunty Trina, are you okay?" Kim asked.

"Bruce, that skank aims to ruin our business," Katrina said. "And what did she mean by 'groundwork'?"

"Don't worry about her, Aunty Trina, she's just talking," said Kim.

"We've only had one murder at the inn that happened to benefit that witch," Katrina spit sarcastically. "I wonder what other exciting tidbits we can look forward to in the near future." Katrina poked at an ice cube with her straw.

"The chick's ruthless," Bruce said. "Nothing seems to stop her. We'll just have to keep an eye open for the next few days, that's all."

"I can't imagine a guy wanting to take her home," Kim said, her coy expression aimed at Spike. "It's hard to find a good woman these days, isn't it, Spike?"

"Now do you still think the adorable Ms. Hodgkins is still such a prize?" said Katrina.

"Well, I–I was starting to have my doubts about her," said Kim. The young woman avoided her aunt's gaze as she poked a swizzle stick at the cherry in the bottom of her glass.

"You know," Spike said, never addressing Kim's hinting, "if she shows up where she's not wanted you can always charge her with trespassing. If she causes any trouble, you can get her with harassment."

"Why not tell Klonski what we just overheard?"

"I guess you could, Katrina or–" Spike said.

"Or, we can just create a few surprises for her of our own?" said Bruce.

"Yeah, but what if she gets hurt?" Katrina said with a mischievous gleam in her eye.

"Wait a minute. What did you have in mind?" said Bruce.

"Just thinking..." Katrina didn't realize she was smiling.

"And what delicious thoughts were they?" asked Kim.

"Don't worry," said Katrina, "when I settle on one, you'll be the first to know. Anyway, if Klonski says we can leave, I'm checkin' out even if I have to go alone. Or maybe I'll take off on a photo shoot with Lou."

"Huh?" Bruce said.

"Just seeing if you were paying attention." Katrina winked at Kim. "I'll leave you here with Hodgkins, and Lou and I'll take off to Tampa–with his camera."

"You'll take off with his camera all right..." Bruce mumbled. Kim and Katrina started to laugh.

"And I'll take off with Suntan Man who's heading our way as we speak," said Kim. "We staying for another?"

"In that case, he can pay for your drinks, Kim," laughed Spike.

It was near one a.m. when they headed back to the Tudor Inn passing through orange groves and open back roads. The top down on their sports car offered a view of the night sky profuse with clusters of twinkling stars, a sight virtually unknown in most cities.

"I'm beat," said Kim.

"Guess that means we're done for the night," said Spike.

"Yeah, I'm bingoed after all the... Let's do something tomorrow, okay?"

As they turned left onto the inn's winding drive, Spike pulled up on the grass and turned down the radio lest they wake the occupants of the now dimly lit Tudor Grove Inn.

"Konrath's car's back," Bruce said, referring to the first auto parked to the side of the driveway. "And, Dukette's car's gone. Wonder how he made out at the cop station?"

"We'll probably know tomorrow," said Katrina. "Spike, you better put the top up just in case the scheming Miss Hodgkins shows up tonight and decides to booby-trap your car," she advised.

"Or a raccoon comes out of the trees and craps all over the upholstery," Bruce laughed.

Spike raised the top and turned off the car.

"Are there snakes in there?" Kim asked, glancing toward the thicket that separated the inn's property from the next yard. "Who are your neighbors? Did you meet them, Aunty Trina?"

Once out of the car, Katrina yawned and stretched away the effects of her tall body being cramped in the back seat of the convertible.

"It's a couple in their late-sixties I guess. That's what Song said. She met them about a week ago–when we were moving in. She says they seemed nice." Katrina yawned again and tripped over a small rock. Dropping to a sitting position, she chuckled, "I'm melting." Her companions laughed when Katrina threatened to turn them into toads as they continued to walk off. Katrina rose, dusted herself off and ran to catch up with her uncaring cohorts, never being aware of the pair of eyes peering at her through the cluster of trees that lined the winding driveway.

"G'night, Aunty Trina, tomorrow's another day," Kim whispered as she left her aunt outside the door of her suite.

"G'night, Kim. I'm sleeping in, so amuse yourselves in the morning and I'll catch up with you when I get up. Sleep tight." Katrina opened the door, hoping Bruce hadn't dropped off to sleep yet. "I'm glad you're awake," she said, seeing his eyes nearly closed. She locked up and approached the bed.

"Not for long." Bruce pulled the covers over his head.

"I hope the motion detector works right." She knew she had to talk fast as she was losing her audience.

"You still worried about her?"

"Well, I hope she's smart enough to back off, if suddenly the whole front lawn lit up."

"She won't do anything." Bruce's voice was fading. "We'll talk to Klonski in the morning. G'night."

"Yeah." Katrina dimmed the lights and double-checked the lock on their bedroom door.

Jessie Hodgkins was not Katrina's only concern for now. What truly bothered her was the thought of a killer who might be occupying a room in their inn. While brushing her teeth, Katrina mulled over the events of the last few days. The faster her thoughts ran through her mind, the harder she bore down on her brush until her gums started to smart. "I better go to bed. Right now I'm even dangerous with a toothbrush."

Just before climbing into bed, Katrina stopped and eyed the pair of curtained windows sitting behind the bed and her nightstand. Katrina approached them, then knelt and felt along the baseboard below. Puzzled, she stood and again studied the curtains. Parting the left drape, Katrina peeked out at the front lawn. The lone streetlight stood sentry at the end of the drive, casting a hazy glow on the vehicles parked to the right of it. Everything looked serene but felt sinister. So what should I do, she thought, camp out at the window all night and wait for stuff to happen? This is nuts. I'm sure Jessie's busy doing other things right now. Go to bed before you start thinking... Stepping away from the window, Katrina opened her nightstand and fished around in the dark for a cassette to plunk in her player. It was odd that it took her several minutes to recognize the feel of hard plastic.

Lying down, her head touching the cool, cotton-encased pillow, Katrina realized how tired she was and adjusted the volume on her headset to a comfortable low. A quieting, male voice came through, reminding her that, "if you think you can or if you think you can't, you're right."

Katrina chided herself for occasionally opening an eye, making sure things were still in the dimly lit room, or that sufficient air-conditioning could be felt circulating about. She struggled between the urge to sleep and with the idea of staying awake. Katrina got up. Tiptoeing back to the left front window, Katrina parted the curtain once more and peered through the small slit she allowed herself. Reassured that the motion detector hadn't been tripped, she stood pondering the night, when outside detection range, Katrina made out a shadowy figure gliding slowly down the drive toward the dim lamplight. Katrina gasped as she blinked and refocused her eyes. "Mindy Konrath returns." Quickly she released the curtain and felt a pounding in her chest. She tried to speak but her fright propelled her to the door in effort to rush the hall and scream about the ghost she just saw. While wrestling with the lock, a thought jarred her back to reality. Katrina stopped–her heart still thumping. Instead, she yanked a pair of jeans off a hanger and slipped them on. She needn't wake Bruce. She would handle this herself. Hastily, Katrina slid on sneakers and grabbed a flashlight out of the closet. Her heart continued to thump, but this time, it wasn't due to fear but to the prospect of excitement. She didn't expect to find Mindy, but Jessie.

Katrina padded down the dim lit staircase, extra glad for the seashell night-lights plugged in along the way. With a right at the bottom step, she detoured to the gift shop. Katrina scanned the racks by the beam of her flashlight. She found what she wanted. "I never thought I'd need these," she mused, tearing into a plastic bag containing fisherman's netting. And she fought the

123

urge to grab a pitcher of cold water and ice cubes. There just wasn't time.

Katrina stole through the darkened first floor, crept out the front door and down the porch steps. She sneaked across the front lawn, careful not to trip the motion detector. Now at the grassy parking area, Katrina moved silently between the cars and the wooded area. Halfway down the drive, she saw her target. Katrina's ghoul was standing at the edge of the graveled driveway with its back to the novice ghost buster. Katrina moved closer, continuing to use the grass to muffle her steps. With her prey in sight, the huntress loosened the net and gripped it in her hands. As her ghost stepped closer, Katrina jumped up with netting held high, screamed, and charged the figure. The netted and tackled spook let out a mournful cry. A short distance down the road, Katrina heard fleeing footsteps, a car door slam and the sound of a vehicle starting up and speeding away.

CHAPTER 13

Katrina couldn't believe it as she rolled off Kim. "What? What is… ? Why-y are you running around in the dark dressed like that anyway?" Katrina eyed Kim's white gown. It was cut low off the shoulder.

"Which question would you like me to answer first, Aunty Trina? You almost killed me, jumping me like that." Kim winced as she rose to a kneeling position.

Removing the netting that clung to the pretty woman, Katrina helped her niece up, not knowing what to do first–help untangle the net from her hair, inspect her for bruises or give her hell.

"My dress is torn," Kim wailed, looking down at her flowing gown.

"Never mind the dress, are you hurt?" Katrina threw the nylon netting aside and grabbed the flashlight. "Move close to the lamppost so we can see better."

After hobbling toward the light Kim inspected her knees and arms, insisting that her aunt quit fussing over her as she was fine.

"Then why are you limping?" Katrina demanded.

"My leg got banged up, that's all."

"Well, I'm glad you're all right 'cause now I'm going to kill you. But before I do, I want to know what's going on out here?" Katrina's voice was slowly escalating from a whisper to a shout.

"Sshhh, you'll wake them all up." Kim looked over at the inn. "Can we sit down on the steps? I need to get off this leg." Kim gathered up her flowing gown and started across the front lawn.

"Stay close to the trees, the detector… " Katrina advised as she lit a path before them with her flashlight.

"I almost forgot. That's all I need is for Spike to wake up and start asking me all kinds of questions."

A few moments later they were sitting on the steps.

"Let's hear it," Katrina said. "Just please tell me you're not Mindy Konrath's murderer. I couldn't handle that right now."

"First, promise you won't tell Spike about this," Kim said in a nervous whisper as she glanced at the front door behind them. "What if someone's listening now?"

Bracing herself for the worst, Katrina wondered what could be so awful–or sinister that her niece demanded an oath of silence from her. "Kim, what have you done? And who was that in the car that took off? Are you nuts goin' out to the road at this hour dressed like you just jumped off the cover of a romance novel." Katrina was becoming angrier each moment. "I'm so pissed at you–you've really outdone yourself this time."

"Yeah, well I heard about some of the zingers you pulled at my age. Besides," Kim declared defiantly, "I didn't do anything wrong."

Katrina realized her emotions were running wild and tried to calm down. She'd have to if she were going to find anything out. "Quit stalling and talk." The two women sat on the bottom step in near total darkness, one anxious over what she was about to hear, the other nervous over what she had to tell.

Kim sighed in resignation. "Well, I'm not sure where to begin but..." It didn't matter. The sound of a turning doorknob followed by soft creaking ended any immediate revelations. "Remember, not a word."

"What's goin' on out here?" It was Bruce. He quietly closed the heavy door behind him. "Can't you guys sleep?"

Bruce couldn't see the perturbed look Katrina gave him as he felt around for the top step. He sat down.

"Ah, no Uncle Bruce, we couldn't sleep so we came out here to talk."

"In the dark?" he said. "How can you see anything? Want me to turn on the porch light?" He started to rise.

"No!" Kim said. "We... uh... didn't want to wake anyone so we just used a flashlight. You know, Aunty Trina, this fresh air has made me tired. I should be able to sleep now. Oh, can I use the flashlight?"

"You're not going in yet, are you, Kim?" Katrina said, her words sharp. "He isn't staying, are you, Bruce?"

"Am I missing something?"

"It's okay, I really am quite tired." Kim faked a yawn. "G'night, see you in the morning." The faint rustling of new cotton could be heard as Kim gathered up her torn gown and tried to stand. In pain, Kim leaned against Katrina. Steadying herself, she turned and hobbled up the remaining porch steps. The faint click of the wooden door reinforced Katrina's frustration. Katrina groaned.

"Did I mess something up?" Bruce asked, puzzled.

"Sort of." Katrina sighed and fanny-slid her way up to the top step. "Did Kim take the flashlight? I can't see a thing. Little brat."

"So what's going on?" Bruce asked.

"I wish I knew," came the wistful response. "I wish I knew."

"Or do you mean you can't tell me?"

"What makes you think there's something to tell?"

"Katrina, I was awake, I saw you go out there," said Bruce.

"Great. Why didn't you offer some help?"

"Because I wasn't sure what was going on. I wanted to see what you were up to."

"Like maybe I'm the killer and I had some clandestine business to conduct."

"We're all still suspects, you know." He smiled. "But no, I don't think you're the killer. I wanted to see if, well, maybe you'd lead us to the killer."

"So now I'm bait?"

"Calm down, you're the one who went out there in the first place," said Bruce.

Before Katrina would tell Bruce more, she wanted to know how much he'd seen. After all, she had promised her niece secrecy, but Katrina realized Bruce, with the aid of the streetlight, had seen most of what transpired.

"I don't s'pose you heard the car take off," she said.

"What car? Are you still on that silver car thing?"

Katrina relayed what she had heard, thus adding the fact that she hadn't seen the departing auto or who belonged to it.

"Bruce, what about Kim? S'pose she got herself mixed up in some mess? I'm worried about her."

"What makes you think she is?" Bruce yawned.

Katrina pointed out how she swore she heard Kim on the phone earlier and how she quickly changed topics when questioned about it.

"Also, at the club, I noticed instead of going to the ladies' room, like she said she was, she headed in the opposite direction where the phones were. So whoever took off when I came out could've been who she was talking to. It's too coincidental to be otherwise. Plus, what's with the low-cut gown? Why would she wear something like that in the dead of night to meet...?" Katrina dismissed a possible explanation as she realized that some younger women get all dressed up just to wash a car. Kim was one of them.

"So what do you think?" Katrina asked her beau who had started to nod out.

"Huh?"

Katrina tsked then shook Bruce. "You don't know what you just missed. Jessie Hodgkins was running across the front lawn half naked." Katrina giggled when his eyes fluttered open.

"Why didn't you wake me?"

"You snooze, you lose." Katrina stopped. "I thought you said you didn't like her."

Bruce knew where this was going. "G'night, I'm going to bed."

Joseph Klonski glanced at his watch. It was only nine-twenty a.m., and he felt as if he'd already put in half a day at the office. Between granting the Dukettes' request to leave the area after

128

noon, agreeing with Spike's idea to do a saliva print on Konrath's car phone, dispatching Lewis to the scene of a hit and run, he found himself looking forward to his invite for a late breakfast at the Tudor Grove.

"Thank you, Mrs. Versay," he said into the phone. "I need to make a stop at the inn anyway... I'll see what I can do about removing the police line so you can use the dining room... You're welcome. By the way, is Mr. Konrath there? I'd like to speak with him... Yes, I'll hold." Klonski waited and inserted some last minute notes into a folder on a case he closed the previous night. He took a last sip of bitter coffee and threw the half-filled paper cup into the trash. "Yes, Mrs. Versay. When he comes down, tell him I'm on my way and I need to speak with him. Yes, bye."

*   *   *

"Let me sleep," mumbled Katrina." "The inn's closed today." It was her turn to do the cover pulling. "I'll get up when I want and get my own breakfast.

"Klonski's comin' over," Bruce said. "Don't you wanna talk to him?" He finally succeeded in luring Katrina out from under the blankets.

"Did you call him?"

"No, Spike did." Bruce relayed the information obtained over coffee he took that morning with the rest of the early risers, Song, Tim and Spike. "So I thought you'd be upset if I let you sleep through Klonski's breakfast visit."

"You're right. I'm getting up." Katrina sat up in bed and stretched. She brushed the hair out of her eyes. "Hey, why's your mom having him over so often? Think she has 'it' for him?"

"You never know," Bruce said with a shrug. "I'm going down. Klonski'll be here soon."

"Wait, Bruce. Did Spike say anything about last night?"

"No."

"Is Kim up yet?"

129

"I'm not sure." Bruce was through playing fifty questions. "Get ready and come downstairs."

"Save me some coffee," Katrina called to her now exiting mate. "Or you'll reap the consequences."

Bruce poked his head back in the room. "I think I'm gettin' scared." He closed the door behind him.

As she dressed, Katrina made out the murmur of voices and clatter of dishes escalate, as if to herald the final wake-up call for all late sleepers to come to breakfast. A soft tap on her bedroom door revealed a sleepy-eyed Kim standing out in the hallway.

"Aunty Trina, you going down for breakfast?"

"Yeah, I'm almost ready. Come in. Does Spike know about last night?"

"If he does, he hasn't let on," said Kim. She was dressed in a midriff top and slacks. "But listen, I have to tell you something." Kim's voice dropped to a low whisper and she motioned her aunt away from the door. "I don't want anyone to hear this. I lost an earring. I think it was yesterday. Anyway, I was looking around on the floor for it and then in the closet. I heard murmuring–like a phone conversation–in the room next to mine–so I sorta listened. Anyway, I finally could make out Bob Konrath's voice. He," Kim said, her eyes widening, "said something about cremating his wife's body."

"And?" Katrina waited for more.

"And what? Aunty Trina what else is there? He's cremating her so they can't dig her up in case they need more evidence. In the movies, the murderer always has the body cremated,"

"The key word is movies," said Katrina with a wave of her hand. She ran a brush through her hair. "They do a lot of things in the movies. Maybe that was her wish or... or maybe it's a religious thing." Katrina eyed herself in the mirror, all the while studying the dark circles under her eyes. "Whoever named it beauty sleep wasn't kidding," she told her reflection. "Oh, don't forget, you have a little story to tell me later, right?"

"You ready, Aunty Trina?"

"Yeah, let's go down." Katrina heard a new voice downstairs. "Is that Klonski?"

"Sounds like him." Pausing before opening the door wide, Kim turned to her aunt and started to giggle. "Aunty Trina, you know who Klonski reminds me of?" Answering her own question, she replied, "Grama's undertaker." They both laughed as Katrina locked her suite and paused before starting down the stairs.

"He wasn't bad-looking."

"Aunty Trina, everything looks good to you, lately."

"Well, his son was a fox. I told you, you should've gone for him. I had it all lined up for you. At least his father would've had someone to do his hair for him."

Tim poked his fork at a sausage link on his plate and looked up as Kim and Katrina entered the temporary dining area. They were giggling. "Crissakes, they even wake up stupid," he mumbled before sipping his coffee.

"G'morning," Katrina half-heartedly greeted the diners. "G'morning, Lieutenant Klonski. Mind if I sit next to you?" Katrina plopped down in the empty seat next to the detective.

"Song's sitting there," grumbled Tim.

Yep, Katrina thought, she wants him, and hubby, Hotstuff, doesn't even know it. "Listen, you guys," Katrina announced, "the inn's closed. The only people I'm waiting on is Lieutenant Klonski, Spike and–where's Mr. Konrath?"

"He hasn't come down yet," Bruce offered. "What about me?"

Katrina got up from Song's place at the table, but before leaving she whispered in Klonski's ear, "Before you leave, we want to talk to you."

The lieutenant nodded and Song returned to the drawing room with a brimming platter of bacon and scrambled eggs. Bob Konrath appeared in the doorway right behind her.

"Oh, Mr. Konrath," Song chirped. "I didn't even hear you. How are you this mornin'?"

Bob Konrath mumbled an answer and Song welcomed him to sit at any unoccupied setting at the main table. "Things are a li'l informal today, Mr. Konrath. We've closed the inn in respect to–well, because of the situation and all." Song was obviously uncomfortable with the topic of Mrs. Konrath's death. "Here Lieutenant, here's a nice platter of bacon and eggs. Please help yourself." Tim looked up in mild surprise but immediately went back to his toast.

"Joe, Song claims the police tape may come down today, is that so?" Spike asked the detective sitting across from him.

"It looks good," Klonski said. "I just want to make one review before I authorize it."

"Thank you, Song." Bob Konrath accepted a cup of coffee from the woman and turned his attention back to Klonski. "Lieutenant, if you don't need anything more from me, I'd like to see about leaving sometime today. I have funeral plans to make and I'd like to be with my family."

"Have you decided where your wife will be buried?" Katrina asked, shooting a look across the table at her niece. "I mean, have you a family plot or anything like that?"

"Katrina, maybe Mr. Konrath doesn't want to talk about that right now," said Song.

"It's all right, Mrs. Versay," said Bob. "I'm glad she mentioned it. I wasn't sure how to broach the subject. You see," he seemed to consider his words, "I am having my wife's remains cremated."

A barely audible gasp could be heard from Song. Katrina and Kim followed in like fashion. "I don't know how this is going to sound," Bob laid down his fork and faced Song. "I wanted to ask you, well, if you wouldn't mind if I scattered her ashes on the grounds of your bed and breakfast property. She just loved your inn and I thought this would be a suitable resting place for her. Think about it and let me know before I leave."

Looking across the table at Song, Katrina tried to catch the woman's attention. It was no use, for the woman seemed preoccupied with her own thoughts and appeared to be playing with her food rather than eating it. "Song and I will discuss it later, Mr. Konrath, and let you know before you leave."

"Speaking of leaving, Mr. Konrath," said Klonski, "I need to talk with you after breakfast, but before I leave if you don't mind. It will only take a few minutes of your time. I will also have an answer for you as to when you can leave the inn."

"Lieutenant," Kim asked, "when can the rest of us leave? We were thinking of going..." Kim stopped speaking, cleared her throat and sipped at her water. "I'm on vacation and I was thinking of the few days Spike and I have left to do things. When do you think we can go?"

Klonski noted the look Katrina gave her niece. "As soon as I know, I'll let you know."

"Are you any closer at catching the killer, Joseph?" Song inquired demurely.

"We're making progress, Mrs. Versay. That's all I can tell you right now." Klonski glanced around at the table, and all the diners, seemed to tense. He noted this as he fished in his pocket for his trusty notebook. Tossing the pad on the table, he reached for a pencil and made a few quick jots as though he didn't trust a vital bit of information to his memory.

Katrina wondered if Klonski had ever falsely accused any one before and asked him so.

"Are you worried about that happening on this case?"

"He's answering a question with a question," thought Katrina, typical cop.

"Well, I know I wouldn't be too happy about it," piped Kim.

Klonski assured them he seldom made wrong accusations. "If you're not guilty you have nothing to worry about."

"Well, I'm goin' out for a cigarette," Tim declared, and got up from the table never even offering to clear a spoon.

Stopping, he watched Katrina reach in the pocket of her cutoffs and withdraw a vitamin pack.

"How come you're not any smarter from all those vitamins?" Tim asked, not waiting for an answer, and knowing she'd have one he didn't want to hear.

133

"So I can keep up with you, honey," she called to him as he left the room. Even Klonski snickered this time.

"You bring one for me?" Bruce asked.

Katrina had.

"Well, I guess I'll go upstairs," Bob Konrath announced, pushing his chair back as he rose. "Lieutenant, I'll be in my suite when you're ready for me. Thank you, Mrs. Versay, for another great meal." Nodding to the others, he walked past the reception desk toward the door.

"He dresses nice," Kim said, referring to Bob Konrath's attire of relaxed denim shirt and neatly pressed khaki pants.

Katrina didn't pay special attention to Bob's attire, but did see a chance to confront Joe Klonski. "Lieutenant, we've a few details to clue you in on. I wanted to wait for the guests to leave before we began, as they may or may not be of importance."

Klonski noticed that "the guests" consisted only of Bob Konrath and wondered if that was significant. Song appeared annoyed and Katrina speculated whether it was because of the forthcoming topic or because it interfered with her pampering of the detective. Song announced she would leave and return with another pot of coffee.

Klonski motioned for the small gathering to come in closer and Bruce promptly moved to fill the vacated chair.

Bruce opened the conversation relaying the details, overheard the other night, made by the conspiring Jessie Hodgkins. Klonski asked several questions, made notes and inquired after the man Jessie had met that night.

Katrina continued with an account of the previous evening's late night activities, only revealing the part where a vehicle drove off after hearing her approaching footsteps.

"What were you doing out at the end of the drive so late at night?" Klonski asked, watching her expression.

"I couldn't sleep so I took a walk on the grounds. I came back to the porch and Bruce joined me. He was wondering where I—"

Klonski held up his hand, indicating for her to stop. "I'll ask him about that." Klonski did and Bruce confirmed Katrina's story. The lieutenant wrote more notes.

Song reappeared with coffee pot in hand and walked over to the detective, promptly refilling his cup. Song was oblivious to any tension in the air, as the detective looked up just long enough to smile at her. Song splashed coffee over the rim of his cup.

Regaining her composure, Song continued refilling their cups, looking disappointed that her son took the seat next to Klonski. After setting the pot on the hot plate, Song proceeded to pick up dirty dishes from the table.

"Katrina," Song said, seeing a chance to be included in conversation again, "your poor blueberries are gonna go bad. When will ya use them? You know, every time I see them they remind me of... well, the incident at breakfast on opening day."

"I know, I hate making the dish now as I don't want my mom's family recipe associated with the death of Mrs. Konrath," said Katrina. "I'll figure out what to do with them later."

Klonski looked back across the table with a questioning expression.

As if reading his thoughts, Katrina offered, "Oh the blueberries," she waved a hand in the direction of the kitchen. "Bruce found them on the front porch just before the paramedics got here. You'd think the courier would've knocked instead of just dumping them off at the door. They could've gone bad out there."

"Aunty Trina, that's what they're trained to do," said Kim.

"That's progress for you."

"Or," added Spike, "they knocked and we didn't hear it, because at that very moment a murder was being committed."

Klonski noted all this on his pad. He then met with Bob. Satisfied with the outcome of his latest visit to the Tudor Grove Inn, he thanked his hosts for breakfast and left. He got what he had come for, and was pleased that Bob Konrath consented to his taking saliva samples off his car phone and that he merely balked at the idea of having his mouth swabbed, a standard procedure for the collection of comparison saliva samples.

"You know, Kim," said Katrina, "I can get into trouble for lying to Klonski about last night." They were alone in the drawing room.

"You didn't lie. You just left out a few things."

Katrina looked toward the foyer. Song, Bruce and Tim were out on the front porch talking as Klonski backed down the drive.

"Okay, Kim," Katrina whispered across the table as the pair collected dirty dishes, "no more putting me off. I want to know about last night."

"Remember your promise..."

"Yes." Katrina was losing patience.

"Well, I can only tell you so much and I'll tell you the rest later," Kim continued, aloof. "That was Lou, the photographer, out there last night." Kim stuck a clean fork in the remaining scrambled eggs and emptied it into her mouth, caring not to smudge her freshly reapplied, red lipstick.

"What?" Katrina stopped and studied her niece. "This gets better all the time. What could he possibly want from you out there in the dead of night? Never mind. I almost don't want to know."

"Okay then, you don't want to know." Kim smiled smugly.

"By garsch, you girls almost have the drawing room cleared," said Song, breezing in to join them. "Thank you. Oh, Joe is so nice," Song gushed to her helpers. "And," she continued in a whisper, "he's nice lookin', too."

"He's also quite married," Katrina trilled back. "He has a wedding band on his finger."

"Oh, Katrina," Song said lightly, "why would you say such a thing?" She nearly floated out the front drawing room door.

"Did Klonski say we can use the dining room?" Katrina asked, walking behind the woman, soiled tablecloth in hand.

"Yes, but I just don't want to go in there yet." Song's smile clouded.

"I'm with you there. I know–let's send Spike in first. He can scope it out, then we can all go in together."

"I guess," Song said, continuing down the hall to the kitchen.

The reception phone rang as Katrina crossed the foyer. "Kim, can you see if someone's on the phone? I've gotta shake out this tablecloth."

Kim didn't need to be asked; in a heartbeat she was at the front desk. "Tudor Grove, may I help you?" Katrina heard her niece coo into the phone. "Just a moment." Kim put her hand over the mouthpiece. "It's some lady about reservations." Kim handed her aunt the phone as she stepped back in. "I'll be out in the backyard," whispered Kim.

Minutes later a smiling Katrina sprinted down the back stairs.

"Hey you guys," she called, walking toward the patio grouping and its occupants, "we got a reservation for Thanksgiving."

Katrina approached the gathering, relaying the latest information and joined in the conversation. No one appeared to be discussing unpleasant business, for it seemed that everything that could have been said, was indeed discussed with Lieutenant Klonski and afterwards. Of course, Bob Konrath sitting there may have had something to do with it.

"Well," Bob stood up and announced, "I need to go into town on some errands. If Klonski returns with his verdict, please tell him to leave a number where I can reach him."

"Did he say when you were able to leave, Mr. Konrath?" Song asked. "Would you like to join us for dinner?"

"That's not necessary, Mrs. Versay. Thank you anyway." With a somber farewell, Bob turned and walked toward the back door of the inn.

Katrina watched as the man slowly walked away. He was, according to her definition, a distinguished gentleman; tall, well groomed, poised, and soft-spoken. He carried himself with an air of dignity, and she laughed to herself as she caught herself thinking both words, "distinguished and gentleman," in the same sentence.

Tuning herself back into the ongoing conversation, she heard Bruce describe his upcoming plans for the restoration of the chimney.

"I'd like to have it completed by early November so we can start using it."

"Oh, nothing's better than a roaring fire with cocoa and marshmallows," Song offered.

"Nothing's better than a roaring fire, a fluffy rug and a hot drink," Katrina said dreamily, referring to her favorite orange-flavored liqueur–and other things.

Kim hid her grin in her hand, while Katrina turned her head in effort to catch up with her daydream.

It was Tim's coughing that broke the spell. "That stuff tastes like alcohol."

"It is alcohol," said Katrina. "What's it supposed to taste like, chocolate milk?" Katrina realized her voice escalated, and softened it when she answered in defense of her favorite cognac. "It's delicious."

"It's expensive." Tim countered.

"Of course you wouldn't appreciate it, it's meant for the discriminating palate," said Katrina, with an air. She smirked at Kim while biting back a laugh.

"Give me a beer any ol' time," Tim snapped.

Bruce eyed the two, sensing what was going on. Song showed signs of anxiousness, typical when Tim and Katrina were about to get into it. Kim hung her head down, trying to ward off the giggles and Spike watched in amusement.

"I wonder," Katrina leaned toward Kim and whispered, "If that man ever knew what a woman wanted?" She added, "Wanting to bolt from his chamber doesn't count." The pair laughed and Tim shook his head, reaching for another cigarette.

"Isn't it a beautiful day?" Song said. "Just look at that blue sky." It was her attempt to lighten the cloud of contention.

Katrina looked up at the heavens. It was a beautiful day, but she wasn't in the mood for pondering cloud formations, and switched the topic to more relevant matters. "So Klonski said we have to stick around another day or so?"

"Anyone for lemonade?" Song offered. Everyone was, and Song rose and went inside.

Spike waited till Song was out of earshot and contemplated the results of the saliva test. "This may detain Konrath if they play around with the results."

"Why a saliva test, Spike?" mused Katrina.

"I thought you said they used a rape kit?" Kim asked Spike who was sitting across from her. "No one was raped."

"No one has to be. They just use the swabs from the kit to perform the saliva tests," he answered.

"Well, you didn't say that."

Tim chuckled while blowing smoke.

Katrina resented Tim laughing at her niece. "Who knows, Tim, maybe Song gets upset over talk of murder 'cause she botched the job and got the wrong person."

Tim stopped laughing. "Maybe it was you, Katrina," he said, his eyes narrowing. "Maybe you tried to kill me. After all you set the table. You must be disappointed that I'm still here."

"Yes, and Kim was·my accomplice," said Katrina. "She made out your place card."

"Klonski seemed to jump on that blueberry issue," Bruce added thoughtfully. "I wonder if he ever talked to our neighbors?"

"Well, he hasn't said much to me," said Spike. "My being an off-duty cop doesn't make me privy to anything. Maybe it's just as well."

"Mom's coming back, let's change the subject," said Bruce.

"Yeah, Tim, your wife's coming back." said Katrina. "Go help her with the drinks."

As Katrina figured, Tim sat back and watched as his wife struggled down the back steps, screen door snapping shut, barely missing her. "Nevermind, I'll do it," Katrina said. "Anyway, if she did try, I wonder what took her so long?"

Tim snickered at Katrina as he watched her walk away.

The resentment between the two did not go unnoticed by the others.

CHAPTER 14

"Damn," Klonski muttered as he hung up with Theresa Dukette's mother. He was furious. He had never given the Dukettes permission to leave, but they had. He called Theresa's mother hoping to reach them, but the couple had left an hour ago. He was angry with the police lab, too, for failing to get clear prints off some of the glass evidence.

Klonski was on his way back to headquarters when he turned and headed for Theresa's mother's home. Minutes later Klonski was cruising past her driveway. The yard was indeed free of vehicles. He thought about questioning the mother, but would do so as a last resort. Klonski called his office and requested a plainclothesman in an unmarked car cruise the street and notify him the moment the Dukettes returned—if they returned.

Klonski turned his car around and backtracked toward the inn. While driving, Klonski went over what he had learned that morning. The only thing on this case that worked in his favor was spotting his sidekick, Lewis, earlier at the local greasy spoon. Leaving him with the saliva samples and orders to start on them "yesterday," saved Klonski a trip and allowed him to move on to finding the Dukettes; that's when his momentum ceased. He was determined to regain the initiative.

Katrina set the tray of glasses down on the counter top and answered the ringing phone. "I'll meet you in an hour," she said into the handset. "No, I think Klonski eats there. Is there someplace else? How about—forget it, I was gonna say the doughnut shop… The bowling alley, how about the bowling alley? Our cars won't be easily spotted. Okay then, one hour. Make sure no one sees you. Gotta go, someone's coming." Katrina hung up the phone.

The screen door squeaked open. "Garsch, that's some walk from the patio tables to this kitchen, I'll tell ya," Song puffed. "Just rinse 'em and stack 'em in the dishwasher, Katrina. I'll run a load later. I'm goin' back outside for a while."

"Sure." Katrina didn't care about the dishes and focused on getting away from the inn–alone. She needed to sneak out without having to answer questions. Her solution was simple. She told Song she needed to get a pair of pantyhose, and asked Song to tell the others.

An hour later Katrina pulled the van alongside the bowling alley. There were few other cars in the lot and this made her uneasy. She parked between two, hoping her van wouldn't be seen. Katrina turned the vehicle off, got out and hurried across the parking lot toward the front door.

Unknown to Katrina, parked a few cars to the left of her vehicle, sat a lone figure, waiting and watching her. The figure quickly snapped some photographs.

"Meet me in the restaurant," were the orders she received over the phone. "It's quiet there, we can talk."

Katrina spotted her clandestine caller. She went to his table, set her purse on the floor and pulled up the chair across from him. He rose slightly. Katrina looked straight into his green eyes as they sat down.

"Thanks for showing. I need to get some things straight," he said coolly, his suntanned hands wrapped around his coffee mug.

She nodded, but remained silent, recalling the first time she'd met him. He reminded her of someone, but she couldn't remember who.

"Can I get you something?" he asked.

"No thanks, I have to make it quick. They'll have the dogs out after me."

"What excuse did you use?" He waited for an answer.

She continued to look across at him and noticed his thick, styled brown hair and well-groomed moustache.

"Decent... " she heard herself saying. "Oh, I thought–of a fairly decent excuse actually. Um, I said I was going to the

142

store." Katrina sat up straight in her chair and cleared her voice. "I think I could use a glass of water."

He signaled for the waitress and Katrina glanced toward the window. A little nagging voice told her all along who he resembled but the truth was, she was trying to forget.

"Are you all right?"

"Uh, yes. Did anyone ever tell you look like… ?" and before Katrina could stop the words, she uttered the name of her all-time favorite hunk, who used to reside in Hawaii, drive a hot red, sports car and wear an awful lot of Hawaiian print shirts.

"Once or twice," he flashed a near perfect smile, "except he's a few inches taller and a few million richer."

The two enjoyed their newly acquired friendship and sat talking and laughing for nearly an hour. Several times he reached over, stopping short of touching her hand. She stared at him most of the time studying his playful, boyish grin. She was grateful for a chance at meaningful conversation. He was thankful she didn't hit him with her purse when he explained. The couple rose from their table. He approached Katrina, and hugged her gently. The photographer out in the parking lot was using lots of film, taking pictures through the window with the aid of a powerful zoom lens.

He's a few inches shorter and a few years younger–he's adorable. She smiled at the thought. He'll be perfect.

The two meandered out of the restaurant and chatted as they sauntered toward the front doors of the bowling center, oblivious to the commotion out in the parking lot.

"You go ahead, I need to call back at the inn. It's better this way, if you know what I mean." As he turned to walk away, Katrina watched him, all the while thinking, but I won't hesitate conducting my own background check, just to see how perfect you really are.

"Hey, Lover Boy, is this yours?" It was the hefty Officer Casey calling to him across the bowling alley parking lot.

Adjusting his eyes to the bright mid-day sun, Lou located his sunglasses in his shirt pocket and quickly put them on. "My camera, how the hell did you get that?" asked Lou.

"One of your jealous girlfriends. You hear the one about the guy who had so many girlfriends, he forgot where he laid them?" Casey laughed at his own joke.

"That joke's as old as you are. So what happened?" the photographer asked the cop. "Let's move over to my car."

"Well, some woman called in a report, said she saw a blonde breaking into a car in this parking lot. Of course I came out right away. I found your girlfriend, Jessie Hodgkins, hiding in the shrubs snapping away at you and your friend."

"And you let her go?"

"I had to. Whoever called, left, and I couldn't very well file a complaint without the complainer. Besides, there was no break-in. The call was bogus. So, I did the next best thing, I got your camera back for you," said the white haired cop. "You can thank me any time you like."

"What's her story this time?"

"Said you forgot your camera last time you were with her and that she was gonna return it to you."

"That call wasn't bogus, Casey, she got into my car and helped herself to my camera."

"She's used to gettin' her way, and if she doesn't well–you know the rest. Hey, here comes your girlfriend." The officer nodded toward the bowling center.

"Don't say anything." Lou turned his back to the building.

"She's not lookin' this way. What, you tired of that one already?" The stout officer looked over at the woman heading for her vehicle. "You're picking 'em older these days. She's at least in her thirties."

"I'm not picking anything. It's not what you think."

A van started up, backed out of it's parking place and exited the lot.

"You can turn around now, she's gone. So-o, what are you hiding from? I got time for a good story."

"Nothing."

"Well, if it's nothing I guess you don't need this," Casey smiled as he tossed a plastic container up in the air and caught it.

"There's nothing on there to worry about. You think Hodgkin's would give it up if there was?" asked the photographer.

"And I thought it was my charm."

"Just give it to me."

"I thought you said..."

"I don't want to involve any... Jessie just thought she'd get something on me to cause trouble with."

"Here, pretty boy, catch." Officer Casey tossed the container at him. "You owe me, dude–you owe me good, Lou."

The metallic blue luxury coupe headed west on Highway 60, exiting the town of Lake Wales. Patiently awaiting the opportunity to accelerate from a city crawl to an open road cruise, Bob Konrath turned off the air-conditioning system and hit the window buttons, opening all windows full. As the sunroof opened, he glanced up and saw the magnificent powder blue sky above. Steadying the steering wheel with his left hand, he rolled up the denim sleeve with his free hand, exposing a suntanned arm. As his gold watch glistened in the sunlight, he reversed the process and freed his right arm of the warm material. With both hands now on the wheel, he gave the car more gas and felt the coupe respond as it surged forward. The intoxicating freedom of the open road prompted the need for music and he flipped on the radio, eschewing the task of fumbling through compact discs. Recognizing a tune from the early seventies, he cranked up the volume and got lost in the song's heady lyrics involving a hotel named California.

In spite of this freedom ride, he felt miserable. Passing citrus groves and farmland, not wanting to invite trouble, he lowered the speed of his vehicle and the volume of the radio. He didn't want to get stopped. He didn't want to speak to anyone–especially about Mindy.

He stared blankly at the road ahead. He thought of her and was jarred by the harsh mental impact. He closed his eyes and gave his head a quick shake as if to change the tape his mind was playing.

In a short time, Bob was on the outer fringes of the approaching small town. He slowed his speed again as he entered the downtown shopping district. Seeing a parking spot, he maneuvered his car into the horizontal space, rolled up the windows and turned off the ignition. He examined his manicured nails and looked at himself in the mirror. Not drawing a conclusion about the state of his appearance, he reached up to the visor, closed it and now glanced in the rearview mirror. He was surprised to see Wren Dukette and his wife in the distance, and he wondered at the coincidence. He relaxed, relieved when he thought that Klonski must have let Wren go, a good sign.

Bob was about to leave his car when he took one more look in his rearview reflector. He noticed the Dukettes had stopped in front of a hardware store and looked around. Theresa pointed to a building across the street, turned to her spouse, looked at her watch and then started in the direction she had indicated. Wren, he noted, started walking away, occasionally glancing back at his wife, and watched her go off in the opposite direction. Bob continued to observe. Wren, reaching the corner, stopped and looked down the street. Bob noticed that Theresa had entered a store. Looking back at his subject, Bob saw Wren change direction and, instead of turning the corner, Wren crossed the east end of the street, and disappeared around a building.

Curious, Bob wanted to find out what was going on. He locked his doors by remote and hurried off in the direction he'd seen Wren take. Bob entertained the idea of catching Wren engaging in activities implicating him as the killer of his wife, Mindy. His thoughts haunted him and he was more determined to see what his subject was up to.

Bob picked up his pace as Wren went out of sight. Following alongside the building Wren had passed, he soon reached the corner. Bob peered around the side and saw him again. Wren was walking quickly and finally took a right and entered a small shop. Crossing the street, and staying undetected, Bob counted down five storefronts. He stopped. He wasn't sure which one Wren had gone into. Noticing a row of newspaper boxes, Konrath moved in close, feigning interest in the morning's headlines. Bob inched over to a nearby pay phone and pretended to make a call, all the while watching the shops across the street. Bob guessed that Wren was either in the bakery or at the florist.

When a teenaged boy approached giving him a questioning look, Bob started talking into the mouthpiece. He covered the phone with one hand and told the boy, "I'll be on a few more minutes," and was relieved when the kid took off.

Hoping he didn't miscalculate the store his subject entered, Bob shifted the phone to his right ear, looked down at the ground and continued listening to the silence. Refocusing his gaze across the street, his patience was rewarded; Wren Dukette strode empty-handed out of the Floral Fantasy, and headed down the street in the direction from which he had come. Bob quickly hung up the phone and followed the man once more, carefully maintaining a safe distance between them. He figured that Wren ordered something to be delivered and wondered what and to whom. His subject now headed in the direction of the store his wife arrived at earlier.

Bob decided to give up the chase but contemplated going to the florist on his own. Maybe he could discover the nature of Wren's business, maybe even get a glance at the order pad or computer screen he pictured the clerk working on.

Bob parked on a bench just outside an Italian deli and inhaled the alluring aroma of garlic and spices. Trying to decide his next move, the only conclusion he came to was that the shop behind him, with it's familiar scents, was making him hungry. Bob abandoned the bench and the idea of further sleuthing. He got up and headed for his vehicle.

As his blue hardtop rolled past the dubbed "Floridian's Store," in poor judgment, Bob glanced at the front doors. Two people were leaving. He turned his head quickly as he passed the specialty store, hoping the Dukettes hadn't seen him.

"Damn," he cursed at himself. But then he realized he had nothing to hide. Thoughts of the cruise back, east on U.S. 60, lifted his spirits. Maybe he'd get word that he could head west once more, back to his home in Tampa.

CHAPTER 15

Lieutenant Klonski walked across the wide front porch and thanked the couple for their cooperation. As he descended the five steps leading to the concrete walk, he turned and waved, using that gesture to take another look at the couple. Mrs. Swanson raised her hand in a half-hearted wave and her husband, Thomas, had already gone back indoors.

The detective continued down the front sidewalk and cut across the remaining lawn toward his car. He glanced up at the thicket separating the Tudor Grove property from the Swanson's. The couple claimed they hadn't seen anything and Klonski believed them. Out of curiosity, he stepped over to the bushes and peered through. He could barely make out the outline of the bed and breakfast establishment. He also noted that in several areas, there appeared to be sparse growth in the unruly bushes and trees, though not unusual in a thicket of this sort.

Klonski looked down at the gravel shoulder beneath him as he dug in his pocket for his keys. Locating them, he walked to the front of his car where he noticed a fairly fresh set of tire marks in the gravely border. This could have gone unnoticed, except that the stony surface had been stripped away as though a vehicle had accelerated rapidly and noisily, given the long, deep burn in the soil. Surely the Swansons would've seen a car parked here in the daytime, Klonski mused, or heard it during the night— their bedroom window overlooks the front lawn and the road. He started to doubt their claims.

Walking back to his car, he glanced up at the Swanson's old house. The front parlor curtain moved back into place. Klonski got into his car and drove away. Several yards down the road he pulled over in front of a vacant field, took out his pad and jotted down questions he hoped he'd be able to answer. Slapping the notebook shut, he caught sight of his glum expression in the mirror. The job was taking its toll on him. But then, he usually felt this way during a complicated case.

"So where were you?' Tim asked Katrina as she peered into the kitchen, hoping to return inconspicuously.

Katrina avoided his question and looked out the back window.

"Where did you go? Everyone was lookin' for you." He slurped down the last bit of his chocolate milk, eyeing Katrina over his glass.

"I went to the drugstore," she said. "Where is everyone?"

"Song's out back, sleeping. Spike's walking around somewhere. Bruce and Kim went to take naps. Konrath's still out. And I'm here."

"How astute," Katrina said of his latter observation as she looked through the refrigerator for a snack.

"How the hell do you get into these things?"

Katrina whirled around to catch the man holding up a beige, prune-like ball of synthetic. "Put them down, you're gonna snag them, you shit. Why are you going through my bag anyway?" Katrina slammed the icebox door and ran across the kitchen to rescue her pantyhose. "I'm gonna have to hurt you," Katrina yelled as she grasped at the hosiery, trying to free it from his hand. Tim held on as Katrina pulled, stretching the leg several inches. "Look what you're doing. Let go of them."

Tim was clearly enjoying the game of tug of war with Katrina's pantyhose. Not letting go, she took advantage of her position and kept the leg taut in her hand as she closed in on the man, proceeding to wrap the garment around him. Slipping up over his shoulders, it snapped around his neck.

"Boy, this tempting," she whispered at her captive, slowly winding the stretchy hosiery around his neck one more time. "One good tug and you won't bother me anymore."

His throaty laughter transformed into a cry for help and Katrina immediately ceased her mock strangulation. She looked

150

up at the kitchen door. "Uh, Spike–how long have you been standing there?"

"Long enough for him to see that you're the killer, and that it's me you're after." Tim started to loosen the hose.

Katrina unwound it from Tim's neck. "Look what he did to my stockings." She held up the disfigured garment and looked at them. One leg was nearly stretched to the floor. "Now what am I supposed to do with them?"

"Wear them," said Tim. "They should fit you real good."

Spike watched from the doorway.

"You see, I told her she couldn't have me and she didn't take it very well."

"Don't you hate when that happens?" Spike chimed in.

"You're both sick."

"I'm going up to my room," said Spike. "You two have fun." He left the kitchen and proceeded down the hall.

"So, Katrina, where did you go besides to buy those things?"

"Your wife's whereabouts are your concern, my business is my own. And you still owe me for these." She held up a bag containing the damaged goods and started to leave.

"Not when it concerns my son."

Katrina froze. Wheeling around she faced Tim. "What are you talking about?"

"I know where you were so long and it wasn't the store."

"Where was I?"

"You were with some guy."

Katrina couldn't tell if he was fishing or not. "Oh yeah, was I having a good time?" Her thoughts ran wild. How would he know–or who could have told him?

"The caller said she saw you at–"

Katrina didn't allow him to finish. "You don't have to say a word. I know who it was, I only wonder how she…"

"How she what?" the man asked smugly.

Katrina left the kitchen and stomped down the carpeted hallway. "The wrong person got it; it should have been Hodgkins."

151

Katrina reached her second floor suite, unlocked the door, and entered quietly. Finding Bruce asleep, she quickly tiptoed across the plush carpet and took a seat at her writing desk. Katrina found stationery quick enough, but had to search for a pen. Puzzled, she shuffled through labels and paperclips, until an idea presented itself. She would look into it later. Katrina glanced at Bruce who had just issued a clipped snore, then turned and readied a dull pencil. "Kim," she wrote across the paper. "Taking a nap. We need to talk as soon as I'm up. Have news. For your ears only, Aunt Trina."

Leaving as quietly as she had entered, the aunt crept slowly down the hall and shoved her note under the second door on the left. As she turned to head back to her suite, the door to Spike's room opened, startling Katrina.

"You scared me."

"I see that."

"Uh, where's Kim? Is she in her room?" asked Katrina.

"Yes, why are you whispering?" he asked, doing so himself.

"Bruce is sleeping. I don't want to wake him."

Spike nodded. "Yeah, Kim came up earlier. Said something about taking a bubble bath and a nap. She needed time alone."

Katrina wanted to make an inquiry but figured it best not to. "Well, I'm sorely in need of some sleep myself," she continued in hushed tones, "while it's still quiet, that is. See you later. Spike, please help yourself to whatever you need."

"See you later, Katrina."

A bubble bath did sound good. As she returned to her suite, Katrina reminisced about the regular soakings she indulged in before becoming part owner of the inn. Somewhere she read that the bath was a dying luxury and that Floridians preferred showering over bathing. Katrina smiled as she silently vowed to do her part in keeping the tradition alive. Now, however, sleep took precedence over bubbles and Katrina settled for flopping on the bed and nodding out.

Klonski returned to the dingy police station and found his assistant, Sergeant Lewis, occupied with a phone call. Catching Lewis's attention, he motioned for the younger detective to join him in his office when he became free. Lewis nodded and turned his attention back to the paperwork before him, and continued with his phone conversation.

Flipping on the light switch and hanging his jacket on an old wooden clothes tree, Klonski looked around his office and decided to put in a request for a paint job and some new furniture. Somehow the room he occupied at the station looked more dismal and smelled more musty than usual and he wondered why it would matter after all these years. Sitting at his desk, he glanced at the picture of his long-suffering wife and realized it had been a while since he took her out for a good time. All those erratic hours he put in at the job–she never complained, at least not lately. He pondered the possibility of her tiring of it all and decided he wouldn't blame her if she did. Pulling out a directory, he found the number of a florist in town and dialed, quickly placing an order for a dozen salmon-colored roses for his wife. He knew she preferred these over red–she only hinted several hundred times.

The light to Lewis's extension went off, and Klonski hurried through the clerk's query of what sentiment should appear on the card. "Just say something nice," he ordered and hung up the phone. He didn't need his subordinates taunting him with stupid remarks–not that it would bother him–he convinced himself.

Klonski fixed his gaze upon the door he purposely left ajar. "Come in, Lewis, what have you got for me?" The young detective unclenched his fist from a knocking position and pushed the door open instead. "I'd like the particulars on the Konrath case first."

Lewis pulled a wooden chair away from the wall, positioned it in front of his superior's desk and plopped himself into it. "Well, I have some bad news and some good news. At least I think it's bad news."

"I'll give you that first. The saliva samples taken from Konrath do not match the ones from the rear kitchen pane of the Tudor Inn–or whatever they call that place." The detective pulled forth the report and handed it to Joseph. "The good news is, I tracked down the party you asked me to and I got an I.D. on him–"

"Damn," Klonski interrupted his assistant while perusing the report before him, "so Konrath isn't our stocking-masked man. Well, there's another theory that bites it. Anyway, it was only a hunch." The lieutenant signaled for Lewis to proceed but interrupted again. "What about the other guy? The one you got I.D. on. Did you question him yet?"

"No, it took some time just tracking him, Joe." The young man wanted to remind Klonski that he wasn't superhuman. "But I did call and a woman answered. He wasn't in anyway. I'll get out there later and wait for him if I have to."

The old-fashioned doorbell jangled and the women looked up from a floral arrangement she was creating. "That was fast," she said. "I'll have more deliveries for you–probably by mid-afternoon."

The young deliveryman closed the door behind him and made for the water cooler. "Man, it's gettin' warm out there," he gurgled as he talked and swallowed at the same time. "What happened to autumn?"

"It is unusually warm today. Want to take your lunch break now?"

"I guess," he said as he looked at his watch and headed for the refrigerator in the back room. "Want me to bring you something?" he hollered to the rotund women as he extracted a brown lunch bag and waited for an answer.

"Grab me a vegetable juice."

Yep, Mona's on another diet, he thought as he brought it to her.

"Just set it on the counter, please."

The young man unfolded a chair he grabbed from the storage room and parked it in front of his boss' workstation.

"This gonna bother you if I sit here?" he asked, digging his hand inside the crinkling sack.

"No, go ahead, I need to develop willpower." The woman sighed as she cut off a huge piece of blue and white, gingham-checked ribbon and maneuvered it into a lush, full bow. "Another baby boy has made his entrance into the world last night," reflected Mona as she skillfully attached the bow to the white bassinet planter she'd been arranging. "So, Paul, what's going on out there? Anything exciting?" She stepped back and smiled as she surveyed her latest creation.

"Not really, just the usual weekday activity. Traffic's not too bad." He chomped down on his sandwich.

"Oh, you'll never guess who placed an order today."

"The president?" he answered between chews.

"No–really try this time, Paul," the woman implored.

"Give me a hint."

"We've had a few orders from this party. Let's see–oh, they are not typical requests." She shook her can of juice thoughtfully.

"You're bored, Mona. I give up."

"Come on, Paul–all right, one more clue. The deliveries are made at different and weird locations—and," Mona couldn't contain herself, "they have exotic pet names."

"Oh, good ol' Adonis and L.G. Why didn't you say so?"

"What do you guess L.G. stands for?" the hopeless romantic asked as she gazed wistfully past her employee and out the front window.

Paul witnessed the amazing metamorphosis of a no-nonsense, take charge woman into a starry-eyed schoolgirl. Crumpling his bag in front of her face did nothing to break her trance. "Probably Lucky Girl," he said sarcastically as he chomped on an apple. That worked.

"What? Men are all alike," she fumed and threw her head back as she sipped on her can of juice and swallowed. "It's a wonder any babies are born at all. You people have no idea what love is about." Mona stopped. "'Course it doesn't take love to make–"

"Settle down, cupid. Look, any guy who calls himself Adonis, assuming he is a guy, must have a real ego problem, or–"

"Or what?"

"Or–he's a dud." He shook his head and smirked up at Mona.

The woman returned smile for smile. "Maybe he doesn't call himself Adonis," she winked. "Maybe L.G. does!"

Bob Konrath entered the front door of the inn. Everything appeared still. He wondered if they heard from Klonski yet? He followed the hand-hooked runner to the kitchen.

"Mr. Versay, where is everyone?" he asked Tim, sitting at the kitchen table.

Tim jumped, threw a lit cigarette into his near empty glass and waved his hand through a cloud of smoke. "Jeez, you scared the hell outta me." The man chuckled and coughed. "Bob, you didn't see me smokin' in here did you?"

"Smoking? I don't know what you're talking about."

"Thanks. They'll have me tarred and feathered–that's on a good day." Tim looked out the rear window at his wife fast asleep on a lounge. "I outta wake her up now."

"Yes, she'll get an awful burn."

"No," snickered Tim. "I'm hungry."

Bob shook his head slightly. Turning serious, he asked if anyone had called for him during his absence.

"Not that I know of, but we were all outside for a while. Song will check the answering machine for you when she gets in."

"That won't be necessary. I'll take care of it upstairs. Thanks anyway." Bob excused himself and left.

Tim scowled at the man as he left the kitchen. "Mr. Proper Ass. Guys like that give us regular men a bad name."

156

Tim belched for emphasis. "One week with me and the guys," he pondered while scratching his distended belly, "and he'd be a new man."

"Lieutenant Klonski, I am beginning to lose my patience with this situation and if need be, I will assert my rights." Bob Konrath listened with angst as he paced as far as the telephone cord would allow. "I have a wife to bury and a family to get back to–not to mention my need for a decent period of mourning. Of course I want her killer caught and this case solved. I have given you my cooperation." Bob paced the floor of his suite as he listened to Klonski.

"I have good news for you," Klonski's voice lightened. "Your tests came up negative–that is, for our investigative purposes."

Bob brushed the revelation aside. "I'd like to ask why the Dukettes weren't detained? I thought for sure it was a positive sign when I saw them shopping this afternoon."

"Where did you see them?"

Bob described the scene he had witnessed that afternoon. "I don't know if it means anything but I found it a bit odd."

"What was the name of the shop?"

"The Floral Fantasy–I'm pretty sure that's it." Bob looked at the plush, jade green carpeting beneath his bare feet. "After he made sure she was out of sight he changed direction. Do you think that's significant?" Bob caught himself. "I know you can't say; I wasn't thinking."

"Mr. Konrath, just sit tight a bit longer," Klonski said. "We have–let's just say we're making progress. I'll pass along any news as soon as it's made available."

"Please, with all that's going on–well, I don't know how much more I can take," Bob said, his voice weakening. "Goodbye, Lieutenant, and thank you." Bob returned the ornate handpiece to the cradle of the phone.

157

The white wall phone rang a third time as a groggy Song hurried across the room to answer it. "Garsch, Tim, why don't you answer the phone? Tudor Grove, may I help you?"

"It's prob'ly for you anyway," he said.

Song turned her back to Tim and went to the island range, while trying to untangle the cord and allow herself more distance. "We need a cordless. Oh hello, Lieutenant, how are you?" The woman turned to note that her husband appeared unfazed. "Why, that's terrible," Song declared, returning her attention to her caller. "When did it happen?" I see. Will she be all right?" Tim gazed out the window while his wife punctuated the silence with an occasional "ooh" and "garsch."

"I'm hungry," Tim hissed in a loud whisper. His wife continued to block him out.

"Well, when you find out, let us know. Maybe we can do some rearranging upstairs... Oh, it's no problem, Lieutenant, it'll be my pleasure," Song assured him. "Bye, Bye." Dreamily, the woman smiled to herself and headed back across the kitchen. Tim had since gained a renewed interest in his wife's conversation–and demeanor.

Song hung the phone back on the wall and in newly acquired nonchalance exclaimed, "Oh, that was Lieutenant Klonski." She looked at Tim. If he was bothered by her conversation, he didn't show it. Song headed for the refrigerator. Her husband never took his eyes off her.

"Are you fixing me something to eat?"

"Of course, Tim. I'll make you something quick to hold you till dinner. How about a sandwich?"

"Yeah. What did Klonski want?"

"You'll never guess–Theresa Dukette's mother was taken to the hospital a few hours ago. I guess they thought she was having heart problems but after taking several tests, it turned out to be an anxiety attack. I suppose with all that her son-in-law was going through, it finally took its toll on the woman." She shook her head, sad at all that had happened.

"So, at this very moment," Song continued while making the sandwich, "the lieutenant is trying to get in touch with the Dukettes to notify Theresa about her mother. The mother asked for her daughter and Lieutenant Klonski thinks they may return. He wanted to know that if they needed a place to stay, could we put them up? He'll let me know what they decide." Song paused thoughtfully. "Funny thing is, he almost sounded pleased about the whole thing. Anyway," she grabbed a towel to dry her hands, "if they don't stay over, I'll at least have everyone over for a breakfast or lunch."

"Mom, who are you talking to?" Bruce asked, coming into the kitchen.

"Oh-h, Bruce." The woman wheeled around to face her son, and saw that Tim was gone. "Where's your father?"

"He went outside. He's out on the lounge."

"Would you like a sandwich?" Song asked.

"Yeah, what's going on for dinner?"

"I'm not sure—I thought I'd wait and see what everyone's doin' before I make anything. Here, take this to your father and I'll be right out with a sandwich for you."

Song opened the icebox and closed her eyes, allowing the cool air to swirl against her face. She wondered how Tim would react when he found out that the Dukettes might be returning. She started to take a jar of pickles out.

"Hello, Mrs. Versay." It was Spike.

Startled, Song spun around nearly dropping the jar. "Oh, Spike, I didn't know you were there. Did ya manage to rest?"

"Yeah, I did—thanks. What's going on?"

Song recounted the details of her latest conversation with Klonski. "Well, if you need my suite, don't worry, we can double up somehow. Oh, by the way, Kim and I are going out for dinner tonight so you don't need to fix us anything. See you out back."

"Oh, Spike, be a dear and take this out to Bruce," she said, handing Spike a sandwich on a plate.

"Sure. Well, at least your phones work," said Spike.

"Yes… so they do." Song paused. "There hasn't been a problem since… "

"Since…?"

Song looked up at Spike. "There hasn't been a problem with them since the murder."

CHAPTER 16

"Come in, the door's unlocked," Kim said to the knock on the powder room door.

"Are you decent?"

"I said come in."

Katrina cautiously peeked inside the room, finding her niece immersed up to her neck in a peach-fragranced bubble bath. "This can wait, you know."

The young woman waved a soapy hand in the direction of the vanity. "Pull up a seat–would you like some champagne?" By the looks of the makeshift bar assembled on the floor, Kim had started her own happy hour.

Katrina pulled the bench a little closer to the tub and tightened the belt on her terry cloth robe. "I can't believe you left your doors unlocked," she said while sitting down on the pastel cushion.

"Don't preach, I left it open for you."

Katrina didn't dare mention her indulging in spirits so early in the day. Besides being old enough to decide for herself, Kim was on vacation.

"What was so important and where were you this afternoon anyway?" Kim lifted her leg high in the air, inspected her bruised knee and waited for an answer.

"You're in a shit mood, I'll talk to you later."

"Oh sit down. Yes I'm in a bad mood; Spike and I had a fight. We're gonna talk things out over dinner."

In spite of feeling like a traitor, she recounted her meeting with Lou that afternoon, including the fact that a female had already reported to Tim that she'd spent time that afternoon with the photographer. "Now I have some explaining to do."

"You think it was Hodgkins?"

"Who else?"

"We gotta get her, Aunty Trina." Kim's devious expression quickly turned to excitement. "So, what else did he say?"

"He apologized for the commotion the other night and asked how your knee was. He seems nice and is a great conversationalist, but..."

"He's so cool." Water splashed over the sides of the tub as Kim kicked her toes creating more bubbles.

"Don't get too excited–he may be a little too perfect."

"One mother's enough, please. Anyway, why did he tell Klonski that he was scoping you?"

"He had to explain what he was doing here that morning if he dislikes Jessie as he claimed he does. Plus, Lou didn't want it getting back to Spike should Klonski slip. He said he didn't want to get you in trouble–he claims he had to think fast and he just grabbed my name out of the air."

"I'm impressed," Kim purred.

"Yeah, now it's become my problem."

"Oh, don't be bummed. Bruce'll believe you. Have some of this." Kim held up her glass. "You'll feel better."

"I hate champagne."

"I'm offering up a toast, it's bad luck to decline."

"Oh really." Katrina managed a smile. "Good excuse as any, I s'pose."

After many salutations, memories and spirits, Kim emptied the last of the bubbly into her glass. Giggling, they reminisced about a party they had and how a neighbor's husband called the police to break up their bash in order to get his wife home.

Kim tilted her head, sipping from her glass. "Remember," she added, "we invited the cops in? They didn't stay though. If it was Spike, he would have."

Laughter filled the room, drowning out the creaking made by the eavesdropper crouched just outside the bathroom door. The intruder stayed to hear more stories and giggly recollections.

"Well, I gotta get going."

"What's your hurry, Aunty Trina? I thought you had more weird stuff to report."

"I did."

"So," Kim said, "what is it?"

Katrina hesitated and looked at her niece. Laughing, she said, "I... I forgot."

The listener winced as the level of giggling escalated.

"Now I've really got to get going."

"Why, Aunty Lightweight?" Kim teased.

"I need to splash some cold water on my face. Besides," Katrina covered her eyes, "your bubbles are starting to disappear." With that warning and more laughing, the eavesdropper quickly left.

"Excuse me, Mr. Paul Capello?"

"Who wants to know?" the young man asked, loading the last floral centerpiece into his van. Straightening his stance, he nearly came face to face with a tall blonde man standing only inches away.

Producing the obligatory badge, Sergeant Lewis introduced himself. "I need to ask you some questions."

"Wha' did I do?" Blocking the sun from his eyes, the edgy deliveryman looked up at the detective and waited for an answer.

"As yet, nothing that I know of."

Paul slammed shut the side door of the white delivery van. "Look, I gotta get these flowers delivered. They'll wilt in this heat—"

"Well, you can talk to me now or at the station." Lewis spoke with authority. "It'll be much easier for me if you talk here. I like it when my job is easy."

Paul glanced nervously at the storefront. Had Mona seen the man approach him? "Can I at least pull the van down a half a block? I'll run it with the air on. That's all I need is for these flowers to go bad."

Lewis nodded. "But no funny stuff. I'd know where to find you, but I guarantee, if I have to, I won't be in as good of a mood as I am now."

"Don't worry–I just don't want to lose my job."

"I'm not worried, Paul," Lewis replied coolly. "Relax. There's parking three stores down, see you there."

The young sergeant walked calmly in the direction he had indicated and processed several thoughts in his mind. "I hate playing the dick but if he runs, Klonski will rag on me for days," he mused. The white van parked down the street as promised.

Leaving the engine and the air-conditioning running, Paul hopped out of the van, locked the doors of the idling vehicle and approached Lewis. Standing against the warm, red brick of a neighboring store, Paul pointed at the plate glass window. "I'm gonna stand here. Mona knows everyone up and down this street."

Lewis chose a shaded spot under the store's front awning. Asking pertinent questions, Lewis' hand flew across the pages of his tiny, black notebook recording Paul's responses. "Okay, once more; you say you knocked at the front door and then noticed the bell and rang it. That correct?"

"Yeah, and no one answered. Well–I'm not s'posed to, but I make more money when I get tipped, so instead of just leaving the package on the front porch, I went around to the side of the house. I banged on the back door. Nobody answered that time either. Guess I was a little pissed off, you know, like sometimes people are home and they don't want to answer the door, but as soon as you drive away, a hand comes out and grabs the package. There's some cheap people in this world."

"Yeah. Go on."

"Well, with all the cars parked in the drive, I knew somebody was inside. My curiosity got the best of me–since this house became an inn. Anyway, I looked in one of the side windows, you know. I thought I heard voices." Paul envisioned the scene as he relived that fateful morning. "There was a fancy lace curtain, so I kinda could see in but I don't think anyone saw

164

me. Well, I peeked through the holes in those curtains and I saw a bunch of people standing around, but no one was saying anything. I remembered one woman who covered her face with her hand. I saw on the floor a pair of legs sticking out past the people gathered around–what I thought was a woman. Then," he reflected, "I thought they were playing one of those murder mysteries–you know, the kind they play at restaurants and inns and places like that."

"Yes, go on–but slower please."

"Well, I figured I'd lose out on another buck or so, and I just walked to the front porch and left the box just outside the door. That's what we're trained to do. After that I just left."

"Would you say you had a good view of the people–the party?" Lewis studied Paul's face as he gave his testimony, occasionally taking quick breaths to remain calm.

"I have a little trouble with seeing distances–but, no, I guess I could say I'd seen everything pretty good."

"Thank you for dinner after all, Mrs. Versay," said Bob. "I hate to eat and run but again, I have errands and calls to make."

Katrina watched as Bob removed himself from the picnic table they occupied. Every move he made, he did with finesse and bearing.

Song turned her attention to Katrina.

"The bar-b-que came out good, don't you think?"

"Oh yeah–real nice." Katrina gazed across the table, marveling at the picturesque sight in the distance. "Check out the sunset, guys, isn't it beautiful?"

Beautiful it was indeed. The rapidly darkening sky was awash in lavender, rose and orange. Silhouettes of palm trees and other vegetation stood in the foreground, seemingly inviting the round blaze of sun to snuggle amongst them for yet another warm, Florida night.

"Well, we should get this stuff inside now. It'll be dark soon," Song announced, filling a basket with utensils. Tim lit up another cigarette.

Katrina hated the smoke. She stood up in a huff, grabbed a stack of dirty dishes, and headed for the house, soon hearing Tim's crackly laughter.

"Katrina, if you take this basket, I'll get–"

"Mom, she's gone," said Bruce.

"Where's the fire?" said Song.

"I'll put the coals out." Bruce turned, straddling the picnic table bench, and faced his father.

"So, did you talk to her?" Tim asked.

Bruce scratched and shook his head at the same time. "No, I didn't. It probably was nothing."

"You gotta keep a better eye on your woman."

"I'm not worried–besides, it probably has something to do with her niece. She's protective of Kim and it usually ends up getting Katrina in trouble."

"It got dark fast didn't it, Katrina?" Song set the half empty bowl of potato salad down on the countertop.

"Yeah, it did."

"Where did Kim and Spike go for dinner tonight?"

"They didn't say." Katrina licked the last bit of chocolate cake frosting off a sharp kitchen knife.

"Katrina, don't do that, you'll–"

"Don't worry, I'll wash it before I use it again." Katrina purposely avoided her message. "Did Theresa Dukette call yet?"

"I don't know, I'll have to check the recorder."

"I hope not. That is, if Kim and Spike have words, and we have to put them in the same room, they'll probably scratch each other's eyes out before dawn."

"Unless the Dukettes get into town early enough so they won't startle the mother–if she's home."

"So you don't know if the mother's been released yet?"

Song shrugged and admitted not knowing the fate of the panic-stricken woman.

"I guess if those two have a fight, Kim could sleep with me and maybe Bruce can sleep with Spike–no, that won't work." Katrina worked several options over in her mind.

"Don't worry about it now, maybe they won't stay here. The thing is Joe... Lieutenant Klonski was adamant about the Dukettes staying here." Song shrugged again and continued scraping dishes.

Darkness descended upon them as Katrina hung the damp dishcloth on a hook inside the cabinet door. Dimming the lights in the kitchen, she glanced out the back window and saw the lone glow of a burning cigarette.

"I'll be out in the yard, Song. Join us when you're done." Hearing muffled conversation, Katrina knew the woman was involved in a phone call and headed out the kitchen door to the backyard.

"Are the bugs biting?" she asked the father and son team sitting out in the dark. Pulling a lawn chair away from its table, Katrina squeezed herself in between the two men as Tim shot her a questioning expression. "The better to mess with you, my dear," she answered with a leering smile.

"Who the hell are you, the bad broad or the bad wolf," Tim asked.

"Bruce," she ignored the question, "your father seems to be having a problem with my afternoon activities. Even though he has grilled me and you haven't, I'll be glad to make that information public–for those who have found it necessary to concern themselves with my life."

Bruce rolled his eyes while his father coaxed forth the explanation. Katrina obliged and made sure to pronounce the photographer's handsome face, great smile, gift for conversation, "and women are very attracted to him." Katrina winked at Bruce. "So Tim, can you imagine what that must be like?"

"I'm getting a beer," Bruce announced.

"Get me one, Bruce." Tim turned to Katrina as she moved to Bruce's vacated chair. "Who the hell do you think you are?"

"You're just sore that you made more of a story than there was." Katrina turned to see Song approaching. "Your wife is coming. Let's not upset her. Let's even pretend we like each other."

Tim grunted, then drew a long drag on his cigarette.

"I just got off the phone with Theresa Dukette," Song said, sitting down. "They're on their way here."

"I don't want to see 'em again," Tim scowled.

Katrina frowned at the thought of her impending getaway getting farther away. "I guess that means Theresa's mother is out of the hospital, huh?"

"Yes, and her doctor suggested someone be with her," Song continued. "So, being the mother has a nurse stayin' overnight, the Dukettes thought that rather than wakin' the two late at night, they'd check in here, sleep over and have a late breakfast and then relieve the nurse."

"Why's Wren coming with her?" Katrina asked. "I thought he had to get back to his business." Katrina mulled over her own question, finding it odd that Wren would also stay with the mother-in-law. Most men she knew didn't even want to be in the same county with their wife's mother.

"I don't know, Katrina, but I offered to serve a late breakfast for us all. Lieutenant Klonski thought it a good idea." Song's revelation was met with retorts from both Katrina and Tim.

"This is one time I have to agree with your husband," Katrina said. "Why Klonski again? I thought we cleared things with each other first?"

"Is his ass gonna become a permanent fixture around here now?" asked Tim. "He's just mooching free meals from you, Song. Where the hell's Bruce with my beer anyway?"

"Well, I've sat long enough," said Song, uncomfortably. "I'm gonna start settin' up for tomorrow morning." Song stood, shook her shoulders lightly, and started to walk away.

"Wait a minute," Katrina said, "we won't be setting up in the–"

"Don't worry," Song said, inching away from the disgruntled twosome, "we'll dine in the drawin' room. It won't be a big affair–maybe a bit more than a continental breakfast. How's that?"

Katrina, somewhat dumbfounded, mumbled an answer and watched as the women strode off toward the house. Was it her imagination, or did Song seem a bit cocky?

As Katrina watched, Bruce came down the back stairs and headed across the yard. "Here comes your beer."

"I hope you're happy, Ms. Women's Libber."

"They don't say that anymore, Tim. They now call it equality. You know, being treated like a human being, not a slave."

"My wife is my business, so keep out of it."

"Are you two still at it?" Bruce sat down. "Here's your beer, Dad–relax."

Tim guzzled his beer for several moments, wiped his mouth and belched. "You better put a leash on your girlfriend. She's ruining your mother."

"I'm getting outta here," said Katrina, disgusted. "Bruce, don't sit too close to him. You may get some on you." Besides, she thought, the inn's fairly vacant–a good time to do a little sleuthing.

"Honey, look, there's a supermarket up ahead and it looks like it's open. Let's try it."

Wren drove a short distance, turned and approached the well-lit grocery store. Several cars dotted the parking lot and a yellow banner welcomed customers to late-night shopping.

After parking, Wren yawned and stretched. "You go ahead and get started. I want to stretch my legs some."

"I won't be long."

The couple stepped out. Theresa reached skyward then headed across the parking lot. As his wife passed exiting shoppers and disappeared inside, Wren noticed a pay phone left of the automatic doors. He would use it instead of his cell phone.

169

Swiftly passing the plate glass windows, he glanced up at the storefront, and back again at the contents of his wallet. He was looking for a number.

In seconds, Wren found the number, dialed it, and reached an expected answering machine. After leaving an explicit message, he rang off and made for the supermarket entrance. Swatting off a bothersome gnat, he drew a breath of muggy, country air, and composed himself as he waited for the sliding glass door to allow his entrance. Scanning the aisles of the air-conditioned grocery store, Wren located his wife, slid a hand through his styled hair and walked up behind her.

"I feel better, but I could use a cup of coffee."

"So can I if I'm going to stay awake for the rest of the trip. Wren, do you want me to drive?"

"No. It'll keep my mind off having to see ol' what's his face again. Are you sure we can't go straight to your mother's house?"

"No dear, we'll only wake her and the nurse. Besides, it will buy us a little more time."

Wren mumbled as he shuffled toward the checkout counters. "I dread having to go back there."

"Need I remind you," she shot him a knowing look, "you're the one who wanted to play 'payback's a bitch,' were you not?" Theresa turned her attention to the magazine rack.

With a leering smile the man replied, "Yes, but it was worth it." Slowly he returned a tabloid newspaper–heralding the investigation of an actor accused of poisoning his girlfriend so that he could move back in with his mother– to the rack.

* * *

"Tim," Song said as she turned down their bed for the night, "I've concerns about some of the goings on 'round here–I mean other than…"

Loud gargling echoed from the bathroom and the woman doubted she even was heard.

170

The bathroom light clicked off and a yawning Tim strode across the floor, heading for the bed. "I'm tired, can I get in?"

"Yes, Tim. Did you hear what I said?"

"No, rub my stomach for me."

"Okay, but I have to go downstairs soon."

"Why?"

"'Cause Bruce went to bed, Katrina's in the tub, and I promised I'd wait up for the Dukettes."

"You let people take advantage of you, Song. Rub my back."

The novice masseuse half-heartedly stroked her husband's shoulder. "You know, Tim, I kinda wonder about things."

"What things?"

"Well, for instance, how well do we know the gal our son has chosen to marry?"

"She's a pain in the ass. What else is there to know?" He shifted his weight. "You're not doing it right, Song."

Not hearing Tim's protests, she proceeded. "Well, earlier– not that I paid much attention, I heard voices."

"You were eavesdropping you mean."

"Now why would you say–?"

Chuckling, Tim asked his wife to continue.

"Well, I sorta overheard Katrina talking to her niece."

"And?"

"Well, I don't know how to–"

"Just say it."

"I heard her talkin' about wild parties and the cops."

"What?"

"She said that at one of these parties, someone called the cops and they raided the place, causing a neighbor to be chased home by the police for havin' deserted her husband."

Tim laughed in his pillow.

"And," Song said, earnestly, "I think there's something else goin' on."

"This should be good," he said, catching his breath.

"I think they were drunk, naked and playing with bubbles."

Tim roared with laughter and Song insisted he quiet down.

171

Katrina slid deep into the warm, bubbly water. Tilting her head back, she sipped from a favorite long-stemmed glass filled with cognac but failed to escape the dubious thoughts she had concerning her recent clue search. Did I miscalculate, she mused, or was it moved? Nixing the idea of telling Bruce, she wondered whom she should share her discovery with. Would Klonski deem my story foolish? Should I handle it myself? Katrina would unearth the item in question, and this time keep it on hand. Aware that her free time was dwindling, and wanting to enjoy the rest of it, Katrina stopped laboring the issue.

Now focusing on her glass and its contents, she reasoned that it was more fitting to fill a champagne glass with liqueur than it was to fill a beer mug with fine wine. Who makes up these rules anyway? she wondered, and she smiled as gentle thoughts began to drift in and out of her consciousness. Recalling an amusing tale claiming that Victorian lovers did not favor claw-footed bathtubs, she reflected, sipping brandy, "Now that one I can understand."

Katrina set her glass on the floor, settled back, and reveled in the spa like ambiance she'd created for herself. Suddenly, a roar-like noise sounded from down the hall. Recognizing it belonged to Tim, Katrina tsked and hoped this wouldn't be a regular occurrence. "He could be a little more discreet," she murmured, then reached for her shower radio, turning it on low.

Within minutes, the sound of footsteps padding quickly toward the staircase reinforced Katrina's assumption that women did indeed flee Tim's bedchamber, and she giggled as she pictured Song scurrying frantically through the halls in effort to escape.

CHAPTER 17

The escalating voices out on the front porch startled Song from a fitful sleep. Her heart pounding, she listened somewhat relieved that the anger belonged to lovers quarrelling.

The front door opened. "You need your space? Have all you want. Out there's an open road–is that enough space for you?"

"Kim, keep it down, you'll wake the whole place."

"I don't care. How dare you scope out babes when I'm with you?"

"Kim, I don't want to break up altogether, I just want to see other people, that's all. I'm just not ready to settle down." Spike was speaking in a loud whisper.

Song coughed loudly. Immediately the quarrelsome couple spoke in low tones; only problem now was the woman couldn't hear the rest of the argument.

"I'll sleep on the couch," Spike declared.

Song sat up. She listened as footsteps pounded out their fury while climbing the staircase to the second floor.

Spike stood in the drawing room doorway. Upstairs a door slammed shut. "Anyone in here?"

"Yes, Spike. It's me, Song. Please don't turn the bright light on. I was asleep."

"Sorry we woke you."

"That's okay. Just be careful. The breakfast table is set up again." Song clicked on a table lamp and welcomed the forlorn Spike to sit down. "How 'bout a brandy?"

"No thanks. What's going on here?"

Song explained briefly her sleeping on the couch and their late morning meal plans. Faint footsteps coming up the front porch interrupted her and she moved to the foyer, hoping she would be greeting her awaited guests.

"Oh hi, Mr. Konrath," she said. "Come on in."

"Is anything wrong?"

"Oh no, I'm just waitin' for our late arrivals. I thought you were them. Care for a brandy?"

"Maybe I'll have one in my room. I'll be right down to get it. No need to send it up." Bob noticed Spike take a seat in Tim's favorite chair. "Hey, Spike, any news?"

"Don't know. We just got in."

"I'll be down shortly," said Bob.

Katrina released cool water down the drain, making room for more warm strawberry-scented foam. Peace had returned to her utopia and she hummed along with the radio while the force of the faucet created billows of bubbles. Catching a brown wisp of hair and clipping it back up, she slid back into the beckoning warmth of the frothy pink water. Closing her eyes she murmured a triumphant "yes-s" and resumed drifting down the runway of fantasy.

In minutes, quick footsteps, followed by a door slamming shut, jolted Katrina from a place, void of things that bumped in the night.

"I'll ignore it, maybe it'll go away. On second thought, if that's Kim, she'll soon be pounding on my door."

Katrina sighed as she pulled the plug on her bath and watched it swirl down the drain.

Katrina closed the front of her thick, white robe and walked down the hall to Kim's suite. She rapped on the door. Inside she heard sniffling, followed by a demand to "go away."

"Kim, open up, it's me. Don't make me stand out in the hall. Let me in."

More footsteps climbing the staircase revealed Bob Konrath returning to his room for the night. Katrina thought of making a dash for her suite but it was too late. "Oh hello, Mr. Konrath."

"Hi, Katrina," he whispered. "Having difficulty sleeping?"

"Uh... not really." Katrina clutched at the collar of her robe.

"Song invited me for brandy, and I guess I'll take her up on it. Will you be joining us?"

"Um, maybe," Katrina said, thinking, if I'm not busy strangling Kim instead.

"Well, maybe I'll see you downstairs." Bob smiled and headed for his suite. Katrina tried not to stare lest he turn around and catch her.

Mesmerized by the essence of the departed gentleman, Katrina leaned against the door of her niece's room not caring if she ever answered.

"Oh-h, come in." The door opened suddenly, and Katrina fell in, almost landing on Kim.

"What were you doing, pressing your ear against my door?"

"No-o. Bob Konrath just passed through and, of course, I'd be looking like this."

"You still steamin' on him?" Kim scolded while dabbing her runny mascara. "He's probably the murderer."

"I'm that obvious?" Katrina laughed at the thought of Kim disciplining her. "You still look like a raccoon. Wipe under your eyes better."

"Yes, you're obvious."

"I just talked to the guy," said Katrina. "Who happens to be great looking. So what?"

"Yeah, but Konrath's wife just died–is this better?"

Katrina nodded and sat down on the satiny lounge.

"Is Jerkface around?"

"I don't know where Spike is. So what happened? Do you want to talk?" Katrina raised her legs and stretched out on the lounge. Resting her head on the pillow, she let herself become distracted by her own thoughts.

"...and the dish ran away with the spoon."

"Then what did you say?"

"Aunty Trina," Kim pouted, "you're not even listening."

Katrina looked up at her niece. Kim's arms were folded across her chest and her expression was somber.

"Thanks, this is really important to me," Kim said. "What's with you anyway? I've never seen you act like this before–least not that I can remember."

"I'm sorry, I got lost in my thoughts. Want to go down for a drink?"

"Not if Shithead's down there."

Kim was clearly upset and encouraged her aunt to go on ahead. Downstairs, someone announced the arrival of the Dukettes and the murmur of voices convinced the pair to salvage the night by joining in the gathering.

"I'll run back to my room and put on some leggings."

"Aunty Trina, you look fine the way you are. Besides, if Konrath wants to take you with him, you'll be ready to go."

Katrina laughed as she made for the door. "I'll only be a few minutes. Lock up, I'll see you down there."

Bruce stood in the doorway of the drawing room. Doors banging and voices chattering woke him, but it was Katrina's dressing in her tightest leggings and applying perfume that propelled him downstairs.

Everything seemed in order. Kim was ignoring Spike, and Song was playing hostess. Bob was talking to Spike, and Kim was chattering at the Dukettes. Bruce looked for Katrina. Unnoticed, Bruce made his way to the kitchen and heard his girlfriend humming strains of what he recognized to be one of her favorite love songs.

"What's going on?" he asked.

Katrina took a breath and turned on the coffeemaker. "Oh, nothing. Seems this has taken on the look of a party. Why?"

"Just wondering. Is that decaf?"

"Yeah. Want some?"

"Later. Did my Dad come down?"

"Yeah, he was awakened by the noise; he's outside as usual. Also Wren is back–you know." Katrina nodded her head toward the drawing room. "You joining us?"

"In a while. I'm goin' outside for a few minutes."

"Sure," Katrina said under her breath as Bruce left through the back kitchen door.

The mood was tranquil and the dim lighting washed the expansive room in a pale yellow glow. Conversation was light and warmed brandy flowed. Song noted, while serving hors d'oeuvres, her dreaded night duty had evolved into a pleasant autumn soiree. In her heart, she wished Tim would join in and mingle instead of making his occasional trek inside just to stock up on snacks and beer. Bruce, she observed, had been almost as scarce as his father, but Katrina seemed to be enjoying herself too much to care, for she and Kim were hanging on every word the fatigued but still handsome Bob had uttered.

Spike, she noticed, moved over to talk to Theresa, and Song was thankful that other than Kim and Spike having a few quick words, the impromptu gathering had turned out fine.

Missing, however, was Wren. Song wondered where he had gone as she picked up empty platters, glad she had covered the pre-set breakfast table. The others realized this and used coffee and end tables to set their drinks on, leaving her setup virtually untouched.

With dishes in hand, Song padded down the corridor and headed once more for the kitchen.

"Can't right now... gotta go. We'll talk later." Wren quickly hung up the phone. Flustered, he looked anxiously at Song. "Uh, a special occasion is coming up and I want to surprise Theresa— no mention of this to her, please, Mrs. Versay?"

"Of course not, Mr. Dukette," said Song. "I'm not one to spoil a surprise." She scraped dishes and calculated out loud the last time Tim had surprised her with anything nice.

"Is that so?" Wren pretended to be interested in the woman's admission, while quickly punching in a fictitious number. With Song's back still in view, he quietly hung up the phone. "Some men just don't appreciate their wives, do they?"

Wren offered the woman assistance and Song graciously declined. "Well, I could use some fresh air. I think I'll head outdoors for a bit," he said. Song closed the door on the

177

dishwasher and rinsed her hands. "Oh, and thank you for your hospitality on such short notice, Mrs. Versay. I'm sure you went through a lot of trouble."

"Oh, it's nothing," Song said and was quite amazed as Wren took her hand and kissed it.

"Tim Versay is a lucky man. I hope he appreciates it." Wren turned, walked away and let himself out the back kitchen door all the while fuming to himself–the bastard never appreciated me.

The flattered woman stood in shock and wondered if what she was experiencing was the age of the "new man" that she had recently read about. Compared to them, Tim, in her mind, was little more than an "ol' fart."

"Are you sure I can't help with the clean up?" Song heard Theresa ask as she returned to the drawing room.

Assured that her help wasn't required, Theresa left the room, yawning, and climbed the stairs to her recently vacated suite.

Song eyed the remaining clutter as she settled in Tim's wing-backed chair. Not much cleaning needed to be done. Kim and Katrina had cleared most of the mess and had stacked everything on the service cart. Spike, Katrina, Kim and Bob looked tired but content sitting on the couches flanking the fireplace.

"Tonight was fun," Katrina acknowledged to Song. "This place is now starting to feel like an inn. I'll love it when the fireplace works."

Bob Konrath stifled a yawn and decided to retire for the night.

"Any luck getting out of here tomorrow?" Spike asked him.

"I've talked to my lawyer. It looks good. I'll know more in the morning. Thank you, Mrs. Versay, Katrina. Good night." Bob left for his suite.

"Garsch, are the guys still out in the yard?" Song asked Katrina, who nodded. "How antisocial..." Song yawned. "Mr. Dukette's out there, too. I just hope Tim doesn't start with him."

Kim waited for what she felt was a sufficient interval and confronted Spike. "We were having a nice evening. Why did you have to bring up lawyers and stuff?"

"What are you talking about?" he said. "You mean Konrath?"

"Yes-s."

"Kim, I just asked him if he was leaving tomorrow. That's all."

"We were having a nice time and the guy's still grieving. You shouldn't have brought up the subject."

"There you go, Kim, making something outta nothing. I'm going outside."

Song jumped in. "The night turned out good. Let's try to enjoy the rest of it."

Katrina took the cue. "Everything fell in place, it was a nice diversion. Those frozen pastries came in handy, didn't they?"

Kim and Spike shot daggers at each other across the room.

"Yes, now all I need to round off a nice evenin' is a good night's rest and boy, I'm gonna sleep like a rock," Song said.

"I'm going outside for some air before I pack it in for the night," Spike announced, standing and stretching. "You need me to carry anything to the kitchen?"

Song hopped out of Tim's chair. "Can you help me move something, Spike? It's quite heavy. Here, come look in the kitchen." The woman's voice trailed down the hall as the young cop followed.

"What a dork," Kim declared to her aunt.

"Things may look better in the morning, Kim. Everyone's tired and crazy." Katrina stood and stretched. "I just wish Klonski would hurry up and figure out who—"

"Yeah, so do I. Come on, Aunty Trina, I'll help put the rest of this stuff away. I'm going to bed."

Katrina straightened the sofa pillows while gazing at the fireplace. She sighed dreamily.

"Now what?" Kim asked.

"Nothing," Katrina said, smiling.

"No, I mean that," Kim said, ears perked.

Katrina heard it too.

"It was a yelp," said Kim.

"It's coming from the kitchen. Come on."

Kim and Katrina ran down the hall. In the kitchen, they caught up with Song, who was racing after Spike out the back door.

Song yelled over her shoulder, "It's Tim and Mr. Dukette. They've started up with each other. Oh hurry."

Kim and Katrina ran to the door in time to catch the spectacle in full bloom. Out in the yard, Tim with a folded lawn chair held high over his head, charged at Wren, threatening to smash it over the younger man's head. Bruce caught hold of his father's shirt tail in attempt to slow him down. Spike headed Tim off, grabbed the chair from the angry man and proceeded to subdue him. Song ran up to her husband and reminded him of his high blood pressure.

Kim and Katrina stood in the doorway and decided to stay out of the fracas, which appeared finished. Concerned at first, they began to laugh at the sight of the plump man taking one step to Wren's six.

"Now I know what the bull looks like at one of those fights," chuckled Kim.

"I never knew Tim could move out like that," Katrina added. "I feel for Bruce's mom–speaking of bulls, look at all the crap she deals with."

"Aunty Trina, shh–here comes Dukette."

CHAPTER 18

Wren Dukette smoothed back his hair with his hands, climbed the back steps and entered the kitchen. Seeing Kim and Katrina, he apologized for his behavior, and offered to go to a hotel.

Ordinarily, Katrina wouldn't hesitate to throw in a barb of her own–but that was amongst family. Now she felt she owed Tim her loyalty and found herself instead, remaining neutral by assuring Wren that no great harm had been done. "Everyone's on edge, Mr. Dukette–with the murder and all. Just go upstairs and get a good night's rest. Besides, I think Theresa's asleep by now."

Sullenly, he went upstairs.

"What's with this place?" Katrina asked after Wren had left the room. "Are we sitting on an ancient burial ground or something?"

Kim didn't answer, but peeked out the kitchen window. "They're all sitting around Tim. Think we should see if everything's all right?"

Katrina decided against it. If anything was seriously wrong, they would have heard about it by now. "It may just piss him off more if I go out there. Besides, Bruce and his mother may need to talk to the ol' horse butt in private. I think I'll just go to bed."

"I'm with you." Niece and aunt walked the hall, passing rooms and turning out lights as they went along. "What do you think happened out there?" said Kim.

"Dukette probably drank the last beer. Leave a light on for Spike."

"I hope he trips. I wonder who instigated what?"

"Who knows? Don't forget Dukette had the poison on him and has had a grudge against Tim all these years."

"Yeah, but Tim can be a shit, too, you know," said Kim.

The two stood at the bottom of the staircase, whispering. "It seems there's more to that ruckus than a grudge over a job," Katrina said. "Maybe I'm fishing, but it feels like there's more."

"Bruce will tell you what happened. You want this seashell light turned on?"

"Yeah, I'll get the one at the top. That's if Flash saw anything."

"Bruce may see more than he pretends to."

Katrina whispered, "If it doesn't pertain to food or work, he doesn't..." Katrina stopped outside her suite. "You'll be all right in there?" she asked.

"Yeah," Kim said, reaching her door.

"Lock it this time."

"Okay. Another thing–if I can't sleep, can I wake you?"

"Yeah. Good night, Kim."

Katrina waited till she heard the click of the lock before entering her own suite.

Running in slow motion, Song and Katrina flung open the doors to a red sporty convertible. Jumping in the front seat of the idling vehicle, Katrina shifted into drive.

"Hurry–he's gaining on us," Song said.

An angry Tim ran down the driveway and shook his fists in the air and yelled, "I'll get you for this, Katrina!"

"Hurry, hurry!" Song screamed. "I'll miss registration night at school."

Laughing but motivated by fear, Katrina floored the fire red convertible down the drive, sending a spray of gravel and dirt at the advancing angry man. Turning her head, Katrina witnessed the sight of a dirt-splattered Tim.

A crescendo of screams penetrated the barrier of her subconscious, and with a muffled cry, Katrina jolted, sitting upright in bed.

Katrina caught her breath and calmed her heartbeat. She realized Bruce's attempt to comfort her, his hand patting her arm, as he dropped back off to sleep. That did a lot of good, she thought as she contemplated letting out a scream in effort to get attention.

Dismissing the idea, Katrina relaxed herself and groaned softly. "Not only does Tim taunt me during my waking hours, but now he's managed to infiltrate my dreams. Just as long as I don't dream of him..." Blocking her thoughts, she threw the cover back and got out of bed. "I need some water."

Katrina poured herself a glass of water from a pitcher on the nightstand, too ruffled to go back to sleep. She paced the bedroom floor and wondered how she'd function at breakfast. Stopping at the front window, she peered around the curtain and remembered the events that took place the last time she did so. "Least I won't see Kim traipsing around the grounds this time–I hope." Calmness claimed her as she gazed at the serene night. She allowed herself to linger and to enjoy the respite.

"I'll hang here for a few minutes and try again–this should do it." Katrina remained at the window and soon felt her eyes become heavy. Releasing the curtain, it brushed against her face and with a start she batted at it. Jumpy tonight, aren't we? she thought, taking a last look out the window. "Yes, everything's okay, and the tree hasn't levitated across the street," she mused as light traffic drove down the road past the inn. "Go to bed." Katrina smoothed the lace material with her hand. "Light traffic– at this hour?" She flew back to the window and resumed her vigil.

A sports car continued slowly past the bed and breakfast estate. Crouching down, Katrina held her breath as she peeked out the lower corner of the window. "Just as I thought," she told herself as she steadied the curtain. Katrina left the window.

"Who's there?" asked the sleepy voice, responding to the tap on her door.

"Kim, get dressed, we have company," her aunt whispered. "Wear your darks, and don't forget the bag—I'll meet you outside my door. Hurry."

*   *   *

Meanwhile, Spike tossed and turned on the cushiony couch. He had a notion to go upstairs and demand Kim to let him sleep in her bed–on top of the covers. He couldn't sleep, and decided on a beer, thinking he might also have some leftovers.

Dressed in cat burglar couture, Kim and Katrina crept silently down the stairs, taking care not to wake Spike; after all, this was a "girl thing" and vengeance was theirs. Once in the foyer, Katrina produced two filled plastic guns. Kim held up a pillowcase. In the faint glow of the nightlight, Kim briefly locked eyes with her aunt's. No words were needed–it was understood–it was time to move and they clearly enjoyed it.

In a haze, Spike stumbled through the dim kitchen, opting against turning on lights. All he needed was the lighting from the icebox showing him the food and beer.

"Yes-s," the vacationing cop grinned, as he rubbed his hands together and eyed the mini-feast set on the table before him. Spike "rocked on" in his chair and tapped his foot as he drank beer and hummed a rock tune. Pulling back the clear food wrap on a platter of hors d'oeuvres he cursed the wussy inn for being the bane of his vacation. Chomping down on his snack, he dreamed of the ideal situation–being able to put Kim on ice while he played on the beaches of Daytona or Boca Raton. While Spike planned the remainder of his vacation, he popped open a can of beer and brought it to his lips. He set it back down. Through the window he saw a light flash in the back yard.

With the advantage of wearing black, Kim and Katrina sneaked down the front steps and crouched near the front bushes. Watching and waiting, they saw their break and stole across the driveway.

I'm getting good at this, Katrina thought as she took the same route she used the night before. Now halfway down the

184

drive, the pair hid behind the rear tire of Bruce's van. With the thicket of trees a few yards behind them, Katrina glanced over her shoulder. Don't need someone coming up behind us, she rationalized. Looking down to the end of the drive, Katrina spotted the back end of a silver auto. Her stomach knotted as she realized the car was running, suggesting the probability of an accomplice–something she hadn't thought much about.

It was too late for second thoughts, for a tap and a nod from Kim caused her to look out at the front lawn. There it was, Katrina's second ghost sighting of the season. A chill ran through her. This time, this ghoul was a dead ringer of the late Mindy Konrath.

Thoughts of death, poison and bodies immobilized Katrina and she hoped Kim didn't hear her gasp. No time to lose it, she told herself as they watched the ghost glide across the front lawn, rattling chains and moaning hideously.

"If I didn't know better, I'd swear that was Mindy," Katrina whispered. "But then, that's the idea, isn't it?" In the glow of the lamppost, Katrina detected that mischievous gleam in her niece's eyes–she was ready. "Mrs. Corpse is getting near range of detection," came the whisper. Katrina held the two weapons in her hand and nodded.

Kim raised one, two and three fingers. They were off.

Putting out the flashlight, the lone figure moved closely to the right rear window and pressed its stocking-masked face tightly against the glass. He couldn't see anything. The peeper placed the flashlight between his knees. With both hands free, he cupped them on the window, trying to get a better look. "Damn," he mumbled, still not able to see.

"That's too bad," a voice said from behind him. "Considering you shouldn't be looking in windows anyway." The perpetrator grabbed for his flashlight, but the young cop blocked his move. "Take it easy, pal, and you won't get hurt. How about taking off the mask so I can see your friendly face?" Spike glanced about the yard, and the intruder attempted to run.

He grabbed the man. "That was stupid, pal. Now let me help you with the mask."

"All right, all right–just don't tell my wife. Please don't tell my family." The man removed his mask and wiped at his sweaty face. With a tremble in his voice he admitted his identity as Thomas Swanson, neighbor to the inn. Spike couldn't help feel sorry for the old Mr. Swanson, but realized he could be playing the sucker to the old guy's act.

Spike went along with the game and managed to calm the elderly man and convince him to come inside for a drink. "We can talk some and have a beer. You don't want the Mrs. to see you out here, do you?"

Thomas struck up a deal. "Make it a whiskey and I'm yours."

"I'll see what I can do. Let me take that stocking from you." Spike held out his hand.

"Oh no, I don't have many pairs left," the old man said. Realizing Spike had little patience, he handed over the hose and headed up the back kitchen stairs.

Spike was determined to find out what Swanson was doing.

"Say, can I use the bathroom first. You know with all the excitement and–"

"Okay, but you have to be real quiet, Mr. Swanson."

Meanwhile, the counterfeit corpse continued its routine as Kim and Katrina crept behind it. Uttering dull moans of their own made the ghost stop and listen.

"Kim, doesn't Mindy look good," Katrina said, coming forward, "for being dead, that is."

"Yeah," Kim spoke from behind. The spook wheeled around to face her. "She looks too healthy. I think," Kim produced the pillowcase, "she should be more pale, don't you, Aunty Trina?"

The wigged imposter started to run.

"Not so fast, honey," Kim said and stuck out a foot, tripping the ghoul. Staggering to its feet and shaking off its chains, the pseudo-deceased screamed in the direction of the road.

Immediately, the silver automobile screeched out of position and wailed down the road. The actress, quite furious, hollered obscenities at the departing vehicle. Kim, having heard enough, seized the opportunity and raised the white flour-filled sack, dumping it over the screaming woman's head.

"Oops, there goes your ride. Good help is hard to find these days," Kim said.

"Kim, there's still some in the bottom." Katrina feigned a knowing tone.

"How careless of me," Kim said, dumping the pillowcase once more, this time pulling it entirely over the intruder's head.

"I can't breath. Let me out."

"What do you think Aunty Trina?"

"Spin her around a couple of times, she's a dizzy bitch anyway, she'll feel recharged."

Kim yanked the sack off and it loosened the woman's dark brown wig. "That's better. That's a good shade of pale, don't you think Aunty Trina?"

Spitting out flour and rubbing her eyes, the tackled pest moaned and cursed.

"That death rattle sounds better, but something's still missing," said Katrina.

"You mean her wig? Here, catch." Kim grabbed the loosened headpiece and flung it at Katrina.

"Careful, my outfit." Katrina faced Jessie. "What a surprise."

"You're in serious trouble, bitch," the stocking-capped Jessie threatened.

"Kim, it just occurred to me what it was," Katrina said, striking a thoughtful pose. Toying with a plastic squirt gun, Katrina lifted it several inches away from the reporter's face. "Rot, a ghoul needs to be green and rotten." With that, Katrina showered the stunned troublemaker with several sprays of green water.

Ignoring Jessie's screams and threats, Kim felt some fake blood was in order. "Blonde hair, especially bleached, blonde hair is very porous and will wear the color well. Least for a few days anyway." Kim laughed while dousing the head of a flustered Jessie.

"There," said Katrina. "Now you truly look like death warmed over. You'll be the envy of the graveyard."

White, red, green and sticky, Jessie leered at Katrina. "I know people in high places—you're good as dead."

Katrina got back in Jessie's face. "What about your plans to destroy us and see our inn go under? This place was made possible by our parents' hard-earned money, and you had no qualms about seeing our lifelong dreams die."

Jessie backed up a few steps. "I don't know what you're talking about."

Katrina stared Jessie down. "We had the booth right next to you and your friend. And," she said, baiting Jessie, "your buddy in the silver car wasn't as inconspicuous as you told him to be. Kim's right, good help is hard to find."

"That coward, the idiot," Jessie blurted, glancing toward the road and then down at herself. "Look what you've done to me."

"You're lucky—you should've seen the plans we scrapped," Katrina said. But she wasn't finished. "What about the bowling alley?"

"I gave the film over to the cops."

Kim demanded, "What film?"

Jessie felt her head and her hands stuck to the stocking cap. "You've ruined my hair!"

Katrina ignored her. "How about a phone call made to Bruce's father? I had some explaining to do."

Jessie was speechless.

"Come on, I think I'm gonna make a phone call of my own." Katrina grabbed the woman by the arm and headed her in the direction of the inn.

"Let me go! Who are you going to call?"

"You'll see."

Kim took hold of Jessie's free arm and helped escort their captive toward the house. While Jessie fumed about her appearance, the women moved closer to the inn tripping the motion detector. There they were in all their splendor; one tackled, gooey ghoul escorted by a pair of cat burglar-attired bookends.

Spike waited for Swanson outside the spare bathroom on the second floor. While planning his course, the young cop heard a door close. He glanced down the hall. "Can't you sleep?" he asked Bruce who had emerged from his room.

"I heard a noise outside," he said, lowering his voice to match Spike's.

"Damn," said Spike.

"Okay, Miss Hodgkins, down the hall to the kitchen and don't drip on the carpet," said Katrina.

"Aunty Trina, watch her. I'll get a towel."

"Wipe your bare feet on the mat," Katrina said.

Jessie obliged.

Kim returned with a kitchen towel. Grudgingly, Jessie took it and wiped at herself as they continued down the hall.

Spike quickly told Bruce of his catch and revealed his plans. "I can't afford any screw-ups. The old dude won't talk with an audience. Make yourself scarce."

"It won't be that easy," said Bruce.

Spike started back for the spare room. "What do you mean?" He listened to the noise downstairs. "What are those two doing up?"

"Those three," said Bruce. "That's what I tried to tell—"

"I don't believe this. Bruce, take care of them. I gotta see what's taking Swanson so long." Spike entered the unfinished suite and closed the door behind him.

Bruce shook his head and started down the staircase, wondering what to do with the women.

"Tim, he went downstairs mumbling to himself," said Song. She was peeking through the crack in the door and checked her head for loose curlers. "Darn, why did I wear these things? I haven't slept a wink. Come on, Tim, we can hide in the gift shop. We've gotta find out what's goin' on."

"Katrina. Kim. What is going on?" Bruce asked in disbelief as he studied each one. He returned his gaze to his girlfriend.

"I'm calling the cops," Katrina said. "Seems there's been an escape from the morgue. You're looking at it."

Bruce grimaced as he looked at Jessie.

"Katrina, hang up the phone. What have you done to her?"

"Stay out of this, Bruce. This is my gig. Something has to be done about this witch before we lose our business."

Song, not being able to control her curiosity, appeared at the door. She was wearing Tim's brown plaid robe. "Oh-h, Miss Hodgkins, is that you?" Tim now peered over his wife's shoulder.

Jessie, protesting loudly, attempted to get out of her chair, but Kim physically convinced her to stay seated. Creaking floorboards drew their attention to the corridor and Katrina hung up the phone.

Spike paced the floor of the gutted room and waited for Thomas Swanson to finish whatever he was doing. "Mr. Swanson, you all right?"

"Yes, I'm a tad slow, that's all." The medicine cabinet clicked shut.

Spike paced on. Turning over a large bucket, he sat down and rubbed his tired eyes. He leaned forward and rested his face in his hands.

At last Swanson came out.

"Ready for that drink?" Spike said. When the old man nodded, Spike slowly led him down stairs. "Keep it quiet, Mr. Swanson. This will be our secret. I bet you have all kinds of stories you can tell me." The young cop lightly slapped his new buddy on the back.

"This way. Let's go back and hang in the kitchen," Spike whispered, leading the way. "Hey, who turned on..." Spike turned to the man. "They've got major electrical problems," he fibbed. "Lights just come on... Wait here, Mr. Swanson." "I'll see about dimming them...and about that whiskey. "Wouldn't want anyone to see us up."

Swanson mumbled something and Spike hurried down the hall. When he reached the kitchen his mouth gaped. "Great, now what... everyone go out."

Mr. Swanson reached the doorway. "You talkin' to me?" Bright lights blinded him as he entered the kitchen. Focusing his eyes, the man stepped back, his mouth open, and a gasp escaped him as he backed toward the exit. A stunned look crept over his face, gradually changing to one of alarm.

"I...I can't stay–I've gotta go." In a near scream, the old man scurried to the back door then glanced over his shoulder.

"Wait, Mr. Swanson, they're all going back to bed–isn't that right?" Spike cajoled. "How 'bout if we go...?"

The peeper tried the door and hurriedly worked it open. Running down the stairs he headed across the yard toward his home.

"Wait!" Spike called as he followed after him.

"You tricked me," Swanson hissed. "Leave me alone." And the young officer did, as he watched in frustration while the elderly man scurried toward the thicket.

On his way back to the house, Spike kicked at the patio furniture and groaned. He looked up at the rear kitchen windows, and eyed the small audience gathered there. Spike shuffled along, and hung his head. He looked back at the panes. The onlookers slowly moved away, and he wondered why the old man was so frightened. Or was he frightened of someone?

Tina Czarnota

CHAPTER 19

Spike joined the others inside. He examined one, then the next, and the next. Song, with curlers in her hair and clad in a huge, maroon plaid robe, attempted to speak. She was silenced by Tim, dressed only in grey fleece shorts. Outfitted in a black catsuit, Katrina had since removed her dark ski mask and tossed it on the counter top. Kim followed in like fashion, except now she was checking her reflection in the chrome toaster. Mrs. Dukette wiped away a gooey layer from her face and fumbled with the sash on her black satin bathrobe. Wren whispered to his wife, and she quickly removed a black mask perched atop her head and stuffed it into her pocket. Wren, wearing a pair of tight black unitards, ran a hand through his hair, and made sure to avoid eye contact with an aggravated but chuckling Tim. And finally there was Jessie.

"Should I call Klonski?" Katrina asked, but the off-duty cop ignored the query. He was eyeing the flour-dusted reporter, noting her silence as she paced the floor. Spike looked at Bruce. He hadn't even combed his hair, his knotted curls stuck out from his head and he found that Katrina's disdain of her beau's mushy girth was not unfounded. At the present rate, Bruce's abs would soon rival that of his dad's. Bob Konrath was the last to be scrutinized. Like Bruce, he was clad only in blue jeans, and like the rest of the bunch, he seemed unnerved and perplexed.

Frustrated, Spike ran a hand over his face, blinked his eyes and looked back at the inquisitive lot.

"What was that all about?" Kim broke the silence.

"I've a feeling we bungled police procedure," Theresa offered.

Spike pulled a stool away from the island range and sighed as he parked himself. "I guess it's nothing. I'm just feeling the strain of the whole deal." He looked at the odd group. "I caught the guy peeping. I thought if I got him to open up, I'd find something out. It's probably a shot in the dark but it was something."

Tim voiced concern about his hibiscus bushes. The others seemed to breath a little easier. Katrina parked on the stool next to Spike, Song offered Jessie a chair from the table, and Bruce stood against the wall and folded his arms.

"Get Klonski to question him. After all, he was peeping," Kim said.

"No, Kim, I'm still gonna try to strike a deal with the guy and see if he'll talk," said Spike. "Besides, what the hell were you two doing?" He referred to Jessie.

"We were taking care of some business." Kim smiled wryly at Jessie.

Bruce tried to spare the reporter further embarrassment. "I'll tell you about that later, Spike. I tried to get them to settle down or go outside, but before I knew it–"

"We came down," said Song. "Tim and I heard the commotion and I was just so worried somethin' awful happened again. Before we knew it everyone was awake and in the kitchen. Sorry."

"You prob'ly woke everyone up with your fat face," Kim spat at Spike.

Spike thought better than to start with Kim and shot her a dirty look instead. Not sharing the possible evidence he collected from Swanson, or his idea that one of them was the killer, he steered conversation toward the topic at hand but made sure not to reveal much. "I'll talk to Klonski the first thing."

Katrina looked at the bunch, "If it's okay with you guys, let's make this a late morning breakfast. As it is, I feel like sleeping till Thanksgiving."

Everyone agreed and breakfast was set for eleven-thirty a.m.

"Jessie, have you a way home?" Song asked.

"Never mind that, Jessie. Whatever happened to you?" asked Theresa.

194

Kim and Katrina smirked at each other.

"The Halloween party she went to got a little crazy," Kim said.

Jessie fumed, "I'll call someone to come and get me."

"Tim will drive you, won't you dear?" Song said.

"We'll drive her, huh, Aunty Trina?"

Bruce shook his head, and Tim chuckled.

Jessie shook off the sarcasm. "I'll call a friend. He owes me a favor."

After a brief discussion, some of the group dispersed and left for their respective rooms. Katrina and Kim followed Spike and Jessie out to the front porch. There they waited for Jessie's ride to show. Disheveled but somewhat calmed, the reporter felt safer with Spike being there, lest his girlfriend and her aunt should decide to continue their revenge.

Katrina stood on the porch, folded her arms across her chest and faced her antagonist. "Jessie, I'm sorry, but I will be pressing charges against you."

Jessie descended the steps, turned to Katrina, and countered, "You'll be hearing from my lawyer."

"You were trespassing and they could get you for harassment," Spike defended the novice innkeepers. He knew many people, like Jessie Hodgkins, who made a hobby out of destroying other folks' lives. Maybe it was jealousy, immaturity or maybe some people were just that unhappy in their own world. Whatever the case, and in spite of a semi-ruined vacation, Spike liked Song and Katrina and was going to do his best to put an end to the ruthless reporter's attempts of destroying the innkeepers and their business.

Jessie clutched at the sweater Song had lent to her as she made small steps toward the driveway. A white vehicle pulled in front of the inn and parked at the end of the drive. The reporter showed signs of relief and then of frustration.

Spike followed behind her and offered to walk her to the car. "Jessie," he cleared his voice, "I spoke with Klonski. You're over your head in trouble. This could stick."

"I can find my way to the car, get lost."

"Suit yourself." Spike watched and made sure she got into the car. The door slammed and the white car sped off, leaving a small spray of exhaust and gravel in its wake.

Spike turned and headed up the drive toward the house. He wondered what her real stake in all this was.

"I wanted sausage and eggs not bacon," Tim grumbled as he looked over the various platters of late-morning fare.

Song, in a state of sleeplessness, dutifully made her rounds with hot pots of coffee and managed to smile in spite of it all. "I thought we put out enough–"

"Song, there's plenty to eat and everything looks..." Katrina noticed Wren nudge his wife under the table. "Just wonderful," Theresa finished.

"Thank you, Mrs. Dukette," said Song.

Tim reached over the table and grabbed the salt and pepper. Song returned a coffee pot to the burner.

Too tired to comment, Katrina grabbed a fresh bagel from the passing breadbasket. I'd like to stuff one of these in Tim's mouth, she thought, releasing the basket to Bruce. But I was taught not to play with my food.

In a wise move, Song sat Wren and Theresa down at the far left end of the table from Tim. Across it, Spike sat at opposite ends from Kim. A lone setting remained untouched, and Song explained that Lieutenant Klonski would be joining them later.

Other than Spike inquiring about Bob Konrath's discussion with his attorney, conversation was light and superficial.

"What time is Lieutenant Klonski expected to get here?" Wren asked Song.

"Song, I want more of that fruit," Tim said; he discounted the man and waved his empty fruit cup in the air.

"Garsch, Tim, I thought I gave you plenty," Song said. She turned back to Wren. "What was that, Mr.–oh, Lieutenant Klonski should be here soon." She grabbed the cup from her husband and headed out the door.

Katrina shook her head and looked up to catch Bob smiling at both her and Kim. Katrina felt the tap of Kim's foot. In spite of his lack of sleep, Bob looked his usual gorgeous self. Tim's glance bounced from Katrina to Bob and then at Kim.

"How come so quiet this morning, Katrina?" Tim asked.

"I'm tired. Why?"

A knock sounded at the front door and Song, returning to the makeshift dining area, offered to answer it. Setting Tim's fruit before him, she headed once more for the foyer. In the interim, Kim offered refills of food while Katrina made her rounds with the coffee pots. With an opportunity to study their guests once more, she pondered their possible motives and involvements.

No one looked especially suspicious. Tim registered a quizzical look as Katrina studied him. Konrath checked his watch and Katrina looked away when he noticed she was staring. Passing her own cup, the idea struck, I wonder if they're thinking the same about me? As if to confirm her thoughts, she glanced away when she looked up at the few who studied her. Katrina refilled Bruce's cup, unfazed by the newcomers chatting with Song in the foyer. She moved on to Spike.

Song entered the room and ushered in the three new arrivals: Lou, Jessie, and a young, tall, toothy-grinned male. Katrina wondered if the blonde man was the one from the bar the other night. She checked him out again as Song led them to the seating ensemble in front of the fireplace. Katrina then thought the man might be Jessie's accomplice from last night.

Katrina sidled up to the Dukettes but looked over at Kim. Obviously happy to see Lou, Kim smiled lightly as he winked at her from across the room. Katrina wondered why the trio had come, and she moved on to Bob Konrath, glad when he indicated he had had enough.

It was Song who offered breakfast to the new arrivals. Jessie granted Katrina a dirty look and turned her back to her. Katrina smiled. Jessie's hair was streaked with traces of pink coloring.

197

"Do you have sugar for the coffee?" Lou asked. Kim almost knocked over her chair as she moved to oblige, then collected herself should she appear too eager.

Now the reception phone rang. Katrina and Song ran for the front desk, causing a mild collision. "Garsch, did I burn you?"

"It's okay." Katrina whispered, "why are those three here? It feels like deja–"

"Katrina, can you take the pots? I'll get the phone."

"Yeah." Katrina's head was reeling from the burst of activity and the over-consumption of coffee jangled her nerves rather than revived her. She wished everybody would simply go away. She tuned in Song's conversation.

"I didn't know he'd be joining us. Let me get my pad and– sure, Lieutenant." Song grabbed the message log and scribbled quickly. "I hope so–yes, I'll give this to him soon as he gets here. I see… okay, then, we'll see ya soon." Song's enthusiasm waned as she set the mouthpiece back on the cradle. With mild trepidation, she reviewed her message, tore the perforated note from its book and stuffed it in her apron pocket.

"Good news from Klonski, I hope." Katrina waited for an answer. She guessed not as she noted how Song's expression had changed since her brief conversation with the lieutenant.

"Is everything all right?" Theresa noticed it, too.

"Oh yes–yes of course. That was the lieutenant," Song said. "He, uh, he'll be a bit longer." All eyes were on her. "Oh, and Sergeant Lewis will be joinin' us." Song returned to her seat at the head of the table.

"That's it?" said Katrina. "For a minute I thought you had some good news for us."

"Not really." Song pushed her half-empty plate aside and sipped her coffee. "He just said they were makin' progress. That's about it."

Kim echoed, "That's about it," and the room was abuzz with speculation.

Song had heard enough. She went about collecting clutter from the dining table and assured the guests that plenty of food was left and more coffee was on the way. "Don't anyone remove the lieutenant's setup—I'll have to bring another one for Sergeant Lewis."

The gang barely heard Song and went on with its discussion. Even Tim delayed his cigarette break to offer a few of his own suppositions, leaving only after he laughed at Katrina for downing her vitamins with several sips of orange juice and champagne.

"Yes, and take your glass with you," Katrina said. "I just might be tempted to put something extra in your juice."

"Excuse me, Katrina," said Bob. "I'm going out to my car. If I get a call, please have them hold. I'll be right back."

"Sure, Mr. Konrath."

Katrina leaned over and whispered to Bruce, "I'm going to help your mom. Listen to the buzz while I'm gone. Catch the phone if it rings?"

Bruce nodded and went on talking to Spike.

"Aunty Trina," said Kim a short while later. "I think Sergeant Lewis is here. Can I help with anything?"

"Yeah, ask Bruce to open the small table so we can join it with the one all ready set up. We'd like to keep everybody at the tables instead of all over the inn."

"Good luck there—these bottles of champagne going out?"

"Yeah—what do you mean good luck?"

"Tim's out on the porch, Konrath joined him. Jessie and that guy are in the library. Lou's still on the couch. Spike ran upstairs and the Dukette's are roaming around."

Katrina dug deep in the refrigerator. "Kim, would you take these bottles of champagne and ask Spike to open them when he gets down?"

"I'll ask Lou."

"Whatever. Greet Sergeant Lewis and offer him coffee." Kim was on her way. "Oh, get Bruce or Spike to help with that table please."

"Okay," Kim yelled from the doorway.

Song, busy cracking more eggs over a bowl, was deep in thought.

"I hope things get settled," said Katrina. "Kim's ignoring Spike and hangin' with Lou. I know they quarreled, but I wish she'd wait before she starts up with a new one." Katrina transferred fresh orange juice into chilled pitchers. "Why are Lou, Jessie and her friend here anyway?"

"I don't know, Katrina," said Song. "So, Sergeant Lewis arrived?"

"I guess. I better go and see how that table's coming along." Sensing the woman was not up for conversation, Katrina left to survey the progress being made in the dining area.

"Aunty Trina, I need more silverware."

Katrina thought she was catering an event in heaven. A white cloth-covered extension table was in place and Bruce was setting chairs around it. Stepping up to him, Katrina asked lightly, "Okay. What did you do with Bruce? Set him free and go in peace."

"Don't get too used to it, Trina," he said. "I only did this so I can sit back down."

"Figures–Kim, I'll finish setting up. Round everyone up and invite them back to the table. And try to cool it with Lou. Spike is still here and..."

Kim nodded and with that sparkle in her eye she headed straight for the drawing room.

Katrina returned with china and silverware, almost dropping a cup as she made for the empty reception desk. It was awkward having to set a table when everyone was sitting around it. Unloading her hands and flexing her numb fingers, she noticed the open message pad. On the top portion of the exposed page was the carbon copy of the note Klonski dictated to Song. "L," it read. "Know person w/key ingrd. Apricot recp. Will get today. Laeter."

Katrina slowly stacked plates while reading through the abbreviated note once more. What? Why would Klonski...?

Then she caught it. At the top of the note Song had written "from Klonski–Mrs. Klonski."

The phone rang with a shrill, and Katrina jumped. She answered it. Stunned, she listened to the voice on the other line.

"Hello? Hello? Klonski here. Damn it."

"Uh, Tudor Grove–"

"Is Sergeant Lewis there yet?"

"Yes, Lieutenant."

The young sergeant asked to take the call in another room and Katrina heard Song trill her consent as she entered the room with brimming platters.

"Aunty Trina, I'll give you a hand–she's ready with the hot food," said Kim.

"Yeah–thanks, Kim." Katrina collected herself, her thoughts, and the cups as she proceeded to the table. So it was Mrs. Klonski that called and not Lieutenant Klonski. Katrina's mind fast-forwarded, trying to process this sudden bit of information. Song lied about it being Klonski–but why? Plopping herself in the last unoccupied chair, Katrina cringed upon hearing Jessie pleading with Mr. Toothpaste to change seats with her. Don't flatter yourself. I don't want to sit next to you either, Katrina thought. Well, at least it explains Song's funky mood. I don't think it ever registered that there was a Mrs. Klonski.

After he was done speaking to Klonski on the phone, Lewis rejoined the others. Digging a spoon into his fruit cup, between bites, he fielded questions thrown his way, being careful not to reveal any important new information.

"Who would like coffeecake?" Song felt the young investigator's frustration and tried to steer attention away from him. With a few takers, Song was off to the kitchen once more.

Katrina figured this was her chance. Not being able to fake indifference much longer, Katrina followed the woman down the hall. "We need another pitcher of ice water," she said. "I'll get it, Song." Trying to make small talk, Katrina eventually got back on the subject of the phone call. "Did you give Lewis the message?"

201

"Garsch, I almost forgot–I'm glad you reminded me." The woman punched a few buttons on the microwave and watched the red digital characters rapidly count down.

"Who did you say called?"

"Klonski. I told you that."

"Mrs. Klonski, you mean," said Katrina. "That's what your message read."

Arranging hot slices of coffeecake in a covered breadbasket, Song appeared intent in the task at hand.

Katrina asked a second time. Walking around to face the woman, she folded her hands across her chest and waited for an answer.

"Katrina, Mr. Klonski–Mrs. Klonski, what's the difference?" Song's face burned bright pink.

"Look, I don't understand what's going on here, but was it Joe or his wife that called?"

"Both." Song expected the puzzled look and explained. "Joe got on the phone and assured me they were makin' progress on the case, then he asked me to take down a message for Lewis. I said okay, and before I knew it a woman was talkin' over him– into the phone and told Joe that she'd handle it. Klonski said he had to go and the woman gave me the message that I wrote."

"I don't think that was Mrs. Klonski, but a lady clerk at the station. You know, a secretary or someone. Besides what would Mrs. Klonski be doing at the office?"

"I don't know. I just figured it was his wife, being it was a recipe and all."

Katrina twirled a lock of hair around her fingers, her eyes narrowing. "Why would Klonski–or a clerk for that matter– dictate a recipe to you for Lewis?"

"Maybe it's for Sergeant Lewis's wife?"

"This is a murder investigation, not a recipe swap." Katrina noticed Song fidgeting with the cloth covering. "I guess that cake's getting cold."

"Yes, I should get it out there."

"Well, if this was to be a confidentiality thing, you may as well forget it. If I saw that note, everyone saw it. I don't think it was wise to leave it out like that."

Song hoisted the tray and backed toward the exit. "It's just a recipe, Katrina, it's no big deal." She turned to leave.

"Yeah. Okay, I'll be out there in a minute."

"No big deal she says." Katrina stood in the middle of the kitchen and pondered the puzzling message. What's Klonski up to? There's an ulterior meaning to this–but what? There's no way he'd be leaving a note of fluff during an investigation–or any other time for that matter. He seems to be the hard guy, but who knows... Some men are so hard out in public and at home–well, I wouldn't put anything past…"

Katrina was rocked back to the present by refrains of greetings for the lieutenant. She gathered two full water pitchers and returned to the drawing room. Lieutenant Klonski was already seated and Song fawned over the man as usual.

In spite of the diners being satiated, everyone remained at the table. Hanging on to the few words the investigator uttered, no one pestered him as they had his young sergeant.

Not hearing much of interest, Katrina pondered possible meanings of the note. She thought about asking Bruce and Spike. She looked at Bruce on her left, but he was still eating. Spike, to the left of Bruce, gawked past Katrina and broke his gaze at Klonski to look back at her. The chilling thought hit her again: One of these people is a murderer and it could be as close as the guy on my left–my boyfriend. A murmur rose from the group.

"I knew you'd do it," Song said.

"I said I may have a break in the case, Mrs. Versay," said Klonski. "We'll know in due time."

"Can I get you anything else, Joseph?" Song asked.

Tim grumbled and went outside for a smoke, while Klonski continued eating. He studied each individual.

Katrina stared at the lieutenant and wondered if he would answer her questions. Maybe it'll get Song in trouble for leaving the note out, especially if it was to be confidential. But then again, she struggled, still staring at Klonski, if it botches the investigation, he should know. And then there's the other issue...

"Katrina, you seem lost for words this afternoon," Klonski said. "Is everything all right?"

Uneasy about being zeroed in on, she blamed her contemplative mood on sleeplessness. Person–key ingrd.–apricot recp.–today–laeter. No–later. Katrina ran the message through her head. Song always said she was bad at spelling–wait a minute... The reception phone rang again and Katrina jumped up to answer it.

"It's for you, Lieutenant," she said.

"Lewis, take it please." Klonski sipped coffee while the younger officer picked up the phone at the front desk.

All ears cocked toward Lewis as he said, "I see, uh huh, very well...gotcha...I'll wait." After jotting some notes in his pad, Lewis flipped its cover shut, and tucked it in his pocket. He glanced down at the desktop. Phone still in hand, he turned to Klonski and signaled a knowing look and continued to hold. After a return to conversation and a few short comments, the sergeant hung up and returned to his seat, casting a side-glance at his superior.

Lunch was soon finished.

"As usual, that was a great meal, Mrs. Versay," said Klonski. "Thanks again–seems I'm going to owe you one."

"That would be nice."

"I need to use the phone in the library," Klonski told his hostess as he produced his note pad. Lewis followed close on his heels.

"I'll take these out to the kitchen." Katrina picked up a small stack of dirty cups and trailed the two investigators.

"Lewis," she whispered just loud enough for him to hear, "I need to talk to you."

"What is it, Katrina?"

The two detectives followed Katrina's lead and entered the library. At the door, she surveyed the corridor, closed the door behind her, and whispered the need for discretion. Katrina set the cups on the table, and told the two men about the phone message being left on the desk and the probability of everyone having seen it.

"And you feel that's of importance, Katrina?" Klonski asked.

"Well, if it was confidential information regarding the case–I thought you should know that it isn't any longer."

"And?"

Katrina sighed. "Well, I just thought you should know, that's all."

Klonski's look was stern. "Are you sure that's all?"

"Sorry I said anything."

Klonski stood in front of her.

Katrina leaned over at Lewis and softly said, "Keep talking." Padding over to the front library door, she quietly opened it and peered out. Greeted by the mingling of chattering voices and clinking dishes, Katrina pulled back and gently shut the door behind her. Assured that they were not overheard, Katrina felt that all was secure. However, standing in the foyer, a lone person hid, pressed up against the wall, catching key pieces of her conversation with the investigators.

Tina Czarnota

CHAPTER 20

"Just wanted to be sure no one was listening," said Katrina.

"Suppose you tell us what's on your mind." Klonski remained standing and Lewis readied his notebook once more.

Katrina grew nervous. She entertained the idea of Klonski not thinking her revelations warranted his time and told him so.

"I invited you all to share anything you felt may be of importance. If it isn't, no harm done."

Katrina exhaled. She looked up at the lieutenant. "It's about that message you left earlier. I don't think that was a recipe you dictated to Song. I think, well, it was a code or something. You know, a message with an ulterior meaning." She sighed. "Okay, go ahead, this is where you tell me not to concern myself with police procedure, right?"

"Sit down," Klonski said. Katrina parked herself on the couch while Klonski lowered himself in the club chair opposite her. "You said a code?" She nodded. "What might this code or other meaning possibly be?" The man sank back in his chair and listened as she offered knowledge regarding preventive and holistic medicine.

"So, you think this... this code has to do with natural medicine?" asked Klonski. Katrina nodded.

"Also, I want to know what action I can take against Hodgkins–"

"You assaulted her," said Klonski.

Katrina reminded him of the reporter's intention to get a story, no matter what. "My witnesses overheard her. Besides, It may have been in self-defense. She is a suspect in a murder–"

"So are you."

Katrina shifted in her seat. "You know I didn't do it. Besides," she went on, "she harassed us on our property. I

207

understand if enough charges are racked up, we can at least get a restraining order against her, and..." Katrina brightened. "I've an idea how we can finally get her to leave us alone."

"What might that be?"

"If I heard right, I understand she could be made to undergo psychiatric evaluation, is that so?"

"Possibly."

"Well, if it all sticks," Katrina said, pausing to gauge Klonski's receptiveness, "maybe we could make a deal."

"Katrina, that all has to be dealt with, in the confines of the law, you understand."

Which translates to–don't expect any favors just because I've become a permanent fixture in this place, she thought as he stood, thus signaling the end of their discussion.

"Shame on you for thinking otherwise, Lieutenant." Katrina stood.

"Well, it's obvious how you feel about the woman."

"No kidding," she murmured. "Oh, wait." Katrina leaned over the coffee table. "There's something else."

Klonski and Lewis watched as Katrina carefully put the cups in the center of the table. Moving to the bookcase, she reached up into a vase, and took out a small, bagged item. Setting it next to the cups, Katrina returned to the couch. Klonski reclaimed the leather chair. Sitting forward in his seat, the officer eyed the objects before him. Lewis opened the door and checked the hallway.

Katrina began her account with the supposition that her own quarters had been violated. She told of how the front curtain moved–without logical means. That her nightstand and desk drawers had been disturbed and how her favorite pen was missing, only to be found on the floor. Katrina noted the bagged item on the table and how she had kept it hidden. "I'm the only one who knew about it. Following a hunch," she said, "I checked on it and sure enough, it also was moved."

"And, you have an idea who or what is behind all this," said Klonski.

Katrina sighed in relief–he was taking her serious. "I do. And," she said, "the top cup, which I handled carefully, was used by that person." Nervously, she went on. "It's pretty dry by now. It should make a good specimen." She waited for the pensive detective to speak. He didn't.

"Now," she resumed, indicating the bag. Klonski held up his hand.

"Lewis, bag and tag these two, please." Klonski stood.

"You'll do it?" Katrina said. Sergeant Lewis moved to retrieve an evidence collection kit.

Klonski granted her a terse look.

"But it comes under the realm of…" Katrina rose from the couch. "Thanks Klonski. Now, I've got to get back to work."

Katrina grabbed the remaining stack of cups and left the library. Unable to close the door tight–the detectives could do that–she headed for the kitchen. Song and Kim were probably in there cleaning and she thought of several excuses of why she was late pitching in.

The solo figure was pleased that Katrina's footsteps faded in the opposite direction and was also pleased that she left the door ajar, which made it easier to overhear more of the detective's conversation.

"That's right, we'll need your testimony after all." The eavesdropper noted Klonski's voice. "You've got what we need to wrap this sucker. So this time, I need everything. No "I forgots' or any other crap. Understand? We'll see you later–be there."

Klonski hung up the phone and lowered his voice as he briefed his sergeant. "Okay, Lewis, later."

Having heard enough and wanting to stay undetected, the figure slid up the stairs to the second floor.

The young man dialed the unfamiliar number scribbled on message paper, and waited for an answer.

"Who's this?" came the obviously altered greeting.

"You told me to call you. Who's this?"

"I have something you want."

"Oh yeah, what is it and who's it from?"

"You're sloppy, Romeo," the voice said.

"Hey you son-of... Who is this?"

"Doesn't matter–play ball and I guarantee your fiancée won't learn about that night a few weeks ago. I'll even throw in a sweet deal so you won't have to work two jobs anymore, Pauly. Don't you get so sick of running around like a dumbass, never getting ahead? I like you, Pauly–you remind me of... never mind, just meet me tonight at seven. You know Slow Gin's bar?" His listener said that he did. "Go there and wait for me. Come alone, grab a brew, I'll be along with these cool pictures you'll want. Come alone-I'll know."

A click, then a buzz rang in the young man's ear. Slowly he hung up the phone and pondered the offer and orders from the anonymous voice. Macho but challenged, the delivery man knew he had to take care of business. In a few hours he'd be off work and would meet with the clandestine conniver. Shaking his head, he returned to work knowing he'd have a hard time keeping his mind on his job.

"Thank you, girls, for helping," Song said. "Katrina, we're just gonna have to convince Kim to stay with us," she chirped while hanging a towel on its hook.

Kim smiled and asked how the two women expected to spend the rest of their day. She parked herself at the kitchen table and glanced at the clock. "It got late," she said stifling a yawn. "I think I'll hang for a while, then take a nap. After last night, I'm dead."

"Last night? These last few days have been none stop crazy," Katrina declared, pulling up the chair opposite Kim.

Song joined niece and aunt at the table, and yawned as she pulled her seat closer to the table. She caused a chain reaction amongst them and decided then that the kitchen would be closed for dinner that evening. "Trouble is, Tim will be squawkin' all night about it."

"Tough," Katrina mumbled into the table as she rested her head on folded arms. Looking up, she suggested borrowing some yellow police line and draping it around the kitchen. "Just tell him you're sick to death of cooking. Besides, the Dukettes are at her mother's place and Konrath's supposed to get clearance to leave today. That leaves the six of us and a little chance at freedom.

"Well girls, I'm gonna join Tim for a quick nap," Song said. "I'll see you later."

"Later," said Katrina as she and Kim remained at the kitchen table.

Katrina looked tired and glum as she stared out the kitchen window. "So, did Lou say anything before he left?"

"He just said something about calling me, and when this mess was over, maybe we could get together."

"Well, with Spike still in the picture, there's not much he could say. I wonder if Mr. Teeth is the guy from last night?" Katrina changed topics but Kim understood.

"Which one? I doubt she'd lower herself to be with Mr. Silver Coupe, especially after he botched his assignment."

"Lucky for him–a white car picked her up though. Oh, who knows?" Katrina conceded.

"You gonna miss your buddy?" Kim whispered lest Bruce be lurking about.

"You mean Konrath?" Katrina sighed. "Well, he was nice to look at." She hesitated then continued. "But he's newly widowed and I'm–"

"He knows where to find you." Kim smiled suggestively and quoted Katrina's mother as having said, " 'If it's meant to be yours, it will be yours.' "

Katrina laughed. "She was talking about a job interview I went on." Katrina stood up and said she'd join Bruce for a nap. "Oh, Spike moved back into the Dukette's vacated room."

"Good. Wait up, I'll go with you."

211

"Kim, check the kitchen door and I'll get the front one. Being everyone's nodded out, no sense leaving the place unlocked."

Kim locked the back door and scurried to catch up with her aunt who was securing the front entrance. "Where did Konrath go?"

"I'm not sure," said Katrina. "He said he'd get some rest while he waited for his lawyer to call. If he's still upstairs or not, I don't know. He has a key."

Kim nodded and got in step alongside her aunt. They trudged up the stairs to their respective suites. "Kim, what time did Missy Hodgkins leave?"

"Sometime after you joined us in the kitchen. I noticed on one of my trips to the drawing room she was still hangin' on that guy she came with. Lou sat as far away from her as he could. It was obvious he was avoiding her," Kim said, quite pleased. "He was talking to the Dukettes and had his back to her and Toothpaste Face."

Katrina chuckled at the name assigned to Jessie's friend. "This is where I leave you."

"Catch you later, Aunty Trina," said Kim. She opened her door and went inside.

"Mrs. Dukette, this is Sergeant Lewis. May I speak with your husband please? The young detective listened as he leafed through a file on his desk. "Did he say what time he'd be back?"

He listened as Theresa told him that Wren just went off to the drugstore for a prescription for her mother, and that he should be back in another half-hour. She offered to tell Wren that Lewis called, but the detective declined.

"I'll try back later, Mrs. Dukette. Thank you."

"Did you sleep any?" Song asked the refreshed young woman now joining her before the vacant fireplace.

"Yeah, I needed to," said Kim. Her hair and makeup were perfect. Song realized how pretty Katrina's niece truly was. "Where's everybody?" asked Kim.

Song stretched out on the couch. Kim noted the look of contentment on the woman's face. "Well, Tim went to the store– I think for cigarettes. Bruce wanted to get to the hardware shop before it closed. Spike," she hesitated, "left a bit ago but didn't say where he–"

"Did anyone make plans for dinner tonight?" Kim asked, ignoring the mention of Spike.

"Garsch no. We discussed a few ideas but left it open. I hope they come back soon. I'd be tempted to leave without them."

"Is my aunt still upstairs?"

"I'm not sure. I woke, got dressed, came downstairs and saw the notes on the kitchen corkboard. I figured while Tim's gone, I'll enjoy the solitude."

Kicking back on the vacant couch, the young woman gazed at the fireplace before her. "You know, I think Bruce should get the downstairs bathroom going before he finishes the chimney."

"He said he wants to do the outside work first as we're losing our daylight earlier. What I really like is the idea of the fireplace workin' by Christmas," said Song.

Kim hopped to her feet. She walked to the large front windows, and peered out. The sky was showing signs of darkening. "It's a little grey out. Want me to open the drapes more?"

"Okay. Let's get as much of the daylight as we can."

"Looks like it might sprinkle." Song uh-huhed and Kim grabbed the curtain drawstrings. Taking another look at the impending twilight, the young woman drew back the thick fabric, inviting more light into the drawing room. "There she is. My aunt must've gone for a bike ride." Kim scurried past the front desk, through the foyer, and down the porch steps. Katrina was walking her bike up the graveled drive, trying to catch her breath.

213

"Where were you?" Kim asked. "I wish you told me you were going for a bike ride, I would've gone too."

"I started out..." puffed Katrina. Resting the bike against the house she motioned toward the front porch. "What I really wanted to do was peddle into town–"

"Are you suicidal?" chuckled Kim.

"Well, you see how far I got." Katrina regained her breath. "I told them guys if they were going to a store, I needed to go. Well," she exhaled, "I woke up and the place felt like a morgue– no Bruce, no noise and no one around. You know, this place spooks me when it's dark."

"I was here," reminded Kim, parking herself on the top step next to her aunt. "Song was around too."

"I didn't see her. Anyway, I looked out the window and the driveway was deserted. Even Konrath's car was gone."

"I bet he would've given you a ride if you asked him." Kim smiled deliciously. "Would you have gone?"

Katrina purred, "Yes, and I'd never have let him out of his car."

They both laughed.

"Let's go inside," said Katrina.

"Look at the time, you guys." Katrina paced, occasionally peeking through the drapes for any sign of approaching vehicles. "I don't know about you, but I'm starving. I should've never left my car at our old house."

"Well, there's not much we can do until one of the guys gets back," said Song.

Katrina went to the front desk and pulled out the meager telephone directory. "I'm calling a cab. Anyone with me?"

"Katrina, wait a few minutes, maybe they'll be back soon," said Song.

"Okay, a few minutes. Then I'm outta here."

"Aunty Trina, I'll go with you."

Sitting in the last booth at the dingy old bar, the dark-haired deliveryman rolled up his shirtsleeves to conceal the floral logo of his daytime employer. It was five to seven. Paul waved an empty beer bottle at the bartender. The waiter nodded. Anxiously, Paul surveyed the length of the tavern towards the door. A lone, drunken couple sat at the end of the bar and he wondered how long they'd been working on their inebriation.

"Here you go, buddy—want this here on your tab?"

"Sure," said Paul. He watched the cowboy-booted bartender walk away, kicking an old jukebox into commission as he clicked back to his domain behind the bar. A twangy warble quavered through the dank saloon, and Paul couldn't decide if the scratches or the vocalist sounded worse. The cowgirl yodeled a song about some fellow running off with her money, her mother and her dog. Shaking his head, he laughed under his breath as the record began to skip, thus eliciting a loud "son-uva-bitch" and another kick from the bartender's boot. A hearty pull on the plug ended the cowgirl's dilemma.

Several minutes passed. In his anxiety, Paul emptied the bottle.

"Hey, buddy, bring me one more of these when you get a chance."

"Sure thing, pal," the waiter said.

Paul wondered when the mysterious caller was going to show. The clock on the wall of the smokey room confirmed the time on the young man's watch.

"Here ya are," said the waiter. "I brought ya some pretzels."

"Thanks, dude."

"Say, you expectin' company?"

Paul nodded, wondering if he had been set up.

C'mon, Kim, the cab's here," said Katrina. "Song, you sure you don't want to join us?"

Declining, the older woman set her mug of cocoa on the coffee table and sank back against the cushy, floral couch. A blissful sigh escaped her lips and Katrina understood perfectly well.

"Enjoy the peace and please tell Bruce–or someone–to come and get us at Pasqualino's. It's on U.S. 27. We'll be waiting."

Stretching her legs out in front of her, Song assured them that she would, and set her attention back to the splashy-colored pictures of her craft magazine.

Paul glanced at the blurred characters on his watch and confirmed his suspicions when eyeing the yellowed wall clock–both had become difficult to read. His contact arrived several minutes ago and it was getting late. "Damn it's after seven-thirty," Paul slurred. "I gotta go. I've gotta be somewhere at eight."

"So what? We have a deal?" The eyes behind the phony, thick-framed glasses were fixed on the young man sitting across the table. Again the negotiator fanned a thick wad of bills in front of him and repeated the terms of the proposal. "This will be, say, a retainer followed by several increments of like kind–that is when you finish your part of the deal. And as a li'l bonus, I know people who can set you up so you'll be runnin' a department, not friggin' flowers." The gaze penetrated like a laser.

"This is heavy," said Paul. "It's makin' me nuts. I'm s'posed to meet him at eight..."

The eyeglasses and wig were becoming aggravating and so was the deliveryman's indecisiveness. "But this is all part of the game now, isn't it?"

"Man, I hate this," Paul said.

"What do you hate? The chance for a better life–or paying off a mountain of bills? Or maybe it's the adventure you fear? After all, you won't be peddling daisies anymore–"

How do you know so much about me anyway? Paul stared down his opponent through glazed eyes. "I don't even know who the hell I'm talking to–"

216

"That's the beauty part, Pauly. You don't need to know me. You're not gonna have to look for my face in every crowd you encounter. I've made it so easy for you, Pauly. And if it's the decision part you loathe–let me do that for you." Firmly grabbing the deliveryman's wrist, the negotiator stuffed the wad of bills into Paul's relaxed hand and with black-gloved fingers, tightened them over his now clenched fist. In a daze, the deliveryman's grasp remained firm and he watched the raincoat covered arm pull back and hide an exposed dark sleeve.

"There, Pauly. One down and one to go till you're a richer and smarter man." Continuing in a low tone, the disguised figure repeated the plan. "Leave now and go meet with the wise detective. Remember your lines and what you're to tell him. And just as I knew you came alone, I'll know if you don't follow through with the rest of your agreement. Don't look so surprised. Oh yes, this was your idea," came the hissed threat, "I have ways of convincing the cops, but you're smart. I'm sure I won't have to resort to this. Have a rich life, Pauly, you'll be receiving some nice things. Stay tuned–you'll be hearing from me. Now go."

Not looking back, Paul tossed his head back, clearing the dark hair from his eyes. Shuffling past the bar and its tender; dazed and confused, Paul headed out the tavern door.

"Hello, Song, this is Theresa. Has my husband been out that way?" Whispering into the phone, the anxious woman went on, "I don't want to alarm Mother. Wren has been gone some time now and hasn't called. I'm a bit worried." Theresa listened. "Well, if you hear from him, please have him call me."

"I'm waiting for Tim or Bruce to get back," Song said. They've also been gone a while now. Maybe there's a good card game goin' somewhere." Song chuckled, trying to ease the tension.

"Well, I'm thinking about calling the nurse back for a few hours so I can leave for a bit. Wren and I were supposed to go for dinner later, and I think Mom should have someone stay with her. Well," Theresa hesitated, "if he's not back soon and the nurse can make it, would you like me to swing by and pick you up? Maybe we can dine out together."

"Thanks, Theresa, but call first should Tim come back by then. I know Katrina and her niece are gonna need a ride from that Italian place on 27. I'm startin' to get pretty hungry myself. Or maybe I can whip something up right here. Call when you know what's goin' on."

Song paced the kitchen floor, a myriad of images flooding her mind. Up till now, she hadn't been very concerned about her husband's tardiness, but Theresa's phone call, the emptiness of the inn and the blackness of the night served to unnerve her. Poison, murder, and faces in the dark propelled Song across the room to hurriedly pull down all shades in effort to shroud herself in the security of the kitchen's bright lights. She decided she just might accept Theresa's offer. Song flicked off all but one light as she left the room, wondering why Theresa would believe her husband came back to the inn.

Stealing across the near vacant lot, the cloaked figure, favoring dark shadows, looked back at the staggering form of the deliveryman fumbling with the keys to his car. Stripping off glasses, wig and face putty, the caller stuffed them deep into a raincoat pocket and continued to note the moves of the unsuspecting young man. A light rain caused the asphalt lot to glisten and the perpetrator yanked up a raincoat collar, pleased that nature had cooperated. A last look assured the stalker that the subject had made it inside his car. The schemer cut through a neighboring lot and got into a parked car. Paul started his vehicle. The plan was launched.

The perpetrator followed a safe distance behind Paul's car, smiling when it almost went off the road. Once back on track, the deliveryman drove along and began to pick up speed. Bouncing off dips in the winding road, the lead car shot ahead, its wheels chirping and smoking as they skimmed the wet pavement. The trailing driver dropped back, and watched Paul's car shoot around a corner on two wheels. Smug with content as the plan further developed, the stalker leered as trees and ravines whizzed by. Things were going well. With a sudden squeal of brakes and a swerve to the left, the lead car's brakes locked. It shot straight ahead. Maneuvering the curve, the trailing vehicle safely barreled past, just as a loud crash was followed by the glare and heat of a car exploding into a huge fireball, as it rolled over and over into the beckoning ravine. The tranquil star-studded night was no more.

Welcomed but yet shocking, the catastrophe finally sank in and the victor rolled to a stop in the middle of the country road. The deed was done. "I can't believe... What have I become?" the lone motorist cried out to no one. Shaking while guiding the auto onto the shoulder, the guilt-ridden hugged the steering wheel. "Sorry, dude–I had to. Sorry."

Shrugging off the suffocating raincoat and jamming it under the front seat, the driver jerked the vehicle around and headed back toward the accident. Paul's death had to be confirmed. In the distance, sirens could be heard as the burning wreck continued to spew forth billowy smoke. A couple alighted from their truck and ran to join three people attempting to approach the blaze. A loud, horn blast and fierce headlights glared, announcing the approaching rescue vehicles. Following a short distance behind came the paramedics.

Several yards down the road, the driver stopped and turned around once more. After a deep breath, the loner tailgated another passing vehicle... Lights flashed, hoses were engaged, and gawkers fretted as the scenario played itself out like a bad dream. Just as it builds and a scream is eminent, it peaks–and a covered stretcher is removed by sullen-faced attendants, guarded from onlookers by the harsh commands of the commissioned officer. An utterance escapes as the nightmare ends but the sweating persists.

A surfacing thought confirms "it was tragic," but also reassures "it's over," and a weight lifts as the impact subsides, giving way to a renewed psyche. The guilty one parks near the accident site. Every drama needs "a wrap."

"Hello, Mrs. Dukette" Song said, toying with the phone cord. "Has your husband returned yet?"

The responding voice was strained. "Mrs. Ver. . .Song, the agency nurse just arrived. She'll stay with Mom a few hours. I'm going out to see if I can find Wren. This isn't like him not to call."

"Theresa, I just got off the phone with Sergeant Lewis." Song hesitated. "Why don't you come out to the inn? Leave a note for Wren to join us–"

"I need to get out of the house, Song. I'm going stir crazy staying in." Theresa rambled on. "I'll go for a ride, get some fresh air and a dinner. Hopefully, I'll meet up with my husband. Song, why don't you join me?"

Song sighed deeply into the phone. "Theresa, I think you should come over."

"Is everything okay," she asked. What did Sergeant Lewis want anyway?"

"I know about as much as you. All I can say is if something's goin' on, we'll soon find out what it is." Song excused herself, hung up, and quickly checked the icebox inventory.

Katrina returned to the table at the restaurant. She had to call the inn to find out if Bruce was coming for her and Kim.

"You got the answering machine?" Kim asked.

"No, Song answered. No one came back to the inn yet. Not Spike, Bruce, Tim or even Konrath." Katrina pulled herself closer to the table. "Sergeant Lewis called, Song's worried, Theresa's worried and Song asked us to come back."

"Mrs. Dukette's worried? Why?"

Katrina set her coffee cup down. "Wren's also been gone a while. Theresa called and asked if anyone saw him."

"Where the heck are all the guys?" Kim asked. "Was a spaceship dispatched from the planet Babe to kidnap all our men?"

"Right, Kim. What woman of superior intelligence would come down to kidnap Tim?"

Kim chuckled. "I'm sure they'd want him as their love slave. Did Song say anything about Lou?"

"No. Are you ready?"

Kim nodded as she took a last sip of water. "I called a cab. It'll be here soon."

Katrina and Kim tipped their waitress and left the eatery.

"I thought we were going out tonight?" Kim pointed, "There's the cab. He pulled off to the side."

"Let's return to the inn first and see what's going on," said Katrina.

Kim nodded and the women climbed into the back seat of the waiting vehicle. Winding their way back to the inn, the cabby updated the two with sketchy details of a fatal accident occurring several miles north of the restaurant. "They're not releasing the name of the driver pending identification of the next of kin. Word goin' around is it's a kid in his late twenties."

Tina Czarnota

CHAPTER 21

Theresa Dukette pulled into the driveway of the Tudor Grove Bed and Breakfast, never paying much attention to the two cars parked just down the road.

The inn looked inviting with the front porch lit. Theresa noticed the absence of the wreath at the main entrance and wondered if new guests were expected. She knocked at the door and soon heard footsteps coming to answer. Song opened the front door.

"Garsch, were you out here long?"

"No," Theresa said, stepping inside.

"How about a brandy?" Song asked.

"Not at the moment, thank you. Are you sure this is a good time for me to drop by?"

"Of course." Song peeked out the front door before closing it. "Oh good, it stopped raining. I hope you're still hungry." She waited for the woman to look away from the hall mirror. "I just set out a hot and cold spread–there's plenty for everyone."

"Well, actually I thought about getting dinner out to... are you expecting company?"

Without answering, Song guided the woman toward the drawing room. "Have you heard from Mr. Dukette?"

"No, although I had the line tied up for a while. He may have tried to call."

"Well, you can stop worryin'. He called just a bit ago. He said he tried phoning but the line was busy. He tried again and the nurse said you left, probably to come here."

Theresa relaxed with relief, which was quickly replaced with anger as she wondered where her husband had been for so long. "He's got some explaining to do," she said as she entered the room.

"He's safe," said Song. "That's what counts."

"Yes, of course," agreed Theresa.

The backdrop was set once more; several lights were dimmed, couches beckoned and the aroma of Song's amply stocked buffet table filled her senses.

"Song you must be so proud of your inn," Theresa cooed. "This room is done up so beautifully, I could be happy spending hours in here alone."

Song guided Theresa past the Victorian downbridge lamp, briefly touching its cream-hued fringe. "Well, you just might get your wish."

"Excuse me?"

"Uh, you might want to grab a dish–and get started."

Theresa filled her plate with spicy chicken wings and moved on to the crudités. "Did Wren say anything about meeting me?"

"I'll be right back. I'll put on some coffee," Song said. "Please make yourself at home."

In a swift movement, she left the room, leaving behind a perplexed Theresa.

"I don't know about this one," the young sergeant said. He glanced back at the thicket of trees shielding his view of the Swanson house. "Klonski takes his career pretty serious–and so do I."

"It's not like I'm asking you to tamper with evidence or–or..."

Lewis looked at Lou. "Hey, this is my job. If Klonski senses the least bit of dickin' around, he'll demote me to meter boy."

"I need this for my resume, Lewis. Besides you owe me one." Lou was trying out for acting. He had an idea how playing a part in finding the killer could help him.

"I owe you? No, I think you got it the other... Look, just put it on your resume, leave my number and I'll vouch–"

"It doesn't work that way. I need the actual experience if I'm ever gonna break in."

"I don't believe this." Lewis dug his heels into the wet grass.

"Hey, I think she's looking for you." The rear window shade was slowly pulled down. "Whatda ya say?"

"Okay–okay, but if Klonski walks in, you stop the charades," the sergeant said as they walked toward the inn, "and hopefully you won't have to peel me off the wall. Now let's get in there, Lou. We've a murder to wrap up."

Song transferred the aromatic brew to a white carafe, and looked up as the two men opened the back kitchen door. Her gaze shot down at their feet.

"Uh, wipe your shoes, Lou," the detective said.

Her "thank you" was punctuated with relief and she quickly informed the men that Theresa had arrived. "Sergeant Lewis, please go in there and talk to–"

"Have you said anything to her?"

"No, only that her husband called. I didn't get a chance to tell her why I invited her. Garsch, I feel like I've tricked her."

"If nothing else, you've invited her for company. You did just fine."

Song managed a smile as she repeatedly straightened the items on her filled service tray. "Please go talk to her, then I'll serve coffee. Actually," she grimaced, "I should serve some stiff drinks."

"Talk to her about what?"

Three heads shot up and looked toward the voice, which belonged to an annoyed Theresa Dukette.

Sergeant Lewis walked across the kitchen and gestured to the woman. "Let's talk in the drawing room–after you."

Lou remained standing near the island range and leaned on its counter top. Song sighed and tightened the carafe lid once more. "I can't wait till this mess is over."

"Don't worry, Mrs. Versay," the photographer said, "it will be–tonight."

225

Heavy footsteps pounded up the front porch and familiar coughing announced the arrival of Tim. Song scurried across the sitting room to greet her husband.

"Better get out of his chair," Lou told Sergeant Lewis, and the young detective moved to the floral couch where Theresa sat sipping brandy. In the far left corner, Lou sat alone at the chessboard and studied the room. The stage was set. Dim lighting accentuated by the glow of tall, thick candles set in the barren hearth afforded an eerie, yet beckoning tone. Heavy drapery, the kind found in vintage black and white mystery movies, were pulled tightly across the expansive front windows. Nervous suspects clutched brandy snifters.

"What's goin' on?" Tim asked. He was damp and smelled of smoke. "Another party?" No one answered him.

Instead Lewis questioned the man on his whereabouts for the last few hours. Song was glad to relinquish the task to the young detective.

Bored with the details, the handsome photographer strutted across the room and peered around the front curtains. Moving to the drawstring, he cracked open the fabric, affording himself a view of the driveway. He needed this to pick up his cue–and to check out when the babe returned.

The solitary figure pulled away from the crash site, hoping he'd been observed in the crowd of spectators. He was pleased. He had his alibi established; besides, he didn't kill Paul. He just helped Paul help himself. Driving the off-beaten roads, the con planned the next move. All he wanted to do was make a call, head to the airport and be free. But if he left, the police would link him to the murder. In the end, there was only one choice.

The anxious photographer blocked out the mutterings of Song, Tim, Theresa and Lewis, and pondered the points he hoped to make. He paced as he mentally practiced his delivery. Drawing strange looks from the others, Lou decided to rehearse in the library. Peering out the side window, he noted the vehicles

parked in the drive. He saw Bruce's van, and recalled that Tim
mentioned he had traded vehicles with his son.

Lou saw a beam of headlights and quickly left the mini-
repository He hurried to the front door and locked it. Getting into
character, Lou moved past the gang in the drawing room and
took his place at the chessboard. With microphone in check, Lou
dimmed the corner light and began his spiel.

"What the hell's he doing?" was the last thing Lou heard
Tim say. Now he had their attention.

"You may be wondering why you've been asked here
tonight..."

Tim laughed, reminding the others that he lived there. Song
shushed at him.

"Well," Lou's narration continued in forced eloquence,
"tonight is the eve of the solving of," a ceremonial rumble
punctuated, "the incident at Tudor Grove."

A female voice murmured something about heaven's sakes
and the young sergeant shook his head as he envisioned his
badge growing wings.

Attempting to drown out knocks on the front door, Lou's
voice boomed: "To your dismay, the front door will open,
revealing to us this evening the mur..."

"Why are you sitting in the dark? Why didn't you answer the
door?" The voice was cold and demanding.

"Oh garsch, it's Katrina," Song said. "And Kim."

Mumbling ensued. Tim laughed and suggested that Lou's
apartment was located near a toxic dumpsite. Katrina made
threats with a light switch and Kim purred, "Cool."

"Silence!" said Lou as he begged for patience and promised
the saga would unfold. Katrina shook her head and poured
herself a cognac. Kim winked at Lou and sat on the vacant
couch, facing him.

"Kim," her aunt started, "about Lou–I think maybe you..."
She was too late. Her niece was intoxicated with Lou. Great,
Katrina fretted. Florida won't be far enough when her mother

finds out about this one. Katrina took another sip. For that matter, neither is Russia.

"I'm hungry," Kim said. "Aunty Trina, want me to get you something to eat?" Bouncing off the couch, Kim was on her way to the buffet table. "Isn't this exciting?"

Lewis hid his face in his hands; Theresa managed a forced smile, and Tim hollered for another refill.

"I heard car doors slam, Kim," said Lou. "Everybody in their positions." He dimmed the chess table light once more and with a somewhat perfected opening, he again announced that the murderer would walk through the front door.

With the predictable fumbling of the front lock, the small group waited.

First came a thud, then a curse.

"What happened?" Theresa wanted to know.

"Why is it so dark in here? Katrina, I said I didn't want a surprise birth... What's so funny?"

Katrina assured Bruce that there was no party and there were no gifts. "So where were you?"

"Oh good–food. There was a bad accident," Bruce mumbled and headed for the table. "Hi, Lou. What are you sitting in the dark for?"

"Oh garsch, Lou. Is my son the killer?" Song said, frightened.

"They found the killer?" All heads turned toward the door.

Song relinquished her place next to Katrina. "Oh, Mr. Konrath, come and join us." Kim elbowed her aunt.

"Thanks, Mrs. Versay, no need to get up. I'll pull up a chair," said Bob. "What's going on?"

Song hopped up, but instead, went to the chess table. Bob shrugged and took Song's seat. Bruce caught Katrina's smug look as he settled for a seat on the opposite couch. Just then, Spike peered in and entered the room. He added to the acrid smell of smoke that hung in the air.

"Bruce, wanna sit next to Katrina?" Tim asked.

"No," Katrina answered for him. "He doesn't." Tim chuckled, anticipating more action. Someone shouted a greeting at Spike and obvious attempts at conversation were made while Bruce fumed and Katrina ignored him.

"Why are you boys all damp…?" started Song.

"And smell of smoke?" asked Theresa."

"There was a bad accident, someone got charred," said Spike.

"I told you there was an accident," Bruce said to Katrina.

"From mid afternoon until evening–tell it to yo mama."

"Tell me what, Katrina?" said Song.

In spite of the tension, the gang chuckled. Song tsked and went back to business. "Look, Lou," she said, "why don't you put that away for now and get a nice brandy, or I'll fix you a plate of food." She further cajoled but Lou didn't hear her.

He realized he'd lost his audience, for Wren Dukette just arrived, and the group was abuzz over the car accident that occurred earlier that night. Lou temporarily abandoned his place at the mike and made for the buffet.

"Sergeant Lewis, telephone," Song chirped, answering the phone as it rang. She set the instrument on the front desk and the detective immediately left for the library. Someone complained again about the smell of smoke and, Tim got up and went out for a cigarette.

Lewis returned to the drawing room and headed straight for the chess table and its occupant. Background chatter included Kim's urge to go dancing, Wren's plea for a peaceful night's rest, and Spike's plans for the remainder of his vacation.

"You have just a few minutes–Klonski's on his way," Lewis said.

Lou almost dropped his plate. He chewed fast and set his dish aside. "Lewis, call for attention, they'll listen to you," the photog piped as he swung the mike before him.

"This is your gig. I'm not–"

"Attention, everyone. Please return to your seats. I have an update." Lou was pleased with his choice of words–everyone wanted an update.

Repeated scenes of dimmed lights, background effects and cliché deliveries were met with demands for information. "As I promised earlier, we would reveal the identity of the guilty party, and I'm prepared to do that–"

"Just say it," Theresa called out.

"Let him talk," said Kim.

Lou waited for silence as Lewis tapped on his watch.

"Okay. Everyone has their suspicions of who the guilty party might be. That person or persons may be here tonight–or they may not. But," Lou roared, employing sinister flair, "but–" he scanned his audience, "it is in fact each and everyone of you who is guilty."

Gasps and protests rose. "Give me your attention and I will elaborate..."

"This outta be good," Wren said.

Lou cleared his throat. "Very well, I shall start with," he searched his audience, "I shall start wi-ith Katrina."

"Great," she answered.

"You, my luv, are guilty–of–the ease in which you become infatuated." Someone yelled "get down" as Lou approached Katrina. She questioned his state of mental health.

"Oh yes," he continued. "You crave male adoration and bask in the gaze of masculine attention..."

Tim's hysterics almost drowned him out.

"Bu-ut," he whirled around, "it's no wonder as–Bruce, yes you, Mr. Bruce, have a penchant for painting instead of passion. You'd rather work on chimneys than chivalry, and roam hardware stores instead of romance."

"Now we come to the incorrigible, the horrible, the one they set their standards by, the chauvinist's chauvinist–Tim Versay."

Spike yelled, "Yeah."

The photog faced down the grinning man. "You are guilty of running employees out of their jobs, running your wife around in circles–"

"Hell, that's what women are for–they've been doin' it for years," said Tim. "Gives them something to do."

Katrina got up and threatened to flip Tim over in his chair, Kim booed, and refined Theresa uttered obscenities at the man.

"Oh yeah, and what am I guilty of?" the voice boomed.

Heads turned. Lou's mouth dropped. "Hey, Lieutenant–"

"Don't give me that crap, Lou," said Klonski. "Are you making a friggin' parlor game out of this murder investigation? Where's Lewis?"

"Oh, Lieutenant Klonski," Song said, up on her feet. "Lou was nice enough to entertain us with parts of a script he's workin' on. Wasn't he?" Song turned to the group and exaggerated a wink. Looking back at her husband she said, "And he was just gettin' to the good part."

Klonski strutted past the group and called for order. Everyone obliged.

"Now let's get down to business," Klonski began. "This is never an easy task. It's the part I loathe but yet enjoy the most, for you see," he eyed each individual as he paced, "in the process, it is necessary to uncover hurtful information about individuals–say, who are on the outer fringes of an investigation. I will try to keep these revelations to a minimum. Another unpleasant aspect is that, in many cases, the guilty party or parties, are people we've come to like and even admire." He paused. "But there is nothing admirable about murder." Klonski scratched his sideburn while he referred to a page in his note pad.

"Why isn't Jessie Hodgkins here?" Katrina asked. "She was in the dining room at the time of the murder." Klonski didn't respond.

Theresa was startled as the dining room door behind her opened. All eyes focused on Lewis, who now exited the room. He closed the door behind him. A nod from Klonski and the

231

young detective approached the entrance once more as the anxious group looked on.

Through the partly opened door Lewis said, "This way please."

Moments later, an elderly man appeared in the doorway.

"Why, it's Mr. Swanson–our next door neighbor," said Song.

"The bastard who keeps ruining my plants," Tim spat.

"Garsch, Tim, you don't know–"

"What? That he's a bastard or that he's ruining my–"

"Excuse me." Klonski took control. "Mr. Swanson, please enter and make your identification."

Everyone eyed each other as Swanson set his gaze on one individual. "It's him, that's him–that's Adonis." A trembling finger pointed in the direction of Bob Konrath.

"Are you certain?" Klonski said.

"I'd recognize him anywhere, 'cept he has more clothes on this time." The old man recounted the night of the rain dance. "He wacked me a good one, Lieutenant."

"Just a minute," Bob countered. Klonski requested he remain seated. "I never hit you, you babbling old man." Bob loosened his collar and continued. "Maybe I'm guilty about the affair–but I didn't hit you."

"Who's Adonis?" Song chirped.

Bob looked down at his feet, then faced the detective. "I, I was having an affair with–"

"In this house?" Kim wanted to know. Katrina's mouth dropped open.

"Yes, in this house–before you people moved in that is." Slowly, the man disclosed most of the details about an affair he was having with a real estate woman he met at a conference in Tampa. "It was a perfect setup–different times, different places. But that's in the past. I don't see her any longer. Besides, my indiscretion does not make me a killer. Wait a minute," he said as the old man was ushered back into the dining room. "If I didn't hit him, then who did?"

"It was Mrs. Swanson," Klonski said. "Tired of her husband's peeping, especially at a naked young woman, she decided to help him out of his addiction, so she clocked him one—thought it would scare him off. He thought it was you, Bob, who hit him."

"Well, now that some questions are getting answered, let me ask this," Bob said, and Klonski nodded. Bob looked up at the man leaning against the fireplace. "Wren, what were you doing the afternoon you and Theresa went shopping? You know, the day you took off before Klonski gave his final—"

"Wait a minute, I'll handle that," Klonski said. He rephrased the question slightly, but Wren refused to talk.

A ruddy flush crept over Bob's face as he blurted out several questions. "What were those phone calls about, Wren? You make sure your wife turns the corner and you run to the nearest phone. Why? What about sneaking into the florist? And how did that poison get in your pocket? What about Tim?"

"What calls?" Theresa asked.

Song put a comforting hand on Theresa's shoulder and also wanted to know about the calls.

Wren scowled and the lieutenant looked at his watch. It appeared he was waiting for something.

"Let's not get into that now." Klonski flipped through his notebook and asked for a chair. Lewis positioned one to the right of Tim.

"Katrina, you asked why Jessie was not present tonight. Well," Klonski said, "she was ruled out as a suspect." A gust of wind tapped bottlebrush branches against the front windowpanes. Klonski listened then went on. "She may be guilty of harassment, mischievous conduct, and lack of cooth, but she is not guilty of murder."

"Well, I want her prosecuted to the fullest extent of the law," said Katrina. "If that's what it takes to make her leave us alone."

"We'll talk about that later," Klonski said, eyeing Katrina. A stronger current of air swirled around the estate, this time

233

whistling through the near hollow chimney. Several candle flames flickered then resumed their sentinel-like pose.

Katrina looked at the others. "Yeah, right. Now I'm the killer..."

"You do have ample motive," said Klonski. "Not for Mindy Konrath but for the man you love to hate, your fiancé's father." Several gasps followed this. "You see, Katrina, you would never have murdered Mrs. Konrath; as it was revealed to me, you had a certain pity for her. You favor the less fortunate, you love the underdog, but you cannot tolerate the rude, the snobby, the arrogant."

"Where did you get this stuff?" Katrina demanded. She couldn't believe this was happening.

"Remember my pledge for discretion? Let's just say we find volumes in background checks."

"I can't believe you suspect I did it." The silence was heavy. Unlike before, this was no parlor game.

Klonski continued. "Being one of my main suspects, I admit I had you singled out as one of my stronger possibilities. You see, I began to study your association with Tim Versay. You made it known that you are disgusted by the man."

"Not really, I just..."

"Often, one will display overt displeasure or total avoidance of a person he is enamored with, to throw off suspicion. But," he held up a forefinger to his lips, "it became apparent that this was not the case with you. You care about this man but by the same token, you guard your relationship with his son vehemently–you don't want him to become his father."

Klonski took a sip of water; the others took deep breaths. He moved on. "Now an important clue that, fortunately you picked up on, came the other day." He went on to explain about the message Song took down on the note pad. "Everyone saw it, we were certain–but it was planted for a targeted few."

Katrina was taken aback. "You mean Song was in on it?" She looked at the woman. Song would have made a peacock nervous.

Klonski went on to explain the hunch he played. "I knew, first of all, that whoever poisoned Mrs. Konrath, had to have a knowledge of cyanide and of apricot kernels. A few in this group have an avid interest in natural remedies and vitamins; some of you a fleeting interest. In either case you must understand that those were my strongest suspects. In the same token, if you showed no interest in the aforementioned, that could be construed as a smoke screen; just as the example I illustrated for Katrina a few moments ago.

"But logically, Mindy's killer had to have some knowledge in the area of health, as well as the knowledge of Mindy's interest in health foods, so if she consumed apricot kernels and they were found in her system, it would be no big deal. As," this time the detective scanned the group, "apricot seeds and pits are purported to prevent cancer, for they contain a substance called amygdalin, a supposed anticancer agent. In fact, in some countries, health institutions employ Laetrile, an anticancer drug made from apricot pits."

"What's this got to do with the killer?" asked Katrina.

"In addition, apricot pits contain a substance called hydrocyanic acid, better known as cyanide," Klonski said.

"It can be deadly," Katrina contributed. "But what about the phone call?"

"Purposely we left an obscure message with Song," said Klonski, "who in turn logged it in the front desk message book where everyone would see it. Everyone that is except Tim. His priority would have been more bent on getting a smoke outdoors than a glimpse of the note pad. Anyway," he went on, "it didn't matter for his name went on our least likely list–still a suspect, but not a strong one."

Song gave her husband a look of relief. Tim sat in his chair, grinning.

"Go on, Lieutenant, this is exciting," Kim exclaimed as she rested against the arm of the couch. Klonski, just inches away from the young woman, gave her a stern look but didn't speak his mind.

"Murder is not fun, you dip," said Spike.

"I didn't say it was," said Kim. "I mean it's cool to see the investigation. And I'm not a dip so save it for your next–"

"Let's move on," said Klonski. "Song followed her instructions to leave the message out in the open. At that point, Katrina appeared to be the most likely candidate, out of three or four suspects. We needed to, say, smoke her out. Not, however, as a guilty party but an innocent one."

"Why me, why not Spike or Song?" Katrina said.

Klonski set his water glass down. "Good question. Let's look at it. First of all, I suspected you for an attempt made on Tim, not Mindy. You see, you had motive, knowledge of the cyanide, excellent opportunity and..."

"Not very much to gain. He's not rich or anything."

"No, Katrina, but money isn't always what's at stake or to gain. In a twisted mind that doesn't even figure into the picture."

Tim chuckled about the lieutenant's last comment and Katrina turned a shoulder to him.

"So then, who did it?" Theresa studied the group. "Let's see–so you said that little sleaze, Jessie, is out..."

"Theresa!" Wren said.

"Well, darling, she is a sleaze–sorry. So, who else is out? You ruled Song out, is that correct?"

"Yes," Klonski said.

"Why?" asked Theresa.

"Yeah, Klonski, why not her?" said Wren. "She had plenty of motive; she's married to it."

"Talk about having something to gain," offered Theresa. Katrina caught her attention and laughed in agreement.

Klonski called for attention, reminding the group that an investigation was still in progress and to conduct themselves as such.

"So," Kim picked up the narration, "Jessie, Song, Tim and Katrina are no longer suspects, right? Oh great, that leaves me– forget it, I don't even want to think about it."

"No need to think about it, Kim," said Klonski. "I've eliminated you from the list."

"Phew," Kim said, "but how did you figure it wasn't me?"

Klonski viewed the young woman's curiosity as genuine and therefore indulged her. "You did have opportunity but truly lacked motive and gain. Unless of course you were avenging something undisclosed to us, or say, loyalty to your aunt. But with our investigation we discovered that you were mainly concerned with enjoying your vacation and making your relationship work. You also lack the–"

"Brains to pull off a murder," said Spike.

"You don't fit the profile," Klonski corrected.

Kim turned to Spike. "Maybe you did it. You did suggest Bob's saliva test. Why?" Kim said, heatedly. "Think about it; you're a cop, what better cover... You spent time in Florida. You probably scored, weren't any good, and when she kissed and told, you came back to kill her."

"I thought the peeper did it," admitted Spike. "And, I thought Bob was the peeper. As for Mindy," he sat up, "she was old."

Protests over Spike's admissions drowned out a faint knock on the dining room door. Klonski nodded; Lewis briskly crossed the room, knocked once and squeezed himself through the partially opened door. Closing it, he left behind once more a puzzled group of onlookers.

"Someone's in there," Theresa said. "Someone is in the dining room. Is this session being recorded, Lieutenant?"

Klonski answered no questions.

"If so," she went on, "we have the right to legal counsel."

"Do you feel you need an attorney present?" Klonski asked. Theresa thought about it while Wren waived his right to representation.

"Unless," Wren faltered, "this investigation is bungled..."

"I'm already with counsel," Bob interjected while Bruce just shrugged his shoulders.

Silence enveloped his subjects as Klonski consulted his notes.

"Lieutenant," Song said, wringing her hands, "we all know why we're here tonight. This is a difficult situation to handle. I'm sure the others will agree. Can we get through it quickly?"

"You may leave the room if you wish," Klonski said.

"Mom, let's go to the kitchen," Bruce said.

Klonski objected. "Bruce, please remain seated." The rotund, uniformed Casey appeared at the reception desk and slowly approached the group. "Katrina, Kim–if you'd like to leave... " No one budged. Song took her leave alongside the officer.

The grim-faced detective sat up in his chair as his subjects shifted uneasily in their places. An unidentified officer now stood in the drawing room doorway.

"Let's move on," said Klonski. "A witness finally came forward–rather, was tracked down. At first, said witness denied involvement, but of course, times and places were confirmed and we finally got an admission and a statement. It was time to move in."

The veil of tension never subsided, nor did the sporadic burst of wind cease to threaten the half-burned candles flickering in the hearth.

Klonski stared momentarily at the beckoning glow before returning to his notes. "Where was I?"

"You got a statement from the witness," said Spike.

"Right. Anyway, making our move to the library as obvious as we could, without spelling it out, we proceeded with a phone call; making our conversation audible for any person or persons passing through the hallway. This was achieved, for the events that followed confirmed this."

Sitting tall in his chair, Klonski passed from one remaining suspect to the next, grilling each on his or her whereabouts for that afternoon and early evening.

Bruce's admission was the grand opening of a new super home improvement store and stopping at the accident scene when he noticed Spike's red rental. "Everybody was there. Bob, Wren, my dad and as I mentioned, Spike."

Passing on Spike, as having his whereabouts confirmed earlier, Klonski moved on to Bob Konrath. "I went for a ride–to take care of some business, talked to my lawyer and what has been substantiated, my stopping at the scene of the accident."

"Mr. Dukette?"

"Let's see." He looked past Katrina. "I needed to do some shopping and then passed the bowling alley. I stopped in for a change of scenery and ran into Tim. He didn't see me; he was down at the far end of the bar talking with some of the locals. I had a beer, made a few phone calls and, like the guys, stopped at the accident site."

"You do that quite a bit, don't you?" said Klonski.

"Do what?"

"Make a lot of telephone calls."

"So?" he said, purposely avoiding Theresa's questioning look.

The reception desk phone rang, drawing a perturbed look from Klonski. Instinctively, Katrina jumped up to answer it, looking to Klonski for consent. Waving her on, she quickly lifted the handpiece in attempt to silence the annoying ring.

"Tudor Grove, may... yes, he's here but–"

"Who is it?" barked the lieutenant.

"I don't know," she replied and relayed the short message. "It's for Mr. Konrath."

Klonski waved his consent and the recipient crossed the room to take his call.

"Who is this?" the voice asked, confirming the correct individual had intercepted. "I have a surprise for you."

"That's great," said Bob. "Look, I'm in a meeting right now–I really can't talk." Turning around, he faced the intent group who scrupulously observed the situation. Turning back, he whispered into the phone, "Who is this?" He listened hard.

"I'm still with you," the voice said. "Remember that little shake and bake earlier tonight–well, guess what? Seems my gas

239

line had been cut. A li'l gas, a spark...you know the rest. Good news is I'm okay, so you got one less murder under your belt."

"I saw them carry..." his voice cracked. "Where are you? You're breaking up."

"Don't worry, dude, I'm behind you all the way..."

The realization hit and the man whirled around; he dropped the phone. His mouth agape, he stood motionless as a dark haired, uniformed man stepped forward, laying aside a cell phone. Two uniformed policemen rushed and handcuffed the stunned killer. Klonski read him his rights as the stupified Robert Konrath protested, "You're not Paul..."

The dining room door opened once more. "No, but I am, dude."

With stern confidence Klonski uttered some of his most favorite words in the English language, "Take him away!"

CHAPTER 22

The proverbial bomb had just dropped and the killer was escorted out the front entrance, leaving behind emotional pieces to pick up. Tim needed a cigarette and stood on the front porch watching them haul off the dashing murderer.

The stunned gathering sat frozen, shocked. Katrina pushed herself to peer briefly out the front window to witness a patrol car drive off with Bob Konrath, the object of her admiration.

A soft, sweet voice asked if she was all right. "Yeah, Kim, thanks. Why did it have to be him?" She talked at the windowpane, noticing the group filing out onto the front porch. The patrol car disappeared.

"Who should it have been?" Kim asked.

"You know what I mean. Let's get away from the window. It's getting stuffy behind this curtain." The drawing room was deserted. "I need to go out in the back for a few minutes. I could use some fresh air." Shuffling slowly through the now vacant, posh dining room, Katrina continued somberly past the murder site and out the rear entrance.

"I know how you feel, Aunty Trina. I feel bad, too."

"Head for the opposite side of the inn," Katrina said. "I don't want to run into any of them right now." Slowing their stride when a safe distance was achieved, Katrina further reflected, "Kim, it's not so much the feeling part, it's the disappointment. Here's a guy who's gorgeous, suave, well off and what does he do? What a waste of two lives. She's dead and his life is ruined– not to mention the people who will be touched by this." Kim listened in understanding and suggested they go back inside.

"Klonski may have a wind-up, " she said. "There are a few questions that haven't been answered."

"Song, please round everyone up," Klonski said. "I have a little more time I can spend to clear things up–tie loose ends and then I've got to head back."

The hostess was glad to oblige and promised that fresh, hot coffee would be served.

A few minutes later, everyone had gathered again.

"Is the real estate woman going to be charged with conspiracy?" asked Wren.

Klonski placed his coffee cup on its saucer. "No. Even though Konrath still had been seeing her, she had no knowledge of his plans for murder. Konrath told her he would ask for a divorce and this was the weekend he'd do it. Well," he said as he scratched his sideburn, "he had plans all right. When the two met here, she told him of prospective buyers who had an interest in this estate and its potential for a bed and breakfast. Of course, when you bought, the realtor mentioned that this would be a new venture for inexperienced innkeepers and that spelled opportunity. What a perfect backdrop for murder."

While Joseph sipped his coffee, Kim asked, "Wouldn't that be more of a risk to have his wife die while all these people were here?"

"On the contrary, the confusion would benefit the murderer as there would be ample opportunity to administer the poison, plant phony evidence on preoccupied guests–as was the case with the vial planted on Dukette and plenty of suspects."

Klonski looked at Tim. "I don't know if it was disclosed to you, but the lab found traces of cyanide on Tim's chinaware. That, in addition to Mindy's moving to his place at the table, sparked suspicion that Tim may have been either the killer or the intended victim."

"What I'd like to know," Theresa now faced her husband, "is what Bob was referring to when he saw us shopping that afternoon. Why were you sneaking around–what were you up to?"

"You'll spoil things, Theresa… " Wren said.

"1 don't care, I'm not in the mood for–"

"Okay. I ran down to the florist and ordered you some roses for our anniversary. They were to be delivered, but your mother took ill and we returned here–so I had to call and cancel. I made other calls, too. I was planning a surprise cruise for our anniversary."

"That's wonderful," said Song.

"What actually killed Mindy?" asked Katrina.

"Cyanide," said Klonski. "Konrath substituted ground concentrate of apricot seeds into her capsules. She thought she was taking herbal supplements. And she also drank poison."

Wren extended his hand to the lieutenant, "Well, I've heard enough to satisfy my curiosity, so if we're free to go, we'll be off."

Hugs, expressions of relief and best wishes for the couple's anniversary abounded as the two departed. Meeting Tim out on the front porch, Wren suggested a truce and offered a hand; the smoker grunted. Wren shrugged, and headed down the steps.

"Come on, babe," Tim heard Wren say to his wife. "We've got some celebrating to do."

Theresa giggled. "We're staying at Mom's, don't forget."

"Damn. I almost forgot."

"Serves your ass right, Mr. Romeo," muttered Tim. With knees creaking he went inside.

"They're such a nice couple," Song said of the Dukettes.

"He's a romantic guy," Kim offered.

"He's a wuss," said Spike.

Tim laughed and agreed with Spike.

"What's wrong with a little sensuality?" asked Katrina. "I don't mean the syrupy and nauseating kind, but an occasional employing of the senses..."

A fleeting image of Bob Konrath was soon replaced by Tim's taunting, "You mean like your friend? Yeah, he's a real lady killer."

Spike upraised his palm at Tim; the man looked at him and laughed. Spike slapped him teasingly on the head.

Katrina looked at Bruce and shook her head in displeasure.

"Well, I think that ties all loose ends," Klonski said, downing his last sip of coffee.

Klonski," Bruce asked, "who was the guy in the uniform anyway?"

The group became revived as they prompted details about the crash.

"He's one of my men." The lieutenant reclaimed his seat for a moment. "Bob made arrangements with the delivery kid to meet at this out-of-the-way dive. Of course, Paul tipped us off– he was scared–and the stage was set. Konrath bribed Paul with a wad of bills. He knew the kid needed cash for old debts. Paul let Bob buy him a bunch of drinks and he was flying when he left the bar. Bob dropped back a few minutes, so the kid appeared to leave alone. At that point our man, an ex-demolition derby freak, dressed in a dark wig and uniform, took the kid's place and played with the lock on his jalopy." Klonski explained the plan. "You see, the van belongs to Mona, his boss. So we hunted impound and found a heap that resembled the deliveryman's car. Bob thought it was the kid he saw in the lot but it really was our man. The rest you can figure out."

"Why did he stalk Paul anyway?" Kim asked.

Klonski yawned. "Because Bob found out Paul witnessed the whole scene that afternoon. He delivered your aunt's package. Bob was sure Paul saw him back up to the table and drop the poison at Tim's place setting. He figured if he killed Paul, he couldn't talk, so Bob had to get him out of the way fast."

"Who did they carry off on the stretcher?" Song asked. "What happened to the driver when the car hit the tree?"

Tim laughed as Klonski explained that the driver jumped, of course, and predictably, Konrath turned around in time for him to see them carrying off some old clothes stuffed under the rescue team's blanket.

"Thank you all for your cooperation," Klonski said. "You all contributed whether you liked it or not." The lieutenant looked at his watch.

"Lieutenant, if you have time tomorrow, I need to talk to you about something."

"I think I have a workable situation, Katrina. I'll have more details for you, say about noon, if we're talking about the same thing..."

"I'm sure we are, Joe."

"Did you have a good night's sleep?" Kim recognized the caller's voice. Looking back at the others gathered around the kitchen table, she decided to take her plate to the reception desk and finish breakfast there. "Don't hang up, I'm going up front."

With a smaller crowd to feed that morning, Song opted to have a cozy breakfast at the kitchen table. The dark clouds had disappeared in more ways than one and this time talk surrounding the murder was tolerable. The pall hanging over Tudor Grove had finally lifted.

Dumping another fresh scoop of coffee beans into the grinder, Song pressed the on button and her thoughts swirled inside her head as the blades whirled inside the machine. In her mind she felt relief, but in her heart she wished the incident had never happened.

"Song, you're gonna have powder, not grounds," said Tim. "Turn it off." Impatiently, Tim waited for a fresh cup of coffee to enjoy outdoors with his cigarette.

"Garsch, I guess I got lost in my thoughts."

Tim mumbled something about that not being the only thing lost and grinned at Spike. "So, what are your plans now that you're free?"

The vacationing cop went over an itinerary that included stop-overs at various resort towns where his buddies awaited his arrival. "Besides, Kim's already got my replacement lined up. Didn't take her long, did it?"

Katrina felt compelled to remind Spike that it was he who wanted his space and what was Kim suppose to do, sit and darn socks while he had a good time? Wanting to put bad times behind, however, she said nothing.

"Well, I know what I'm gonna do," she said. "I'm going to Tampa for a few days. Bruce, you still with us on that?"

"Us?"

"Yeah, Kim's coming along. She wants to enjoy the rest of her vacation. And, I want to put space between myself and these latest events. Hopefully, I'll come back with a renewed sense of the place." Chasing down a vitamin with several sips of water, she said, "Besides, with the season coming up, this may be our last chance to get away for a while."

Tim exited through the back kitchen door and headed for the patio furniture. Spike, Bruce, Katrina, and Song lingered at the table. Kim returned to the kitchen and pulled up a stool at the island counter.

"Well," Spike said, glancing at the wall clock, "I guess I should get packed." Kim twirled a lock of hair around a finger, then brushed nonexistent crumbs off her cutoff shorts.

"Spike, I've a favor to ask," Song said. "While you're doing that, could I borrow the convertible for a few minutes?"

The stunned foursome looked at her.

"Sure, Song," he replied. "What's up?"

"Well," she began, "this whole mess has given me a new outlook on life. I realize there's more to it than just cookin' …"

Spike dug into his pocket and withdrew a set of keys. "Catch," he said, and she almost did.

"Katrina, will you go with me? It's just a ten-minute ride from here."

"Sure, but where to?"

"I'm enrolling in private dancing lessons." She waited for a reaction. "When the next semester starts, I should be ready to join a group. What do you think?"

"I think it's great," Katrina gushed. "Don't you think it's a good idea, Bruce?"

"Oh yeah–sure, Mom. Go for it." Receiving her son's approval, she beamed.

With a promise to be ready shortly, Song threw off her apron and scurried off down the hall.

"Well," mumbled Spike as he watched Kim scrape off plates. "I did say I was getting packed, didn't I?" He rose again, this time actually leaving the kitchen.

It was Katrina's turn to be supportive.

"You want to go for the ride with us? We won't be long."

"No, Aunty Trina. I don't feel like it."

Song, exuding excitement, showed up in the kitchen doorway. "Well, I'm ready."

"Go ahead. I kinda want to be alone anyway."

"Katrina, I'll be out in front."

"I'll be right there," Katrina said and turned back to her niece. "Who was on the phone anyway?"

"It was Lou. I told him about our plans to go to Tampa, and he asked if he could join us."

"Sure–that is if you want him to."

"I guess. It will help me keep my mind off you know who. Go ahead, she's waiting for you. We'll talk when you get back."

"If Klonski calls, take a message. Tell him I'll call him when I get back. I still have a few questions."

Song paced a short span of the driveway and looked up as Katrina approached. "Did Tim ask where I was?"

"No, he's still out in the yard–Bruce joined him."

"Katrina, put the top down." Song eyed the red sports car.

"But of course." Katrina stopped at the driver's side before unlocking the door. "Hey, this is your gig," she said and tossed the keys at the woman. "You drive."

"Oh garsch." In a flash, Song had the car idling and the top rolled down. Adjusting her rearview mirror, she moaned, "Oh no." Katrina turned around in time to see Tim advancing down the driveway toward the red convertible. Song heard her name being called. Bruce could be seen walking behind his father, calling after him. Tim quickened his pace.

"Should I see what he wants?" Song asked.

"Floor it," said Katrina.

"What?"

"Give it some gas." Katrina glanced over her shoulder. Not only was he gaining, but he was wearing the same expression she'd seen before in her dream."

"Oh, what should I do?" As though she got an answer, Song hit a button and fifties rock and roll filled the air. Tapping quickly on the volume control, she succeeded in drowning out the sound of her name being called. In an instant, the fiery convertible flew down the drive as Kim laughed and flagged them on with a dishtowel.

Alone on the front porch, Spike watched for the return of his rented vehicle. In the foyer waited his packed suitcase.

"You can wait inside, you know," Kim said softly from the doorway.

"Yeah, I know."

"Hey—were you planning on leaving without saying goodbye?"

He started out toward the road. A gentle breeze rustled the tree's branches while the inn's shingle squeaked along in accompaniment.

"Well?"

"It's easier this way." He avoided looking her way.

"Easier? This was your idea not mine."

"I know...here they come." The red auto pulled into the drive.

"Spike—come in and say a good goodbye." Kim stepped back and allowed him entry.

"Well, I guess this is it." Nervously, he glanced about. "Everybody must be outside."

"Must be," said Kim.

"Look, this is difficult for me to explain, but—"

"This is difficult for me to accept."

Finally he looked at her. "Let me just have some time. You know us, we'll probably get back together in no time. We always do."

"Do me a favor? If you decide we should be on again–call first. I may be busy this time."

She kissed him lightly on the cheek and walked outdoors with him.

Outside, he collected his keys from Song, then took a last look at the expansive, manicured backyard. He hadn't paid much attention to the lush vegetation surrounding the acreage of the estate.

"Guess I was too busy looking for clues and planning my future. I wonder how much of the present we miss while we're worrying about our tomorrow…"

"It's pretty, isn't it?" Kim said, stepping alongside him. "I'll walk you to your car."

Spike shouted one last good-bye. Tim waved briefly, then resumed questioning Song about her ride with Katrina. Spike turned and walked away. Katrina caught Song's eye; it was clear, they both disliked unhappy endings.

"Hi Lieutenant," said Katrina. She was in the library pacing. "Thanks for calling. So what do you have for me?"

"Our department worked out a deal with her," he said. "She'll drop her counter suit if you drop yours."

"No more calls, pranks or trespassing?"

"She knows the consequences if she does," said Klonski.

"No more silver coupes…or white ones casing the place?"

"Just call the police if there's a problem."

Katrina paused. "Klonski, tell her I'll go along with it on one condition." Relaying an additional clause to the agreement, Klonski listened and said he'd get Lewis to run that by her and see what resulted."

"One thing is on your side. Her source is tired of helping her out and she knows it. That's all I'll say on–"

"I don't know what you're talking about," she teased. "By the way, who was in that silver car?"

"A friend... and your prank caller."

"The driver who picked her up the night we floured–?"

249

"Another boyfriend."

Katrina laughed. "Oh, a few more things," she continued. "You never said what you got on the falling bricks."

Klonski reassured her that it had no tie to the case or any work of malice. "The bricklayer didn't fasten them down sufficiently."

"And the fingerprints?"

"About the prints," Klonski offered, "ident confirms that the ones on the cup were as you suspected."

Katrina stopped pacing. She listened hard.

"As for the key in the bag you submitted," said Klonski, "we couldn't get a read off it. Sorry."

Katrina sighed. "Are you sure? I was careful not to–"

"It may have rubbed off when the party slid it under the rug. In the meantime," said Klonski,. "I'd change the locks, the place you hide the spare and I'd keep an eye on things."

Katrina was disheartened. A thought occurred to her and she told him so. "Or is it that you don't want me knowing it's Tim?" Katrina waited for an official retort. Instead, Joseph Klonski chuckled.

"It's not like that," he said. "But maybe you should test for a job in the department."

"The inn can be our front," she teased. "Well, thanks for everything…else. Oh, and Song stressed that I extend a welcome to you and Sergeant Lewis to join us at our "country inn, dead and breakfast" anytime you can't tolerate that greasy spoon in town."

"I'm flattered–I think. Now if there's nothing else, I've gotta go fight the bad guys."

"Goodbye Klonski." A faint click signaled the end of conversation. Muttering softly into the phone she mimicked, "…maybe you should test for a job in the department." She added. "Maybe you're covering Tim's–"

Beeping resounded in her ear. "Hey, someone's still on the line," came a man's voice. "Hello? Hell-o-o?"

"Why are you sitting in the dark?"

"Oh Kim, uh… I just got off the phone a minute ago. What's up?"

"I was out in the backyard–Bruce's dad isn't taking the dancing lesson thing too well. He said something about you putting ideas in his wife's head–et cetera."

The phone rang; Katrina jumped. "If it's Klonski, I'm not here."

"I thought you wanted to talk to him?"

"I just did…" Katrina flicked the recorder into commission. The friendly voice asked for Kim.

"Aunty Trina, pick it up."

"Hi, Lou–fine–I heard you might come with us?"

"Yeah," the masculine voice said. "I want to check on some acting classes out that way. I also heard there's some new talent agencies that opened up. Hey, did you ever think of doing some informal modeling–some runway work?"

"I did a few years ago. I think I missed–"

"Not true. There's an agency that specializes in older… uh…I mean women over thirty."

"I used to like you, Lou. Never mind I know what you mean." Katrina held up a finger for Kim to wait a minute.

"If you don't have your comp sheet, I can do that for you."

"I think I can find my portfolio–but I'll need some new shots. Anyway, are you getting out of photography?"

"Not really, I just–"

Kim was signaling in the background.

"Lou, we'll talk on the way out there. Kim wants to speak to you." She handed the phone to her niece. "Find out when he wants to go." Katrina left the room.

Out in the hallway came the familiar cough. "Oh hell, here it comes."

"Katrina–I want to talk to you. See what you started? I hope you're happy–putting those stupid ideas in Song's head."

"No, I'm not, Tim." She folded her arms across her chest.

"Huh?"

251

"You heard me. You see," she stood her ground, "I just got off the phone with Lou and he tells me he's got a friend that runs an acting agency in Orlando. And guess what? They are casting women Song's age for a revue called <u>Silver Belles and Sirens</u>."

"Ka-a-treena."

"But," she continued, "I had to tell them she's prepaid dancing lessons for the next month. That is," she stared him down, hands on hips, "of course, if you tell her she can't take lessons then she'll be free to–"

"Katrina!" he bellowed this time.

"Garsch, now what is it?"

"Oh nothing, Song–Tim was just heading out for a cigarette, weren't you, Tim?"

"Katrina, Bruce wants to know what time you'll all be leaving. He wants to wash the van and get it ready."

"So he's coming along?"

"Sounds that way."

"Oh good. We'll be able to leave," Katrina said loudly, "just as soon as we change the locks on our bedroom door."

"Whatever...?" said Song, looking from Tim to Katrina.

Katrina walked off to the kitchen. "Ask Kim to join us when she's off the phone," she called over her shoulder. "We'll be in the backyard."

"Okay."

Katrina pulled up a lawn chair and sat next to Bruce.

"I heard you're going to Tampa with us? I was beginning to think I lost you to the construction zone."

"I guess I could use a break from this place." he winked, "I gotta keep an eye on you."

"That's right. I might run off to join a rock and roll band." She paused. "Do you think it's okay to leave your mom alone with him?" she pointed over her shoulder.

"Gee, Katrina, I don't know." Bruce feigned worry. "You suppose it's safe?"

"You know what I mean." She stopped. "Anyway, I just got off the phone with... Hey, what's going on with them?"

She turned and looked toward the inn.

Song came hurrying up to the couple, letting Kim walk behind.

"You'll never guess who called?"

"Who?"

"It was Jessie Hodgkins and you'll never guess what?"

"What?" Katrina didn't need to guess.

"She's gonna do a quarter page article on–don't be upset, Katrina–on me." She spun on, "Oh, I'm so excited. It will be titled," she ran her hand across the air, " 'The Manor and her Matriarch'–or, 'Manor Matriarch Helps Snag Lady Killer.' "

"Are they going to print your picture too?" Katrina asked.

"Yes–I think we'll go with the one of me standing in front of the inn.. or kids, how 'bout the one of me standing in the kitchen.. no wait, I might like the one…"

Katrina raised an inquiring eyebrow at Bruce. "How soon will you be ready?"

"In a heartbeat," he said out of the corner of his mouth.

"You know, Katrina," Song declared. "You really misjudged Jessie. I told you she was a nice girl. You know I think you…"

Bruce leaned over to his girlfriend, "My dad's coming–how soon will you be–?"

Katrina answered emphatically, "In a heartbeat."

THE END

Tina Czarnota

ABOUT THE AUTHOR

Tina Czarnota lives in south Florida and is currently working on Deadwaiter, her second book in the Country Inn series.